MW00915578

Blair Adams
The Package

An FBI Thriller

By **Tony Aued**

Copyright © 2006 Tony Aued

This book is a work of fiction. People, places, events and situations are a product of the author's imagination. Any resemblance to actual persons, living or dead is purely coincidental.

No part of this book can be reproduced without the author's permission

First published December 2, 2006

Printed in the United States of America
Blair Adams Books

All rights reserved.
ISBN: 10 1489558861
ISBN-13:978 1489558862

This book is dedicated to my wife, Kathy; you have always been there to support all my efforts. You are my best friend and I can never repay you for everything you have done for our family.

Special thanks to my daughter, Blair, for her involvement.

In memory of our Son-in-law; known to his comrades as Bama.

Watch for the Sequel

Blair Adams / The Abduction

By Tony Aued

Soon to be released

One

The pilot's voice came on the overhead speaker announcing they were making the initial approach to LAX. They would be on the ground in a few minutes. Blair opened her eyes and could hardly believe that they had already made the trip from Philadelphia back to Los Angeles. The past few weeks seemed a blur. She looked out of her window. The sky was a deep shade of steely blue as it reflected off the ocean. The palm trees were just coming into view as the plane banked to the left on its final approach. The landscape was so different than the East Coast that it almost seemed like another world.

The next thing she heard was the flight attendant's voice requesting that everyone bring their seats and tray tables to the upright position. Hunter's funeral was all she could think about as the plane taxied to a stop on the runway. Could all of this really have happened? Is he really gone?

She started to gather her things from the overhead bin when the passenger next to her asked about the triangularly folded American flag. Blair looked down sadly. "My husband was killed in Iraq."

Passengers overheard what she said and started to repeat it to others on the plane. The woman expressed her sympathy and asked, "When did it happen?"

"He was shot by a sniper a few weeks ago."

"I'm so sorry. You're too young to have lost someone."

Blair had tears in her eyes and swore that she would not cry again after shedding so many tears the past few weeks. She made her way up the aisle as other passengers offered their condolences. She nodded simple thanks and departed the plane to head for the luggage area. She hoped that the long walk would do her some good.

It was a typical day in Los Angeles, sunny and mild. The

5

weather was always great in the spring. Warm winds came across the San Gabriel Mountains often trapping the low-laying fog over the city. People from the East Coast couldn't understand her love for southern California. Blair and Hunter could be on the beach from their apartment in less than ten minutes or climbing in the mountains in a few hours. They both loved the mountains and would take overnight trips to the San Bernardino National Forest when Hunter was home. Now those happy times were only fond memories. As she walked toward the baggage area the thought of their trip to Catalina, and the good times they had mountain climbing made her smile. It was a surprise anniversary trip that he'd planned. He was good at that sort of thing.

She held the American flag tightly as she approached the baggage carousel. The long walk through the terminal helped her gather her composure. She had talked to her two best friends, Ashley and Blake, and they said they would meet her near the baggage area. Blair saw them waiting for her and they ran to greet one another.

Ashley moved from Dallas to Santa Monica about the same time that Blair moved there. They met at The California Kitchen an American Grille, where both girls found their first Santa Monica jobs. They became fast friends and because Hunter was gone so often they looked out for each other. They lived together for a short time when Ashley was looking for another apartment. Hunter was in South America at the time and Blair appreciated having someone stay with her. They both loved jazz and big band music and had similar backgrounds. Ashley was a beautiful girl with long, curly black hair. Blair would often tell her that she would do well in an acting career. Ashley had two cats named Lois and Clark from the Superman comics. Blair was a dog lover but enjoyed Ashley's cats when they roomed together. She wanted to have a dog but it was not approved for her apartment building.

Ashley wanted to live near the ocean and had been to California as a child many times. She loved the beach and Santa Monica was the perfect place. They shared the same California dream.

Blair's friend Blake had moved to Santa Monica before either of the two girls. He graduated from Fresno State University and planned to go to graduate school in Los Angeles. Blair met Blake when Hunter was still in Mississippi transferring from the National Guard to the U.S. Army. It would take a few weeks but she wanted to get into their apartment. Blake lived on the first floor and held the door for Blair and her dad when they carried a load of boxes up. She didn't have a lot to move. Most of the things were hers. Hunter always said he traveled light. Blake helped her move the rest of the items and they became immediate friends.

Blake was a few years older than Blair. He had moved to Santa Monica from Fresno. He loved surfing and he could do it every day in Santa Monica. He would often go surfing in the morning before his classes. He tried to teach Blair how to surf but her fear of the ocean held her back from being able to learn the sport. He was attending UCLA and working on his master's degree. Blair would often get him to do small projects for her when Hunter was overseas. He would make sure she was okay whenever Hunter was on a mission. Blake was a kind young man and always very thoughtful. They both loved sushi and Hunter didn't, so Blake was her sushi partner.

Tears flowed as they hugged. They were Blair's two best friends. They had been there from the start and the three shared good times and bad. Both Ashley and Blake had gone to Bridgewater, Pennsylvania, where Hunter's dad lived, for Hunter's funeral. Ashley had flown out with Blair's boss, Olly, and Blake arrived the day of the funeral. Some of Blair's friends from Alabama and Mississippi also made it to the funeral. Hunter was very popular in college and many of his former classmates drove from Oxford, Mississippi, to attend his funeral.

The bags were gathered by her friends as she clutched the American flag. They walked toward the parking lot in silence, just holding hands, the three of them. Good friends were so important, now more than ever.

Her parents were great during the funeral but they had to return home to Alabama. Her dad had to go back to work and her mom was hoping to travel out to California in a few weeks. Knowing that she had so many friends made it much easier for them. Her mom promised to come to California but Blair wanted

7

some time to figure out exactly what she should do next. Having such understanding parents made everything easier. Her mom and dad held her close every moment.

The three friends entered the parking deck across from the main terminal. Blake had his Honda Civic parked in the short-term lot and they made their way toward it. Her bags were tucked into the trunk as she climbed into the back seat still carrying the American flag. No one could know what she was feeling at this time; she wasn't sure herself what she was feeling. They were married only three years but it seemed so much longer. Hunter played football for Ole Miss where they both went to school; it was where they met. He was injured his senior year and it looked like he would not play again. His love for football and his dream of playing for the Philadelphia Eagles was gone.

Blair had dreams of Hollywood and moving to California had been shared with Hunter. They agreed that after they got married they would move to the Los Angeles area. Since he no longer had his chance of a career in the NFL, he wanted Blair to be able to chase her hopes of making it in Hollywood. She was now in the back seat of a friend's Honda holding his flag. The funeral was over on Friday; it was now Tuesday. Time seemed to be moving in slow motion since the visit from the three soldiers to her apartment that night. She could not put any of their conversation into reality until the actual day she claimed Hunter's body on the tarmac in Philadelphia with his dad, Thomas Adams. *No one should have to do this*, she thought. Life seemed so unfair.

The drive along Lincoln Boulevard through Marina Del Ray and Venice toward Santa Monica seemed to take longer than usual. Traffic along the beach was always a challenge and Tuesdays usually had a lot of tourist traffic headed to or from the airport or beach. Blake turned off of Lincoln at Rose Avenue and drove down to Pacific. He could avoid some of the traffic that would be getting on the Santa Monica Freeway at the Lincoln entrance. They would pass the restaurants along Main Street that were always busy. One of them was the small restaurant where Hunter worked when he was home from one of his missions. He was a bouncer at the popular nightclub off of Main Street near the beach. Blake slowed down as traffic backed up along Ocean

Avenue. As they passed the Hotel California Blair asked him to pull over.

"What's wrong?"

"I need to get out."

They turned to the back seat.

"Are you okay?" Ashley asked.

"This is all so hard. Hunter and I would walk down here many mornings. He loved the beach and so do I." She wanted to walk the remainder of the way to her apartment. They were passing places where she spent time with Hunter and she wanted to see them alone.

The sight of the Santa Monica Pier and the Ferris wheel made her sad. They would rent bikes at the base of the walk under the pier and ride to Venice on weekends. Blair had her roller blades in the trunk of their car and was always ready to skate alongside of Hunter as he rode his bike. Pacific Park was a wonderful place full of memories that caused her to think how her life had changed.

"I just want to walk the rest of the way."

"I'll walk with you," Ashley said.

"Thanks, but I need to walk alone for a little bit."

Blake pulled over in front of the Santa Monica Pier. Blair got out of the car.

"Please be careful. I wish you would let Ashley walk with you."

"Really, I'm okay, just need a little alone time."

"We'll park and meet you."

It was only a few blocks to the Santa Monica Promenade from the pier and her apartment on Arizona. They had stopped near The Lobster House. It was a very nice restaurant on the Pacific Coast Highway just before you walked onto the pier. You could look down on the beach and see the tourists renting bikes to ride along the beach. When Blair's parents would come for a visit she often convinced them to rent bikes and head down the path to Venice Beach.

The pier was Santa Monica's version of an amusement park and state fair all wrapped into one. You could see the sights from

9

sunrise or setting to the palm trees blowing in the wind. There were places to get funnel cakes and hot dogs or ride the famous merry-go-round. The pier was full of vendor carts and gift counters. It offered dining and shopping plus some great sightseeing. It seemed like the homeless also found the pier a good place to spend time. They could panhandle or find a nice spot on the manicured lawn to rest.

Blair always had a soft spot for the homeless. When she was eight, her parents took her to Washington, D.C., to see the White House, Washington Monument and other famous sites. She saw a homeless man begging near the Lincoln Memorial and cried for her dad to give her some money to help him. Her dad took her to a food stand and they bought nice meals for the man and his other friends. That gave her a good feeling. She would often talk Hunter into doing the same thing when they went down to the pier. She had a kind heart.

The walk along Ocean Avenue also took her past places where she would take friends and family when they came to visit. It was good that she had the time to gather her thoughts. She had so many memories that she had to see them alone now for the first time. She always knew that Hunter would be back and they both loved the California way of life. Many times she would have her friends from Alabama and Mississippi come to visit and they would see the California that Blair saw. Even her parents knew that it was a great place for their daughter. Her dad would often say, "Maybe when we retire we'll move out here too." That was Blair's mother's dream. She so missed her daughter.

Blair stopped at the Coffee Bean for a latte. She stopped there every morning before going to work. She had met so many new people at the funeral, many for the first time.

One of Hunter's friends, Brian, was special. He and Hunter had gone to high school together and Brian was the one with him on the rooftop. She wished that she could have spent more time with him and listened to more stories about her husband growing up but there was no time for that. Brian had been in the Army's Special Forces for over eight years when he was rejoined with his friend in Iraq. It was odd that they would be in the same command after not seeing each other for so long. He promised himself that he would spend some time with both Thomas, Hunter's dad, and Blair when he was home. He knew that Hunter would have wanted him to do that.

When Thomas took Brian and Blair to the Philadelphia airport, Brian said he would keep in touch. He seemed like such a nice person and was so close to Hunter and his dad. Blair gave Brian her address and got his in return. His address made her especially sad because it was the same as Hunter's when he was in Iraq.

The California sun was high overhead and watching people head down to the Santa Monica Pier brought back a rush of memories. Hunter loved the beach. It seemed that every time he would come home from one of his missions the beach would be his refuge. The sidewalk that ran along the beach stretched from Malibu to Venice and everyday you would see rollerbladers, bicyclists and walkers making their daily trek along the path. This was one of the reasons she picked Santa Monica as a place to move to. She had made two trips out to California to scout out an apartment and fell in love with the area. One could find every type of restaurant or activity within a few blocks. The Third Street Promenade was always busy. Struggling musicians played their instruments hoping to sell CD's that they had placed in open guitar cases. People passing by would often drop in a dollar or two while stopping to listen to a few songs. On most Sunday nights a local dance studio held their lessons in the street. It was also the place for activists to promote their causes. Blair loved helping any cause that protected the environment. She would stop and pick up their literature and always donated to them.

When they moved, Hunter had to stay behind in Oxford, Mississippi, so Blair was responsible for finding a place to live. She liked it that way because he didn't seem to care and Blair liked making the decision for them. She picked out the city, apartment, and most of the furniture.

The short walk alone was only a few blocks and helped her to relax. When Blair arrived at her apartment, Blake and Ashley were waiting with her suitcases.

"I'll take them up for you," Blake said.

"I just want to go up by myself first," she said.

"That's not a good idea," Ashley said. "Let me go with you."

Blake listened then added, "Blair, you know we love you. Let Ashley go up to the apartment with you."

"I'm going to be okay," she told her friends.

They wanted to believe her. She seemed fine.

Blair said, "I'll meet you at The Pub on Santa Monica Boulevard in two hours. She entered the elevator and pushed the button for the second floor. Her apartment was 21A. It was small but perfect for her and Hunter. She paused outside the door. Memories flooded her mind. It would be the first time back home after Hunter's death. When she opened the door she dropped her bag. Furniture was turned upside down and everything was a mess. Someone had broken into the apartment and ransacked everything. She couldn't figure out why or who, but things were tossed all around. They did not have a television but Hunter had bought her a retro stereo and it was on its side. Hunter's Ole Miss football helmet and the football signed by Archie Manning were in the corner. The apartment was in a safe building and that was one of the things her parents really liked when they saw it. Nothing seemed to be missing at first glance.

What happened, who would have done this? She had been gone for close to two weeks to Philadelphia but Blake lived in the same building and would have told her if they had any break-ins. This was the last straw. She sat in the middle of the floor and broke down. Her door was still open when Ashley came in.

"I couldn't leave you alone. My God what happened?" Ashley bent down and helped her up.

"Where do I start?" Blair said.

"We need to call the police," Ashley told her.

The Santa Monica police showed up in a few minutes because the station was located across the street on the Promenade. Ashley answered the knock. They were very efficient. Not many problems outside of the homeless issue came up. Police officers were always present on the Promenade; it made the locals feel pretty safe. Officer Tuttle was the one to come to her apartment. He knew the girls and had often eaten in The Pub where they both worked. He had also heard about Hunter's death and offered his sympathy to Blair.

"I understand that you've been gone for a while. Did you have anyone check on your apartment while you were away?"

Blair said no one had been there that she knew of. "I don't have any pets or plants so it wasn't necessary to have someone check my apartment," she said.

"You just got home today I take it," Officer Tuttle said looking at her luggage on the floor.

Ashley answered for Blair, stating that they had just picked her up from the airport and came straight to the apartment to put her bags away.

"Was the door open when you got here? Did it appear to be broken? Is anything missing that you can tell?"

The girls nodded no to each of the questions.

"Do you think that there was something special that someone would have been after?" It appeared that someone was searching for something. Blair had no idea why this would have happened. Officer Tuttle filled out a police report and left Blair with a copy. He told her to inventory the apartment and change the lock. She said she would come by the station when she had gone through everything.

They felt comfortable with the officer. They would see him at The Pub. It was a popular gathering place for locals. It was not very big and it was located on the corner of Santa Monica Boulevard and the start of the Third Street Promenade. The location made it a great spot for lunch or dinner and to watch the activity on the street. The owners were from England and Ireland and had fashioned the bar like an old English pub. The long bar was made of beautiful dark mahogany wood with many intricate carvings. There was a large population of English and Scottish people who had moved to southern California and places like The Pub were like a piece of home. Locals would gather daily enjoying each other's company and stories from back home. Soccer was always a big event at The Pub. Karaoke night also drew large crowds.

Blair had found a job there soon after moving to California.

She was originally working at The California Kitchen and stopped into The Pub with Ashley for a drink one night. She met Olly, one of the owners, and they became friends. She could work flexible schedules while trying to get into the film industry. She promised herself that she would work legitimate jobs only, not like the stories of girls who ended up in the porn industry. Her dad made her a promise that if she ever needed anything, he and her mom would be there for her.

Olly treated Blair like a sister. They would often plan trips to Las Vegas or Mexico together when Hunter was on a mission. She went to Bridgewater for the funeral. She loved Blair and saw a lot of herself in Blair. She had moved to Santa Monica from Ireland when she was twenty years old. She was a beautiful, petite blond. She had two young children and lived in a house along the ridge that overlooked the ocean. It was off the Pacific Coast Highway that ran toward Malibu. She would often have Blair meet her at one of the chic restaurants along the coast after work. They'd have a drink and order meals that they would share. She was great fun to be with. . They liked traveling together and Olly had planned a trip with Blair to Puerto Vallarta, Mexico while Hunter had been on a short mission to South and Central America before his deployment to Iraq.

Many of the patrons knew of Hunter's death and had sent flowers and cards to the funeral home. Blair was one of the favorites of the regulars that came to The Pub. Nate always asked about Blair whenever he came in. Nate was a famous barber who would often stop in when he had finished cutting the hair of a prominent Hollywood star. Other patrons also asked Olly about Blair and hoped that they would see her soon. Olly had not talked to Blair for a couple of days since returning from the funeral.

Blake arrived at The Pub and ordered a beer. When he told Olly that Blair would be coming in, she was anxious to see her. He waited at an outside table. There were about six small tables that went around the front of The Pub with a large overhang that protected the patrons from the afternoon sun. Blake saw Blair and Ashley headed his way and knew that something was wrong. He got up and met them part way.

"What's wrong?" Blake asked.

14

Ashley told him about the break-in which made no sense to any of them. He felt guilty because he lived on the floor below and should have checked the apartment for her.

"Blair, I'm so sorry that this has happened. What can I do?" he asked.

"I'm going to stay with Ashley tonight. I just can't go back now."

Blake wanted the girls to sit down and talk. Maybe they should have a drink and some dinner.

"I can't eat," Blair said.

Olly came running over and hugged Blair. "I missed being with you the last few days." She had to return right after the funeral and wished that she could have stayed to help Blair after the luncheon. "Are you okay?" she asked.

Blair told her about the break-in and that she was glad Officer Tuttle was the one to come to her apartment.

"You need to change the locks."

"That's what the officer said. I can't go back tonight. Ashley said that I should stay with her." Then Blair remembered that they left her suitcase in her apartment. "I need some clothes."

"We're the same size; you can wear some of my things," Ashley told her.

It was settled. Blair would walk home with Ashley and the three of them would meet tomorrow to clean up the apartment and get new locks installed.

Blake made the girls sit at the table so they could calm Blair down. Olly brought some appetizers over and a round of drinks. "Did Officer Tuttle have any leads on the break-in?"

"No he said that it seemed strange that nothing looked like it was missing. He asked me to check everything out and call him back with an inventory list. He said there had not been any other problems reported in the past few weeks."

They sat quietly and all three wondered why someone had broken in to her apartment and what they were looking for.

Two

The streets of Baghdad were again filled with car bombs. The constant struggle for power between the Sunnis, Shiites and Muslim factions tore the country apart. Iraqis wondered if a recent meeting in the highly fortified Green Zone would resolve the remaining disputes. Although they had a National Assembly, the struggle for power continued to exist. Brian had just returned that morning from Hunter's funeral and now he watched as bodies were hauled away. So many innocent people who had come to register for a spot in the Baghdad Police Department lay dead in the street.

Brian's driver, Al Azawi, was a Shiite who had worried that assisting the Americans would endanger his family. The American troops were the country's hope for a peaceful resolution while the Iraqi National Assembly worked out the new order. Al Azawi had sent his family to the southern city of Basra hoping to protect them from the constant upheaval in Baghdad. Although the regime of Saddam had been overthrown, there were daily street bombings, and gunfire seemed to come out of nowhere.

Brian found it hard to believe that just a few days ago he escorted Hunter's body back to the States and helped carry his friend's casket from the church to the cemetery. They had been buddies in high school and now his friend was gone. Brian was part of the Army's Special Forces that often guarded both American and Iraqi officials. He was on the rooftop with Hunter when he had been shot by a sniper. They had not seen each other for years before they were both sent to Baghdad. He thought it was ironic that they would serve in the same outfit, but having his high school pal with him sure made the duty much better. The two soldiers always traveled with a German shepherd guard dog. They used him for bomb sniffing details. He looked forward to seeing his guard dog, Xavier.

Hunter was a specialist in the Army's premiere unit and was often sent on special missions. He would frequently be gone for weeks on one of these missions. He had been deployed to the northern city of Tikrit, the home of Saddam. Brian heard that he had just returned from a mission to Tikrit that had a goal of searching one of Saddam's castles. Hunter seemed very excited when his search team returned. He reported the findings to the head of his command in Riyadh, Saudi Arabia. Brian had wanted to ask him about it and what they found, but they never had a chance to discuss it.

It was often the case with this unit that the missions were top secret. Hunter never seemed to open up since that time in San Salvador when his unit was charged with a special mission that included finding gold that was earmarked for the drug traffic bosses. He had detailed the mission findings to one of the men in the company only to learn that the man leaked the information to the news media. The information that was found was of no use since the drug lord had been exposed in the newspapers and he was able to go into hiding. Hunter became very private after that incident with information regarding his mission activities.

Baghdad was hot and the temperature often reached 103 degrees. The sun seemed to be hotter there and the sand never quit blowing. The trip back to his unit was long and Brian wasn't too anxious to get there. He knew he would get requests from the troops regarding the funeral: the weather in the States, and most of them would want some bits and pieces of information about home. They were all dedicated but lonely and he really needed to be alone.

Upon arrival to the camp Brian went to his barracks. He was glad to see Xavier waiting for him. Life in Iraq was hard and having Xavier to look after was a release from the reality of war. Even though Xavier was a bomb-sniffing dog, Brian looked after him like anyone would treat a pet.

Although Brian and Hunter were good friends in high school, they lost track of each other for many years. Brian stayed in Philadelphia and Hunter moved to Mississippi on a football scholarship. Brian had joined the Army and was certain that it

17

would be his career. He heard that Hunter was injured his senior year and that he joined the National Guard soon after that. Brian always knew that his friend would be a football star so he figured that the football injury had to be tough on him. He also found out that Hunter had gotten married and moved to Santa Monica. He'd not met Blair until the funeral, although she and Hunter had made a few trips to Bridgewater to see Hunter's dad. Brian was glad to meet her but sad it was under such painful circumstances.

The funeral was still on his mind; it was hard to shake it off. He went home for a week but only to bury his friend. The Army was gracious enough that they allowed Brian to accompany his friend's body back home for the funeral. After all, they were high school friends and he had been on the roof top when Hunter was shot.

The barracks were highly protected due to recent car bombings throughout Baghdad. The use of German shepherds was important and they never entered until the dogs made sure all was clear. The U.S. troops were always the target of snipers and car bombers. How could such a noble cause turn so sour? It had been two years since the start of the conflict with a strong resolve but now it seemed more like an occupation of a country that did not want them. When he was home, Brian felt a sense of pride. The friends and family members who were at the funeral all expressed gratitude for what he and Hunter were doing. He also sensed an underlying question in people's conversation: Why are we still there? It seemed with each serviceman or woman lost, the country grew more restless with the events and hoped for an end to the struggle.

Captain Montgomery came into Brian's barracks and inquired about the funeral.

"It was a tough one," Brian said.

Montgomery was the commander of their unit. He was always quiet and seemed deep in thought. It was his decision to continue the mission that came under fire while protecting diplomats. The captain was only in his late twenties but had seen enough action in his nine months in Iraq to fill a lifetime. This was his second tour of duty in Iraq. He was from Georgia, and like most of his men, he missed home and his family. Montgomery was a tall thin man and had leathery skin after being in the hot sun for so long. The men always thought it was strange that after most missions he and Hunter would meet to strategize and plan operations.

Captain Montgomery often talked about fishing. He and his wife lived on Lake Lanier, north of Atlanta. It was a man-made lake and had great fishing and boating. In recent years the State of Georgia had added a large hotel and water park close to Buford on the southern end on the lake. There was plenty of wildlife and two championship golf courses. The captain didn't talk about family; just fishing, baseball and his love of the lake back home. He was also a big fan of the Atlanta Braves. If he wasn't talking about fishing, he was talking about the Braves. He never engaged in conversation that was personal. He appeared distant to some of his men. It was rumored that he had been the tank driver that helped local Iraqis topple the statue of Saddam in the Baghdad square that CNN had sent pictures of across the world. He had been Brian's and Hunter's commander for about six months.

Both soldiers sat quietly for a while and reflected on the day Hunter was killed. The mission seemed simple enough: Guard two high-ranking U.S officials as they met with key Iraqi officials. It was to be a short meeting, not more than one hour. Something must have gone wrong because the meeting lasted more than three hours. The security guards were stationed on the roof and around the perimeter of the building for the whole time and became concerned about how long the meeting was taking. Any time they had to guard officials they knew that word would get out and the chance of gunfire would increase.

Terrorists took pleasure in this sort of attack. Hide and shoot from cover. Send a suicide bomber into the fray and wreak havoc. The length of the meeting made it very difficult to protect the officials and not lose any of the men. The decision to stay and let the meeting continue rested with the captain. After the meeting had passed the three-hour mark he tried to get the officials' attention. That's when the gunfire started. Two soldiers were injured on the outside of the gate when a car bomber crashed into it. One dead, two injured and nothing accomplished. Hunter was strong and always alert but when the car bomber hit the gate he stood up on the roof. Brian yelled but it was too late.

They had a helicopter fly in to help quell the uprising. They loaded the injured into the Suburban that they used to transport the officials. The helicopter took Hunter and Brian back to the base. Captain Montgomery ordered a second helicopter to fly in and after all was clear they flew the officials back to their headquarters.

Brian did not want to talk about the funeral or anything else. He had seen too many of their friends injured or die. Iraq had been a tough battlefield. Many of the soldiers wanted to help the Iraqi people. There were many sad sights; children left without parents, death and destruction everywhere. It was hard to reason what they had accomplished when the devastation was so great.

"I know you're tired, Brian, but we do have some things to complete here. I received a request to box Hunter's personal belongings and forward them to the FBI."

Brian had a puzzled look on his face.

"The FBI?"

"They have to inspect everything before it goes stateside," the captain said. "I've looked around and found some of his belongings in his foot locker but thought you might know where more of his things are. Can you to help me look through his things?"

It was never easy to do but wives, parents and children back home needed closure. Getting personal belongings to them often helped with that process.

Brian said, "I will need some time."

"Okay," Captain Montgomery said.

Brian met the captain after mess and they went to Hunter's barracks. He had his trunk at the foot of his cot. He often said he traveled light and thus never seemed to have very many personal things. Like everyone's trunk there were pictures and a few items that never made sense to others except to the individual. Captain Montgomery said, "I've already looked through the items in the trunk."

Brian was surprised that the captain had gone through some of Hunter's equipment. Brian knew that Blair and Hunter's dad would want anything they found. He knew that he had some of

Hunter's letters in a package in his trunk. Hunter said that he was planning on sending some things to his wife and asked Brian to keep them for him. It was a difficult task and hard to look at the package.

The body armor that had arrived too late sat at the end of the bunk and was a reminder of how little protection each soldier had. Brian went to Hunter's locker and took out a package.

"This was Hunter's, Captain." Inside there was a bulky envelope. Brian opened it. It contained letters and some trinkets. *Probably letters from Blair*, he thought.

"Where did you get that package?"

"He gave it to me and he said if anything happened to him he wanted Blair to have it. They're just letters, probably letters they sent to each other."

Montgomery looked at them, "We should inspect them."

Brian thought that the captain was overly interested in the package.

"That doesn't seem right," he said and re-sealed the envelope. "I'll address it and send the package to the FBI in the morning."

"I'll do it for you, Brian."

"That's okay. I want to do this last thing for Hunter."

Captain Montgomery insisted but Brian held his ground. "This is all that I have left to do for him, Captain."

Brian put the package back in his footlocker and lay on his bunk. He knew that he had to send the package the next day to Riyadh. He wondered why the captain was so anxious to get the items off to the FBI. It seemed to him that he was too anxious. He would get the package ready for shipment to the FBI but first he wanted to remove the letters that he felt should go to Blair. The box was sealed and taken to be dispatched to Riyadh for inspection. The second package would also be given to the clerk. Once it was cleared it would be forwarded to Blair.

Once in the mail area, Brian took the package and addressed it to Blair. After all, that's what Hunter asked him to do. *It's probably some love letters Blair sent to Hunter,* he thought. *I'll just send these directly to Blair. She'll want them.* It seemed like the right thing to do. Even though he had just met her she seemed fragile and these might help her in her time of grief. *It's a good thing I was here to do this*, he thought.

To his surprise Captain Montgomery met Brian at the dispatcher's office. "I'm sending the package as instructed Sir."

"Brian, you don't know how important this is."

"It's important to me too, Sir."

Montgomery hadn't been sure about asking Brian to help box Hunter's things. If he hadn't, he would not have known that Hunter had given Brian a package to hold for him.

When Brian was in the dispatcher's office, Montgomery asked to use the computer. He said that he had to forward some important information to Washington. The captain waited until Brian left and asked to see the package going to Riyadh.

"Sorry, I can't do that, Sir." said the dispatcher.

"That's a command."

"Federal law, Sir."

Captain Montgomery left but was not through.

Brian went back to the barracks alone. He didn't tell the captain that he sent Blair some items that did not go in the package for inspection.

Three

Thomas Adams walked back to his car. The funeral was over and all the friends had gone back home. He remembered what his brother had said, that the hardest part was after everyone was gone. He was an ex-Marine and proud of his son. The funeral was held with a full military honor guard. The whole town seemed to come out. Thomas knew that visiting the cemetery was the only way he could make himself believe that his son was really dead. He spent much of Hunter's childhood overseas and had missed seeing his son grow up. By the time he was out of the service his son was in high school and a football star. Thomas wanted to make up for lost time with his son. Now that was not going to happen.

Bridgewater was a small town outside of Philadelphia and ran along the Delaware River. It was a great place to live. It had a population of about 15,000 people and most of them had lived there their whole life. You could walk down the street and know just about everyone. It was centrally located. One could cross the Burlington Toll Bridge into New Jersey and head for the Jersey shore in a few minutes. Downtown Philadelphia was less than an hour's ride. Although many comedians made fun of New Jersey, the shoreline offered a paradise of fun. Thomas and Hunter had gone to Atlantic City on his last visit home. Blair did not like to gamble but knew that Hunter and his dad did. It was good for them to be together. A bonding thing, she'd told him.

Many thoughts entered Thomas' mind as he walked to his car. He thought that while so many friends had come to honor his son yet he felt alone. Like many parents he felt that so much went unsaid and he wished he had it to do over. *You never know what life has in store for you. Parents should not bury their children,* he thought. He thought back that seeing Brian, his son's old high

23

school friend in his dress uniform at the airport, made him more aware of how much he missed the time when Brian and Hunter were playing football for Bridgewater High.

Hunter was a local sports star. It seemed that some schools were interested in him but none of them made him the offer he was looking for. Scholarship offers came in and when he got the one from the University of Mississippi he knew that was the one. He told his dad that although he would be far from home, the opportunity to play for a Southeast Conference school may be the ticket to the NFL. Hunter loved the Eagles and always dreamed of playing for them some day. Many SEC players made it to the NFL and scouts from teams like the Eagles would visit these schools because of their location and reputation.

Blair wasn't a big football fan but she loved fall days on the Grove, the campus center and staging area for tailgate parties. That is where she met Hunter for the first time. It was a warm morning, about nine, and she sat with friends in the Grove near the walk of fame where the football team would pass on their way to the stadium. She saw a tall, strong young man with a number ten jersey over his arm walking by and asked who that was. "Hunter Adams, he's the star running back, and is he ever cute." She made sure she would run into that running back first chance she got. She often told Thomas that story. It made him feel good.

Thomas made Blair promise to call him when she got home. He had hoped to hear from her and that she'd made it back safely. He got into his blue Chevy Impala and headed toward his house. The ride from the cemetery to his house was about four miles. It was a sunny day and flowers were coming up along the roadside.

May was always a good month on the East Coast. The weather was getting warmer and the buds and leaves were popping out everywhere. Mother Nature had created a bouquet of colors that filled the woods with nature's beauty. You could always spot a raccoon or beaver along the creek side rebuilding their fortresses for the summer ahead. It had been an unusually hard winter. Over thirty inches of snow had fallen and there were numerous ice storms. But now the flowers were in bloom and the cherry trees were full of beautiful pink flowers. The ride along Highway 13 was teeming with spring life. The Neshaminy River crossed Highway 13 between Croydon and Bridgewater. You had to be careful because at times the river overflowed onto the highway. A line of Bradford Pear trees full of white flowers came into view as he drove along the highway. *Almost there,* he said to himself. Spring meant the beginning but Thomas felt more like this was the end. He wondered how he could go on. Hunter was his only child and now he was gone. As he rounded the next curve he saw his driveway. It was just a couple of days ago that many friends filled the drive and street after the funeral. He parked in the garage and entered the kitchen through the inside door.

The phone rang. "Hi, it's Blair."

"I'm so glad to hear from you, honey. How was your flight home?"

"I'm sorry I didn't call right away but I wanted to let you know that I was home safe."

"Are you okay? You don't sound so good."

"I guess so."

"Blair, I miss you already. Bet it was difficult going into your apartment."

"Well, it was even more difficult because someone broke in while I was gone."

"Oh no!" Thomas said. "You're not hurt are you?"

"No, but it was so hard seeing our things turned over and messed up. I'm glad that Hunter's college football helmet and trophies are still here. I'd like to send them to you.

"You should keep them."

"No, I want you to have them," she said. "I know how much they mean to you and Hunter would have wanted you to have them too."

"Thanks, I'll cherish them always." Thomas thought his son had sure made a good choice. Blair was so thoughtful and sweet. Thomas wished that he and Hunter were closer when he was growing up. Thomas remembered the story of how Blair and his son met. He loved that story and it made him feel good to think about his son and the things he had done.

After he married Blair it seemed that she brought them

back together. She was big on family and wanted to make sure that Hunter kept close ties with his dad.

"Have you called the police, Blair?"

"Yes, they made a report and Ashley, one of my friends here, will help me go through our things to see if anything is missing. It appears that all the big items are here.

Thomas hesitated to tell Blair. "Blair, I'm not sure what to make of this but my house was broken into the day I took you back to the Philadelphia airport."

"You can't be serious! Why would someone want to do this to us?" Blair started to cry. Thomas tried to comfort her.

"Just like your place, nothing was missing, just appeared like kids looking for something. Maybe they wanted liquor or money. Anyway, I called the Bridgewater Police and Captain Douglas made a report of the incident. It had to be kids."

Blair tried to regain her composure but it was tough. "I'm going to stay with my friend Ashley tonight."

"That's a good idea," Thomas said. "You should be with someone."

"You're right. Are you okay?" Blair asked.

"I guess," he said.

"I'll call you in a couple of days."

"Blair, be careful." He hung up the phone and wondered what the odds were of both of them having a break-in. He still had a few things to pick up but Thomas just wasn't in the mood. It had been several days since his break-in and most everything had been put back in its place. He grabbed a cold beer and headed outside.

The weather had been nice every day except the day of the funeral. It rained so hard that they had to have the graveside service under a tent for shelter. *It must have dropped 20 degrees that day*, he thought as he walked outside. The military funeral was impressive to the small town's folks. There must have been over 500 people in attendance. As taps were played and the American flag was folded over the coffin, a 21-gun salute rang out. Thomas remembered that the sound of the gunfire startled Blair. The Army guard folded the flag and handed it to her. The sight of such a young widow was hard to take. Blair had just turned twenty-three.

Thomas and Blair had to go to the Philadelphia airport to

claim his son's body a few days earlier. Blair was the strength that Thomas needed. She held him tight as the honor guard approached. When Hunter's body arrived at the airport they also had a flag folding ceremony. She insisted that Thomas have that flag. It was the flag that had draped the coffin from Iraq to home.

Thomas walked around outside and gazed into the woods behind his house. The birds were having a feeding frenzy around the berry bush in his backyard. He hadn't been in the large yard since the night of the funeral. He'd sat at a small table on the porch with some friends that night. The house was sort of a renovated farm house that was in his family for years. *That's odd*, Thomas thought, as he looked at the back of his property. He walked to the end of his lot and saw that the fence had been broken. It was a split rail fence that he had put up about ten years ago around the whole yard. There was over 150 feet of fence along the back of the house. As he walked closer he saw that there were tire tracks in the woods where the fence had been broken. Thomas inspected the tracks and headed back inside. *Better call Captain Douglas,* he thought. None of this made any sense to Thomas. It appeared that there was nothing missing. *Why were my house and Blair's apartment both ransacked?* He knew it was strange but there was no answer to the puzzle.

Captain Douglas was an old Marine friend and would know what to look for Thomas thought. He let him know about the fence being broken and the tire tracks. Maybe this would lead to the people who broke into his home. He didn't know how they missed seeing the broken fence after the initial break-in report was completed. He went back into the living room after he talked to the captain and sat in his recliner. He looked at the folded American flag in its frame and sighed. The captain said that he would be over in a little bit to survey the yard. Thomas didn't know what else to do. He just sat in a chair and gazed out the front window.

Four

Ahmad looked at the sky as if he had never seen it before. The nightmare of being in Abu Ghraib prison for the past two months was finally over. He had been picked up in a daily roundup of Iraqis by the military police. He was suspected of being a terrorist.

The prison was named after the town it was built in. Abu Ghraib was an Iraqi city about 32 km west of Baghdad. It had become internationally known as a place where Saddam Hussein tortured and executed rebels. The prison came to the notice of the world when American television publicized several graphic and disturbing photos of Coalition prisoner abuse there. The Coalition changed the name to Camp Redemption and actually located its prisoners in a tent area on the outside of the prison walls. It was also used by the Coalition as a forward operations base.

Ahmad was detained and questioned many times. He knew that the American and British troops who questioned the prisoners would get information from some of them but not him. He was strong of will and would never give them any information. It was important to stay free.

He was driven back to the center of the city with another released prisoner, close to where the American troops had helped the uprising of Iraqis pull down the statue of Saddam. The driver zigzagged through underpasses to make sure that they would avoid anyone who might drop a grenade on them. They passed a Humvee that had soldiers on top of it. Their gunners were going side to side to make sure that they protected the men who traveled in their group. Iraq had forced the Army to change its tactics. It was more of a "plan-on-the-go" type of operation than the conventional warfare that most of the men had been trained for.

Ahmad told them, "I want out. I will walk the rest of the way." He got out of the back of the Jeep and started walking. The soldiers watched him for a few minutes and then headed back to their camp.

After the Jeep was out of view, he changed direction and headed toward a mosque. He entered and went to a side room where he met his friend, El Hassen. Hassen was also a Saddam loyalist who had eluded the Coalition troops although he too had been picked up and spent time in Abu Ghraib prison. The two men were happy to be reunited. They were both loyal to the regime of Saddam Hussein and had unfinished business. They had not seen each other for months but were aware of recent issues that would change their mission.

During the early occupation many Iraqis had been detained at Abu Ghraib and then set free. It was a difficult time for both the American and British troops. The Iraqi army had been scattered throughout the region and there was no local authority to seek assistance from. The identification of the men who were taken into custody was almost impossible to verify.

Ahmad and Hassen entered into the small room where a group of men had been talking. "You are free my brother. Praise Allah! We have much to do."

Iraq's economy was dominated by the oil sector, which had provided about ninety-five percent of its wealth. The eight-year war with Iran and now the fall of the Ba'ath party led these men to plot together. They needed the western influence out of Iraq so they could regain some of their power. Ahmad and Hassen went to yet another room in the mosque. They were greeted by a small group of men. Among them was Muhammad Assar.

"Praise Allah," they said. "Our brothers are free!"

"We have been chosen by Allah for a great task."

"Our brother, Commander Muhammad, knows our discipline. We will be strong for the mission ahead."

Iraq was a nation that had a long history of strife and its factions were dedicated to their causes. From Iraq's early beginning, it was now a nation with a population of over twenty-six million people trying to assimilate into a democracy.

Ahmad and Hassen would be the catalysts to lead the group in their plans to get back into power. It would take a critical turn of events and they felt that they knew where it could be found. Muhammad had details of importance that would send them on a search. The search would gather important documents that they needed to regain a foothold in the country. The Coalition forces had steered clear of the activity in local mosques because of religious implications. It was a time when they had hoped to earn support from the Iraqi people and by honoring their right to worship was just one way to show them the respect that would help to further the Coalition's goals.

****

In another meeting, Afghan rebels met in the southern city of Kandahar, Afghanistan. This was a largely unsettled area, long a stronghold of Taliban support. The Taliban had largely unskilled but highly motivated followers. They had another mission in mind, that of creating havoc on the American troops. Their leader was now enlisting men for suicide attacks on the Americans who occupied their province.

Afghanistan was torn with the al-Qaida and Taliban terrorists taking refuge there. The insurgents would continue to use guerrilla tactics. This group was headed by El Jaafi. He was a direct lieutenant of Osama bin Laden. His band of cutthroats had no morals and he was a bloodthirsty terrorist. El Jaafi was planning to take a small group of his men who were more highly trained on the special mission. Some of these men had lived in the States and found a way to assimilate into normal American lives. They attended universities and some had gone to pilot school to learn how to fly. These men made up the core of supporters. Al Yawer was a pivotal member of this group. He was a licensed pilot and knew his way around.

Al Yawer was a very smart man and El Jaafi counted heavily on his knowledge. He knew that all the men would trust his instincts and orders. They had a special relationship. It all went back to the war with Iran. Although El Jaafi was older, he and Al Yawer would act as one when it came to planning a mission of this magnitude.

The men would never question any commands and Al Yawer offered them the ability to infiltrate and keep their disguise until the time was ready to strike.

El Jaafi knew that with this group of men they could travel to the United States and meet without much suspicion. They made their plans to travel separately so as not to have a problem with the new security that had been put into place at all the airports.

****

Back in Baghdad the meeting in the mosque was coming to a close. Ahmad and Hassen had both spent time in Abu Ghraib prison and were lucky enough to be let free. Ahmad had been able to take the identification of another Iraqi who had been killed in the invasion. He kept that on him and was thought to be that man when he was at Abu Ghraib prison. It was critical for all the Saddam loyalists to either go into hiding or to protect their real identification with a false one.

Ahmad had been an integral member of Saddam's inner circle. He was highly motivated to protect the Iraq that Saddam had built. He had been one of the important figures in helping Saddam hide his gold and critical weapons.

The news of Saddam's capture and possible trial upset him greatly. The thought that Saddam could appear before a special tribunal and that he may face the death penalty saddened Ahmad. The Americans and British had forced the new Iraqi government to deal this fate to Saddam. The charges of killing rival politicians, gassing Kurds, invading Kuwait and suppressing Shiite uprisings were preposterous. Ahmad knew that the death sentence was part of the Iraqi legal system before the U.S.-led invasion two years ago, but he felt that the U.S. and Britain were putting pressure on the new Iraqi government to carry out this deed.

The group of Saddam supporters met in the mosque to plan their mission. They knew from information they received that they must travel to the United States. The group included three men who had lived in southern California and would be able to gain entrance to the United States. Another man, along with Ahmad and Hassen, was Jasim Muhammad. Jasim was born in Long Beach, California. His father was involved in the early development of computer chips. His family returned to Iraq when his father's employer outsourced his job. Many Iraqi men had been to universities in the west. It would help them when they traveled because they understood American culture. When he returned to Iraq, Jasim met with the Ba'ath party heads and became a Saddam loyalist. He was never able to understand why his father had lost his job in the United States and blamed the country for their fate. He would be a key player in getting into southern California. It was once his home and he was a U.S. citizen. He would be the first one to travel and would set up their headquarters. He was a pilot and his training would come in handy. The West Coast offered unusual terrain and a small airplane would help scout it out.

Ahmad wanted Jasim to prepare a safe place for them in Long Beach. He figured that they could travel up the coast to Santa Monica from Long Beach and have easy access to either planes or ships in the event that they had to escape. The men made their plans with the mission clear. Ahmad was the group's leader and he would travel last to the United States through London. Because he had attended university in London he knew that it would be easy to get there and be able to travel from there to California. He would detail the plans to the group of men. They would find the key documents and help their group regain the power that they were seeking.

International travel had changed greatly since 9/11. The United States had employed many airport screeners and required that other countries having flights coming into the U.S. do the same thing. New documents would be prepared for the men. Ahmad would make sure they would get to their destination.

Five

Blair walked into the living room of Ashley's apartment. "Wow, I guess I was more tired than I thought. Ashley, thank you so much for letting me spend the night. I think it was the first real sleep I've gotten in weeks." Ashley's cat, Clark, rubbed himself along Blair's legs.

"No problem. After we get dressed we'll go to your place and see what we can clean up. Together we'll be able to get a lot done."

"We also have to fill out that report for Officer Tuttle."

"We should call a locksmith to change your door lock."

"That's a good idea. Maybe one can come out when we are there later today."

The two girls walked down Santa Monica Boulevard toward the Promenade. They were going to meet Blake. He said he wanted to help put Blair's apartment back together. The three friends met on the Promenade at the corner of Third and Santa Monica Boulevard. It was a short walk to Arizona Avenue and Blair's apartment. There was a cool breeze over the Promenade from the Pacific Ocean. This was normal for the month of May. The walk to Blair's apartment helped as the three discussed the break-in.

They went up in the elevator to the second floor. Apartment 21A was the fourth one on the right side of the hallway. Blair opened the door and they all walked in. "I just don't understand how they got in. Nothing seems to be damaged around the door."

"People who break into homes have tools that help them open your locks. Bet that's what they did Blair." The three looked around for a place to start.

"Things are not too bad," Ashley said.

"I can move some of the bigger things," Blake said, as he

33

turned the table back on its legs. There were three chairs that he put around the table. He looked around to see what he should do next. "I'll get a trash bag so you can put anything broken in there." He was surprised to see that most items were just turned over on the floor. Only a few items were actually damaged.

"I might have to keep those items for insurance purposes."

"You're right," said Ashley.

They had been at it for about an hour and a half and were making great progress when the phone rang. "Hi, I'm looking for Mrs. Blair Adams," said the woman.

"I'm Mrs. Adams," Blair answered.

"I'm Special Agent Jones with the Federal Bureau of Investigation."

"The FBI? What do you want with me?"

"I'm so sorry to bother you at this time; we want to offer our condolences on the loss of your husband. I would like to meet with you to go over some details that are necessary regarding Mr. Adams and his time in the military."

"Why does the FBI want to talk to me?"

"Your husband, like many other American soldiers, may have had details that our department is responsible for closing. This is normal and part of the new Homeland Security effort. It's kind of like a family debriefing."

"I'm still not sure why the FBI would be involved. I don't know anything."

"Mrs. Adams, I can give you those details when we meet."

"I would like some idea of what you're talking about before we meet," Blair said.

"We have to ask you some questions because you had been out of the country with your husband several times during his time in the military."

Blair thought back about the time that Hunter had been wounded in Afghanistan and was sent to Germany. She was so concerned that she got approval from the Army to fly there and see him. He had been shot in the shoulder and also had damaged his teeth while diving over a barricade. Blair started thinking about that trip and some unusual things came to mind.

"If I agree to meet you Ms. Jones, can I bring one of my

friends with me?"

"We would prefer that you met with us alone."

"Us?"

"Of course, I'll have a person from our office with me to record any information that you may provide that can help close our file. Mrs. Adams, I can assure you that we just want to clear up a few questions and then you will be free to do what you need to."

"Can I call you back, Agent Jones?"

"How about if I call you back later, Mrs. Adams. We can set the time for our meeting then."

Blair agreed to be home later for that call and said good-bye.

"Who was that on the phone?" Blake asked.

"I'm really not sure. She said she was from the FBI."

"What does the FBI want with you?"

"I'm not sure but I have to think. Blake, can you stay with me?"

"Sure."

She was more confused than ever and had no idea what to do next. She knew that Ashley would have to go to work and she needed someone to keep her company. Blake could give her some ideas if she only knew the questions to ask. Ashley listened to their conversation. Once they stopped talking, Ashley and Blake went back to straightening the apartment. Blair sat at the table and was deep in thought. Her mind raced back to Germany and her trip there. Hunter had been in a hospital, his right shoulder was in a cast and they had made a mold so they could make him a bridge for his missing teeth. He was feeling much better when she arrived and he arranged to take them on a trip to Switzerland. He wanted to show her the beautiful scenery. He told her they would have to travel as students so as not to create any question as to why an American soldier was traveling around Switzerland. It seemed odd to Blair at the time but Hunter had multiple passports. He said it was to protect him as he traveled out of uniform. Why pretend they were students? Now the FBI is involved. "Oh Hunter, what am I to do?" she cried aloud.

Blair wondered why her husband had passports with

different names. How was he involved with the FBI? She could not stop her train of thought until Blake said, "Thanks Ashley. Do you want us to walk you to work?"

"No, it's only a few blocks."

"I'm so sorry Ashley. I'm just a ball of nerves. Please let us walk with you."

"Blair you're almost done here. You and Blake could finish up in about a half hour. I'll be okay."

"We will come to The Pub and eat dinner after," she said to Ashley.

"That sounds good. I know a lot of people will be glad to see you. Maybe you will get more details from that FBI agent."

****

Agent Jones told Tony Baxter that it wasn't going to be as easy as they hoped. "If she agrees to meet me tomorrow, I might get her away from that apartment so you can go back. It has to be there. We must find the document before anyone else does. This time search her place but don't do any damage. We can't afford any more suspicion. I don't want her to know that anyone had been in that apartment again."

Her colleague, Tony Baxter, had been in the Washington Bureau and had been recently transferred to southern California. Tony was a veteran of the bureau and had received many commendations for his work. He could accomplish the task handed to him, although he felt that he should be in charge. That he had to take orders from a woman bothered him. He would let Ms. Jones set up the meeting with Blair Adams but he would handle the apartment search. Allisa Jones had received an email from Hunter's unit in Baghdad. It was forwarded from the Washington Bureau. Baxter knew she received the email but she did not share it with him. *Damn female boss.* He wondered what information she had and why she didn't share it with him.

****

Blake and Blair finished their work at the apartment and

decided to head to The Pub to meet Ashley for dinner. Everything had been pretty much put back into place and she didn't find anything missing. She would call Officer Tuttle after they ate. The two of them made their way down Third Street and through the tourists in the Promenade. One of her friends was playing his guitar on the corner of Third and Broadway. Blair stopped to say hello. She always supported all her friends and he was close to finishing his first CD. She dropped a ten dollar bill into his guitar case and they continued their walk. The Pub was ahead on the corner of Santa Monica Boulevard and Third. It was nice to be greeted by so many people and well wishers.

Many of The Pub's regulars were glad to see Blair as she and Blake had taken a seat at an outside table. Olly came over and gave her a hug. "I just want to help you, honey," she said. "You take as much time off as necessary. We'll help you with everything."

Olly and Sonia were partners in The Pub. Sonia was from Liverpool and had dedicated an entire wall of The Pub to the Beatles. She had seen them play when she lived in Liverpool and loved their work. Olly sat down with them. Blair informed her about the conversation with the FBI agent, Ms. Jones. Like Blair, she wasn't sure what to make of it but suggested, "You have to meet her and see what she wants."

"I guess you're right. Maybe I'll arrange the meeting here so you can make sure everything is safe."

"Good idea," she said. Blake agreed. "You could even meet her upstairs where it's quiet if she wants." The Pub had an upstairs that had video games and pool tables for patrons. There were about five dining tables and it was usually quiet there during the daytime. Most of the day patrons would either want to eat outside or along the windows in the front of The Pub. The glass windows would often be slid open during the day to let the cool breeze in. Blair felt better about the possible meeting and knew that having her friends close would be the protection she needed. She would suggest The Pub to the Agent as their meeting place when she called back.

Jones told her partner, Tony Baxter, that he needed to be close to Blair's apartment when she called. "I'll call your cell phone so that you can watch to see when she leaves. Make sure she doesn't leave someone behind."

"I know what to do," he said. "Just set the meeting up; I'll do the rest." Baxter resented her. The fact that they did not find the documents they were seeking made their relationship even more strained. Jones wished that he was more cooperative but she knew that he had the experience needed for this assignment.

Blair was pleased that nothing was missing when she gave Officer Tuttle the report and only found some dishes and a few small items off her coffee table broken. "Not enough for an insurance report," she said. "My dad made sure that we had insurance just in case of an event like this."

Blair and Blake finished their dinner at The Pub and knew that they needed to head back to her apartment so that when Allisa Jones called Blair would be there. The walk back to her apartment was good. Things felt more normal after dinner. They went up to her apartment and waited for the agent to call. It was just about half an hour later when the phone rang and Blair answered.

"Good afternoon Mrs. Adams, this is Agent Jones."

"Hello Agent Jones."

"I hope that you have thought things over about meeting me," Ms. Jones said. "Mrs. Adams, our meeting won't be very long and I won't bring anyone else with me if that makes you feel better."

"Yes it does." She was now feeling a little better about the meeting with Agent Jones and the FBI involvement. She knew the location at The Pub would be safe and with just her and Ms. Jones there it should not be too threatening. "Agent Jones I was thinking. I work here in Santa Monica and it would be easiest for me if you met me where I work." She hoped that the Agent would agree.

"That's not a problem as long as we can have about an hour to talk Mrs. Adams. It would be best if there is a quiet place to sit."

"Yes that can be arranged. Call me Blair please; it makes it seem not so formal."

"Sure, and you can call me Allisa if it helps you."

"Thanks, how about meeting tomorrow around three at The Pub. It's on the corner of Santa Monica Boulevard and the Promenade."

"That sounds good Blair. You're sure there is a quiet place where we won't be disturbed?"

"Yes, they have a large upstairs room that is used for meetings and overflow crowds especially during the soccer tournaments." The three p.m. time would also be good because the lunch crowd would be gone and it would be a little quieter.

The meeting was set. Blair called Olly at The Pub to tell her what she and Ms. Jones agreed to.

"Sounds good to me," she said. "We will make sure everything is set up for you and we know the only way out is through the downstairs exit so it should be safe. Were you able to finish up at your apartment?"

"Yes. We got everything picked up and put away, and I have to stop by the post office for a special delivery package before I come to The Pub tomorrow. Blake and Ashley were a great help." She looked at the special delivery note she found on her door when she had returned home. *Probably something from my dad* she thought. He usually sent things UPS but guess he sent this regular mail. *Wonder why they didn't leave the package at the door?*

Six

The plane flight to New York LaGuardia Airport was without event. Al Yawer made it through security checks both at his layover in London and when he departed Iraq. Having two separate tickets with different destinations would stop anyone who was watching him travel. His final destination was easy to plan from London. He exited the London Airport where he met another operative with a second set of travel documents and identification. London had a vast terrorist cell that had started to make plans for bombings in the city. Their plans were to cause local unrest and political upheaval because of Tony Blair's government's involvement in Iraq. The new set of identification was pivotal. This helped him when he boarded his next flight for New York. He would travel to New York using the new ID. The CIA and Airport Security still didn't share information. He knew this and because of this, entering the United States would be easy.

Once he gathered his luggage at LaGuardia, he walked through the airport and stopped at a local sports bar along the Spirit Airline concourse. He ordered a sandwich and sat at a small table along the windows. Another traveler sat behind him and put his small bag next to Yawer's suitcase. He ate half of his food and gathered his suitcase plus the small bag that the traveler behind him had left. Yawer left the airport and waited for a taxi cab. While waiting for his cab, he opened the small bag left for him and found details with a location for him to travel to. He asked the cab driver to take him to an address in the Bronx near Yankee Stadium.

El Jaafi waited in the safe house for Yawer. He knew from calls he received that the transfer in London went well and that he would soon be meeting his contact in the LaGuardia Airport. The house was on the lower side of the Bronx not too far from Yankee Stadium and the subway. Once they were together in the Bronx, travel through New York would be easy with the subway system. You could transfer from one line to another and get anywhere in the Metro area in a flash. The plan was set. Yawer and El Jaafi would travel to Bridgewater, Pennsylvania, and check out the home of Thomas Adams. They would look for the documents that they knew had to exist. It was ironic that while in London Yawer passed another traveler. El Hassen was waiting for his plane flight to Los Angeles LAX Airport. Hassen was familiar with the London Airport because he and Ahmad had spent time there at the university.

****

The flight to LAX was tedious due to the many short flights taken to get to his final destination. While in London, Hassen stayed with friends who had attended university with him and Ahmad. They were also operatives and helped him set up the plans for the rest of the group. Ahmad had traveled a few days earlier than Hassen. When he got to California he found the place that Jasim had rented for them in Long Beach. Once he was settled in they would start their plan to find the documents. They had gone to a local airport and rented a plane to canvass the area by air.

The coastline along the shore from Long Beach to Santa Monica was beautiful. It was not unusual to see small aircraft in flight daily along this route. Most were tourists who hoped to get a glimpse of the homes of the rich and famous movie stars. Homes would sometimes look like they were on stilts on the mountain sides overlooking the ocean. A flyer announcing that there was an airplane or helicopter flight available for sightseeing along the California coast could always be found. Many ex-airline pilots found it financially rewarding to enter into this sort of business. The California experience was different than anywhere else in the world. While eating lunch or dinner in a local restaurant one could find his or herself sitting next to Julia Roberts or Dick Van Dyke. Locals found this normal and part of everyday life, but the tourists from Kentucky or Michigan who came to the area would search for just one celebrity finding. They would buy maps that would lead them through Malibu, Brentwood and Beverly Hills to the homes of the stars.

The men found a spot that would let them land and take off when they returned to Long Beach. Ahmad would wait for his friend Hassen and they would travel together to Santa Monica while the remainder of his group would plan their exit by small plane to a safe haven in the northwest before returning to Iraq. Hassen and Ahmad were key to this important operation.

****

El Jaafi set the plans with his men and waited for Al Yawer to arrive. The lower Bronx was a virtual mix of ethnic people and they would not seem to be out of place there. Jaafi had been in New York many times and was there when the Trade Center was attacked on the 11th of September, 2001. He had done some local reconnaissance for a group of men who had planned to drive a car bomb into the financial district. They were still in the planning stages when they turned on their television and saw what had happened. They had thought up a plan that would have caused much concern and some damage but never did they think anyone could have created such devastating results. They all cheered in their apartment when they saw the damage the planes caused at the World Trade Center and knew that they must leave the area before a roundup of suspects took place. El Jaafi and his group separated so that they could leave the area and possibly make it back to Afghanistan safely. He found it a little more difficult due to almost all the airports on the East Coast being closed after the damage in New York and to the Pentagon. They had to lay low for months until travel relaxed and they were able to return home.

Al Yawer came by taxi to the safe house in the Bronx. He found the group had set up plans for the trip to Bridgewater and their exit back to Afghanistan if they found the information they were seeking. Jaafi knew that he could set the plans for travel to and from Bridgewater but the actual attempt to get the documents that they were looking for would be the plan that Yawer would devise. The group knew that he would get them to Bridgewater. He was a cunning person and had been pivotal in similar actions. He

42

would direct the men as to what their part of the plan would be. No one would stand in his way and if they did, they would not live to tell of it.

Yawer studied the document in the bag left for him at the LaGuardia Airport. It detailed Thomas Adams' address and that it was his son who had been to the castle of Saddam's that held the secret documents they were seeking. The plan would be put into place.

The safe house in the Bronx was an old two-story duplex that was on a quiet street. It was close to Yankee Stadium. Yawer found that the group had rented a Chevy Malibu. They had reserved rooms at the Days Inn outside of Bridgewater. He would study the lay of the land and make sure that they had access to leave the area in case they had to use force to complete their goal. This group of Afghan travelers would meet for a few days to plan their mission and then leave to return home after hopefully finding the documents. If the documents were not there, they would have to travel to southern California and search the home of Blair Adams. When he arrived at the safe house in the Bronx, he and Jaafi finalized their plans.

He suggested that they should travel to Bridgewater prior to their plan taking place to check out the area. They decided to go early the next day. The drive from the Bronx through New York took them along Highway 278 and over the Verrazano Narrows Bridge. They would follow 278 to Interstate 95 that would take them south toward Philadelphia. They had to travel through a few toll roads as they made their way through Staten Island. When they got to Elizabeth, New Jersey, they got on I-95 south. The trip would take about three to four hours depending on traffic. There was a lot of construction along the highway but traffic was light. They stopped in Mansfield Square, New Jersey, to review the area map and have lunch.

Al Yawer had suggested this would be a better place to stay and he and El Jaafi rented a room at the Days Inn just off the highway. They would return to Mansfield Square after checking out the Bridgewater home of Thomas Adams. The ride to Bridgewater from Mansfield Square took less than forty-five minutes. They traveled down I-95 to Highway 276. Thomas' house was just off Highway 13 close to the bridge that crossed the Neshaminy River. Yawer drove their Malibu down the street in front of the Adams' house and was concerned when he saw a local police car in the circular drive. He drove past slowly and tried to observe what was going on. There was another police car in the backyard of the Adams' house. It seemed that some men were looking into the woods but they could not make out what was going on from the street. They decided to return to Mansfield Square and advise their group in the Bronx that they would remain in Mansfield Square. This would have to be their headquarters, and due to the police at the Adams' house they must accelerate their plans.

****

Back in California, Hassen made it to Long Beach and met Ahmad. They knew that they may have to make another trip across to Philadelphia if their search in California did not pan out. They felt that the documents they were searching for would be the key to help their coalition of conspirators gain the power that they were seeking. Hassen was brought up to speed about the coastline. They rented a Ford Focus and would drive up from Long Beach on Highway 405 toward Highway 10 and Santa Monica. Ahmad had seen the area from the air and now was seeing it for the first time from the ground.

They found a parking lot on Fourth Street and walked toward the Promenade. They knew that Blair Adams lived in an apartment on Arizona Boulevard and that she worked in a pub a few blocks away. They hoped that they could find an easy access to her apartment, and if so, maybe do a quick search of the place. Hassen held a picture of Blair that they had downloaded from the internet. They found it when they searched the Hollywood catalog of members of the Screen Actors Guild. She was blond and very beautiful he thought. They had picked up a map of Santa Monica and were happy that most everything was in walking distance. They reached the corner of Third and Santa Monica Boulevard. They saw The Pub where she worked. They noted that it was small but it appeared that it had a second story. There were windows that overlooked the Promenade from the second floor. They also noted that The Pub wrapped around the corner and had about six tables on the street. If things didn't pan out at her apartment they would make a search of The Pub after hours. Hassen suggested they walk the rest of the way toward her apartment. It was only a couple of blocks to Arizona and they saw the address they were looking for. It was a three-story building that appeared to be relatively new. There was a movie theater across the street and many restaurants and gift shops on both sides.

They sat down at a small table kitty-cornered from the apartment and ordered coffee. They noticed that the residents who came and went from the apartment building were using a key card at the door to enter. They also noted that there was a small police sub-station that looked into the front of the apartment building from across the street. They drank their coffee and watched for about an hour. Ahmad nodded to him when they saw a young blond leaving the apartment building. They looked at the picture that he held and agreed it was Blair Adams. She was talking to a young man who came out of the building with her. The two walked along the Promenade in the direction of The Pub which they had seen earlier. Ahmad said, "This may be our best opportunity to gain entrance to her apartment." They paid for their coffees and walked across the street toward the apartment building.

A young couple carrying a lot of bags and a large box were also just going up to the front door. Hassen offered to help and they were very appreciative. The couple had just returned from a shopping trip to the IKEA store in Los Angeles and purchased items for their new apartment. The couple did not know many people in their building but thought that these two young men were very nice to help them. They held the door and helped the young man carry a box that appeared to be a piece of furniture that you had to assemble. They asked if the young couple needed help getting the items to their floor, but they said, "No thanks," as their apartment was on the first floor. As the two men helped the young couple another guest had also entered the building. He didn't talk to anyone but just looked down as the others carried the bags and the box. The man was a tall individual who was wearing a suit and seemed all business. He hurried into the elevator and pressed the button for the desired floor.

Tony Baxter thought to himself, *what a lucky break finding that group with all their packages.* He had been watching the apartment when he saw Mrs. Adams and a friend leave. He did not want to use the tools of his trade and create any suspicion. *I'll just enter with them while they struggle with their bags.* Tony got into the elevator and went directly to the second floor. Apartment 21A was the fourth one on the right and entry was easy for him. Being cautious, he knocked first to ensure no one was still in the apartment. His skill was getting into places he didn't belong. He put his pick into the door lock and was able to quickly gain entrance to the apartment. He noted that the apartment had been put back together and figured that he would have at least an hour for this search. Tony hoped that he didn't need too long since he had already checked most of it out. He wanted to look through the top of the closet and go through the refrigerator. Sometimes people would hide things there. He noticed that a small bag was on the side of the table. Tony looked in and found that there were only a few broken dishes in it.

Downstairs the young couple thanked Ahmad and Hassen for their help with their packages.

"You're welcome." The two men waited for the couple to leave then they entered the elevator. They had noticed that the front door had a list of tenants with their apartment numbers. They checked the list for the apartment with Blair Adams name on it. It was listed as 21A. *How lucky,* they thought. It was easy access to the apartment building and now they can search the place. They knew that Mrs. Adams had gone out so they moved toward the apartment. Looking down the hall to make sure no one was coming; Ahmad put his hand into his pocket and slid out the tool that he carried to gain entrance into the apartment.

Baxter turned abruptly and looked surprised as he heard noise at the door and it began to open. He had no place to hide. He stepped back toward the small bathroom and drew his gun. Ahmad entered the apartment followed by Hassen. The two intruders moved quickly through the apartment entrance and closed the door behind them. The waited until they were inside and then started speaking in Arabic. They could see that it was one large room with a short wall separating the bedroom from the rest of the apartment. Ahmad turned toward the kitchen area when Baxter flew out of the bathroom gun drawn. "Put your hands up. I'm with the FBI."

He didn't see that Ahmad held a knife in his right hand. Ahmad reared back and threw the knife at Baxter. The knife hit him; he was stabbed in the left shoulder. Baxter fell to the floor but was able to get off two shots. The first shot entered through the skull of Hassen scattering brains and blood all over the bedroom wall. The second shot went through the ceiling as Baxter was falling backwards. Ahmad ducked and aimed his weapon at the man on the carpet and fired as Baxter was rolling on the floor. The flurry of bullets struck Baxter in his leg and the right arm. Baxter was able to roll over and return fire. His shot hit Ahmad in the chest. Ahmad fell to the floor clutching his chest as blood puddle on the carpet. Baxter lay on the carpet and passed out from the blood flowing from his leg and shoulder wounds. There was a commotion in the hallway as the three men lay motionless on Blair's apartment floor bleeding.

Baxter had been there for only a few minutes when Officer Tuttle along with two other officers and approached the apartment door. With guns drawn, they carefully entered the apartment to a scene of blood and bodies. They had been called by residents who heard the gunfire. Tuttle could not believe his eyes. It appeared that there were possibly three dead bodies in the apartment. Wasn't this the same apartment that he had been to earlier for a break-in? Who were these men and why in this apartment? Where was the resident he had just sat with? They searched the apartment to make sure she wasn't in there. It was clear that there were only three bodies and no one else in the apartment. Could someone have escaped? He made a call to the station and ordered an EMS unit and the medical examiner to the scene. Tuttle hoped his chief would send more help so that they could search the area for any other possible suspects. They put an APB out for any suspicious-looking individuals in the area. Officer Tuttle checked around the room while the other two officers inspected the three men on the ground. Two men were dead and one was still alive. They searched the men for ID. One man had an FBI identification badge with his name on it. It said he was Tony Baxter, special agent, out of the Los Angeles Bureau. Tuttle knew that the small police force in Santa Monica had handled a few cases but never anything of this magnitude. He also wondered what was going on and how Blair Adams was involved. He waited for the EMS unit to take the wounded FBI man to the hospital. He wanted to start a search for Mrs. Adams.

Seven

Blair entered The Pub and was greeted by Olly who was behind the bar. Regular patrons also waved hello as she approached Olly. "Your guest is upstairs waiting for you. She is the only one up there. Would you like something to drink?"

"Just some ice water, please." Blair never drank any soft drinks. She was a health nut and always ate organic foods and drank bottled water. Her only vice was an occasional alcoholic drink. She loved different wines. She handed Olly the small brown package that she had picked up at the Santa Monica Post Office.

"What's in the package?" Olly asked.

"Not sure," Blair said. "I'm afraid to open it. It came from Iraq, Hunter's old command address. It may be something he sent me before he died. I'm not ready to open it yet."

Olly put the package behind the bar on a lower shelf and said, "When you're ready to open it I'll be there for you."

Blair went upstairs and saw a woman dressed in a dark blue suit looking over some material on the table in front of her. Ms. Jones was a very good-looking woman who understated her features. Her hair was pulled back and she had dark rimmed glasses that didn't quite fit. Early in her career she had been assigned to the New York Bureau and did some undercover work. She had some great success. She had been re-assigned to the Philadelphia Bureau and worked as a special agent for a few years before being promoted to the Washington Bureau. One of her early tasks involved following leads after the planes hit the Pentagon during the September 11 attacks. She was pivotal in finding a terrorist cell that had set up its operation in Maryland not too far from the Capitol. She also worked with the head of the Philadelphia Bureau and they had found an individual who was about to sell state secrets. Ms. Jones was given many awards for her work in this search. She was promoted to special agent in Los Angeles, California. Her main job was to continue a watch for possible terrorist cells along the West Coast from Long Beach to Malibu. She had two agents who reported to her. One was Tony Baxter; the other was Justin Wallace, a younger man in his early 30s. She reported to Dean Curry, the bureau chief in the Los Angeles FBI office. Allisa Jones knew Tony Baxter was watching Blair's apartment so he could search it when she left for the meeting. Justin Wallace was positioned across from The Pub at Hooter's watching as Blair entered. He was her lookout to make sure that Blair was alone when she entered. Allisa Jones was very thorough. She did not want anything to go wrong. Jones felt that Blair may not be aware that her husband had found what could be very critical information in a recent search of one of Saddam's castles. Often family members were unaware of what missions their spouses were involved in. That was the way it was supposed to be. Agent Jones knew that after Captain Montgomery helped search through Hunter's belongings and found nothing that the documents must be somewhere else. She had received a copy of Montgomery's email the day before. It was her hope that Blair may know something to help in this search. How could she get that information without alerting Blair as to the reason for the meeting? Jones was the only person sitting upstairs when Blair walked toward a small table and introduced herself.

"I'm Blair Adams and I'm guessing you are Agent Jones."

"Thank you for meeting me and please call me Allisa. Have a seat, please."

"I'm still not sure why you want to meet with me, Agent Jones."

"I understand," she answered. "This is just a formality to close our files. First of all, I want again to offer our condolences for your loss. I'm sure that this has been a trying time for you and if there is any way we can help make it easier, please let me know."

"This has been very difficult," said Blair. "Not all of it has sunk in yet. I did find out that the FBI will be forwarding a death certificate which is confusing because I figured it would come from the Army."

"It comes from the FBI in some cases, Blair. Due to the Office of Homeland Security overseeing all the agencies, certain documents are forwarded through the FBI." Agent Jones saw that Blair was a bit tense but hoped that by answering some of her questions she could gain Blair's confidence and eventually Blair would, in turn, answer her questions.

Olly came to the top of the stairs and asked, "Can I bring you a menu?" She wanted to make sure that Blair was okay and figured by doing this no one would suspect that she was protecting her. Jones knew that Blair was employed at The Pub and that the owner was her friend. She wasn't concerned with the location of the meeting, she just needed all the information that she could gather. She also wanted to get Blair out of her apartment so that Tony Baxter could make one more search. His first effort brought no answers and was cut short when there was a fire alarm in the building.

"Ms. Jones," Blair asked, "would you like some lunch?"

"Please call me Allisa. Not now, but thank you."

Agent Wallace continued his watch of The Pub from across the street. He wanted to hear from Tony Baxter that the search had been completed. He would phone Ms. Jones with the results but was not to call her unless they had urgent information. She did not want to alert Blair to anything that was happening. This meeting would be a time to gather information and maybe, if necessary, set the stage for a second meeting. They continued to talk about the role of the FBI in cases like this. Agent Jones was explaining the role of her office while getting to know Blair. Although she had a complete file on Blair Adams, she hoped that having her talk about herself would put her at ease and would give her the information she was seeking.

Officer Tuttle entered The Pub. It was not unusual to see him walking his beat during the day. He asked Olly, "Do you know where Mrs. Adams might be?"

"She's upstairs meeting with someone; is everything okay?"

"I have to talk to her. It's important."

Before she could say anything else he turned toward the

stairway. Olly called to him but he didn't answer. He continued up the stairs and when he saw Blair he said, "I'm sorry to bother you but it's very important."

Blair turned and looked startled. "What is it, Officer?"

"I'm sorry to tell you, but your apartment had another break-in."

"Oh no!" Blair jumped up. "I can't believe that my apartment has been broken into again." Agent Jones looked around like someone had just dropped a bomb.

"The problem is much worse this time. There were three men in your apartment; two of them are dead and one is seriously wounded."

"What?" Blair slumped back into her chair and was visibly shaken.

"We got a call from a neighbor on the third floor that some bullets were fired into their apartment from below. We headed over right away when there were more calls about numerous shootings on the second floor. We went down the hall and saw your door ajar. When we entered there were three men laying on the floor and blood everywhere. Two of them are dead and the other guy is critical."

Agent Jones was now standing and found herself asking about the one man still alive. Both the officer and Blair looked at her. She knew that she should not have entered the conversation, but the shock of this event and having Tony Baxter at the apartment caused the slip-up.

Officer Tuttle asked, "Who are you?"

"I'm a friend of Blair's," she answered.

Blair turned back toward the officer. "She's not my friend; she needed to ask me some questions about my husband. She's with the FBI."

Tuttle looked at Agent Jones then back at Blair, "Well maybe she can answer part of this. One of the men that had been shot is an FBI Agent."

Blair turned and looked at Agent Jones.

"I will explain everything."

Officer Tuttle looked at both women. "What's going on?" he said. Before Blair could answer, Jones stood and introduced herself to him. "I'm Agent Allisa Jones of the FBI."

He looked bewildered. "What do you have to do with this?" Blair sat back down and tears started to form in her eyes.

Agent Jones said, "I can explain everything, Blair."

Officer Tuttle said, "I want to hear this too!"

"First," she said, "what about the FBI agent who was shot?"

"He was bleeding badly and we rushed him to the hospital. Multiple wounds to the leg and both shoulders but it looks like he'll make it," Officer Tuttle said.

"What hospital was he taken to?"

"Los Angeles Memorial on Washington Boulevard," he answered. "But before you go anywhere, I have some questions that I need answered."

"Officer, this is an FBI matter," Ms. Jones answered.

"Not so quick lady," Officer Tuttle said. "The murder of two men and shooting of another happened in Santa Monica and it is in our jurisdiction."

"I need to call one of my men to check on Agent Baxter," Ms. Jones said as she dialed Wallace who was still stationed across the street. "Wallace, you need to get to Los Angeles Memorial on Washington Boulevard. Baxter has been shot. I'll call headquarters and meet you there in a little while." Tuttle and Blair looked at Agent Jones and wondered what was going on. Jones said, "Everyone needs to sit down and I will explain."

Olly came up the stairs to see what was happening and saw the three sitting at the table. She also saw that Blair had been crying. She went over and tried to comfort Blair and to see what caused her distress.

"What's going on?" Olly asked.

Officer Tuttle answered, "Blair's apartment has been broken into again but this time three men were found and it appears that they had a shoot-out."

"A shoot-out?"

"Yes, and two of the men are dead and another is in serious condition."

Blair tried to answer but she was still in a state of shock.

"I'll get you a drink, honey." Olly hurried downstairs and got Blair a glass of wine and a cold bottle of water. "Here, take some of this," she said.

Officer Tuttle told Ms. Jones, "It's time for you to do some explaining."

"Blair and I need to talk first."

"Not yet," Officer Tuttle said. "We have two dead men and another in serious condition and I think you set the whole thing up."

"I did not set it up. I did know that one of my men, Tony Baxter, would be in Blair's apartment but I have no idea who the other two men are."

"I would like some answers," Blair yelled. Everyone turned to look at her. She still had tears in her eyes but she had a determined look on her face, one that had not been there for a long time. "My apartment has been broken into twice. My things have been scattered and now there are dead men on the floor. My husband has been killed and I'm not sure of anything. I want answers and I want them now!"

Ms. Jones knew that she was in a tough situation. How much information should she provide and what about the local police and the owner of The Pub? "Blair, I want to level with you."

"You better go back to calling me Mrs. Adams," she said.

"Mrs. Adams, we did have an agent go to your apartment to look for a document that is critical in an on-going investigation of national security. I cannot tell you any more about that. I am sorry that my agent damaged some of your things. We will pay for the damage and cover the cost of repairs to your apartment."

"What in the hell are you looking for in my apartment?"

"I told you all that I can for now. I really have to take care of my injured agent. I will call you back to set up another meeting to answer your other questions."

"I'm going to the hospital with you, Ms. Jones," Officer Tuttle said.

She was not pleased with that but knew that she had no choice. "Okay, you can come along, but this is an FBI investigation. We will share all the details with the local police as we get them but we will take the lead on this."

Blair jumped up and said, "Not so fast. I need some answers before anyone goes anyplace. I have had it with all this crap. I came here to meet you and get some answers but instead you have someone in my apartment searching through my things. I need to know why and I want to know now." This was her second demand for answers.

"I'll be able to give you that information but really I need to attend to my agent. I will call you and we can set up another meeting. I'll give you all the information you want."

"I can't go back home with dead bodies and blood all over my apartment. I'm not sure where I will go now. I need your number to contact you for this explanation meeting."

"You're right. Here's my card with my number. Call me to let me know where you will be. We want to help protect you."

"Now I need protection! What's next?"

Olly was still standing by her side and said, "You'll stay with me." She turned and gave Agent Jones her number.

"I don't want to put you and the kids in danger, Olly."

"You're like my sister Blair. You're coming home with me."

Officer Tuttle and Agent Jones walked downstairs to go to Los Angeles Memorial Hospital.

Olly sat in the upstairs room with Blair. "I'm so confused. Why is the FBI searching my apartment? What is going on? Did Hunter do something wrong? I just don't know what is going on."

"I'll call Blake and let him know where you'll be. I'll take you home with me; Ashley will be here in a few minutes to tend bar. I have some things that you can change into; you need to relax." Blair was understandably upset. She wanted to stay upstairs at The Pub while she waited for Ashley. She needed to gather her composure. When Ashley arrived Olly told her that Blair had another break-in and that there had been a shoot-out this time. "I'm going to take her home with me." They left the bar and headed to the car.

Ashley was behind the bar talking to Chris, one of the locals who always came in around lunch time.

"Where did Blair and Olly go?" he asked.

"I'm not sure why but she took Blair back to her place." Ashley didn't want to tell Chris about the second break- in because she didn't really know what had transpired. It was best to just let Blair's friends know that she was going to be with Olly. It was not unusual for Blair to go home with her. She often would help her with the kids when Olly needed an extra hand.

Ashley was clearing the back of the bar and found a package on the lower shelf. She saw that it had Blair's name on it. *She probably forgot it. I'll just leave it in the back office for her.* Ashley knew that Blair was always leaving things behind. She looked at the return address and saw that it was from Iraq. She guessed that it was from Hunter. She took the package from under the bar and put it on a shelf in the office. She left Olly a note to give Blair the package.

Eight

Jaafi and Al Yawer felt that staying in Mansfield Square was a good idea. They called back to Omar who was waiting for orders in the Bronx. "We will be staying here. The local police seem to be staking out Mr. Adams' house. They have two cars out front and one in the backyard. You and Abdullah need to come to the Days Inn at Mansfield Square and bring weapons. It is the first exit and the hotel is one mile from I-95 on the right-hand side of the road. We are in room 201."

Mansfield Square was a quiet little town in New Jersey a few miles east of Trenton. No one would suspect that the local Days Inn was harboring a group of terrorists. This made it a perfect hiding place.

Jaafi and Yawer were early Saddam supporters and after that long war in Iraq, headed to Islamabad, Pakistan, with Osama when he organized the Taliban and masterminded his terrorist organization. Osama sent Jaafi, who was now one of his lieutenants, to Afghanistan. They would hold regular meetings along with Usman, a key member of Osama's band and a suspected minister in the Taliban. El Jaafi was with Osama bin Laden and Usman in Afghanistan when he was given the task of finding key documents that were said to exist. The information that they held would give their cause great strength. They also found out that a U.S. team that searched one of Saddam's castles was reported to have found this information. El Jaafi quickly put together his team and would not consider the task without his loyal supporter and friend, Yawer.

Yawer told Omar to make sure they were careful when registering at the hotel. The Days Inn was a favorite place for U.S. military to stay while training in the region. McGuire Air Force Base was located to the southeast of Mansfield Square. Omar had attended school at the College of New Jersey located in Trenton and knew the area well. He returned to Afghanistan and became an ally and joined the Taliban.

They made their plans while waiting for Omar and Abdullah to arrive at the motel. They would all travel the next day to Bridgewater and start the surveillance of Thomas Adams' home. They were organizing the search for the documents and planning a trip to California if necessary. They knew through their investigation that the lead U.S. soldier in charge of the mission was Hunter Adams. After capturing and torturing one of the U.S. soldiers involved, they found out that Adams had found some documents at the castle but the Army had never acted on any of the information. Hunter Adams must have been killed before he got the documents to his superiors. Adams was sent on another mission the next morning after the search of the castle. They also knew that Adams was from Bridgewater and that he and his wife lived in southern California. Because this group was very familiar with the East Coast it made sense to start there. "If this takes too long we will split up and one group will go to California."

Omar registered at the desk of the Days Inn and asked for a room on the lower level. When he was at the desk, a group of Air Force soldiers came into the lobby. Omar took his key and headed toward his room. He was given 204 on the lower level and three rooms from the men he was to meet. He and Abdullah moved their bags into the room and called Yawer. The group met in his room and planned their trip to Bridgewater. They wanted to make sure that they did not have a run in with the local or state police, nor did they care if they caused harm to Thomas Adams. They were just interested in finding the documents or eliminating Bridgewater and then heading to southern California.

****

Captain Douglas told Thomas that the tire tracks were very strange. He said kids would not have gone to that much trouble for a break-in. "This was planned," the Captain said. "Thomas, you must have something that is valuable to someone. You have to think and look around. Are you sure nothing is missing?"

58

Thomas Adams again searched his mind as Captain Douglas walked through the house with him. He had a few items that were broken but could not place any missing items. He said, "Hunter had some baseball cards but they are all here and I have a few things from Viet Nam but they have been accounted for."

Captain Douglas told him, "My men made a mold of the tire tracks but they were standard treads for an off-road vehicle like a Jeep Wrangler with seventeen inch knobby tires. The wheelbase was short like that of a Jeep or an older Ford Ranger. We tried to see if your house had any fingerprints but came up with nothing. Thomas, we will have a squad car drive by on a regular basis for the next few days. Either they were scared away or decided that what they were looking for isn't here.

****

Dino Tuchy was mad as hell. "Steve, I can't believe two of my best agents made such a mess and came up empty. What the hell were you thinking of by parking behind the house?" Steve Watkins, special agent out of the Philadelphia Bureau, had his head down. "Boss, we knew that so many friends had been coming to the Adams' house after the funeral bringing food and all that going through the woods offered a perfect hiding spot in case someone came by."

"You and Frank better figure out how to get one more shot at getting in that house. I have to report to the Washington Bureau and they're not going to be happy. It should have been a one-trip mission."

Dino was one of the top special agents for the bureau and heading this task force. He had heard that his friend Allisa Jones, special agent in southern California, had not found anything in the search of Mrs. Adams' apartment in California. He would call the director and report but wanted to get his men into the Adams' house one more time. "Steve, you and Frank should give the search another try tonight. Both of you need to case the property and get in and out as quick as possible. I understand the dumb shit local police are snooping around. We need to resolve this." Frank

Walker and Steve Watkins would head off to Bridgewater and try to get into the Adams home later that evening.

****

Yawer told Jaafi that time was critical. He felt that he and Omar should go to Bridgewater that evening and scout out the Adams house. "If we can make our move we will settle this or head to California."

Jaafi agreed that the plan made sense. He said, "We should all go."

"That would be too many people for this sort of mission. Omar and I can get in and out without much fuss. If Adams is home, we will do away with him. He does not cause me concern; the local police are my only concern." Yawer and Omar took two boxes from Omar's trunk and put them in the Malibu. "We will call you after the deed has been done," he told Jaafi." They headed for Bridgewater and the Adams' house.

****

Steve Watkins and Frank Walker were competent agents and both had been with the bureau for over fifteen years. They did not want their boss upset with them. They also were not used to failure. They decided to head for Bridgewater after gathering a few tools in case they needed them.

Thomas Adams had been alone for quite a few years but the knowledge that his son or daughter-in-law might come to visit or at least call made it seem like someone was always there. He decided to call his brother to see if he was in. Thomas' brother, Bill, was retired and he and his wife had given his great support during the past few weeks and helping with the funeral.

"Thomas, glad you called. Martha is making one of your favorite dishes. Why don't you come over and eat with us."

"I don't want to bother you," Thomas said.

"You're no bother; we would love to have you come for dinner tonight."

Thomas didn't want to intrude but he wanted to get Bill's opinion of the events of the past few days. It was only five-thirty and Thomas knew that Bill and Martha always ate around seven p.m. "Thanks," he said. "How about if I stop at our favorite place and bring dessert."

"That sounds good," Bill said. "See you in a little bit."

****

Steve looked at his watch and told Frank that they should be at the Adams residence about seven p.m. "We should be able to park down the street after we pass by to make sure the coast is clear. Let's get this done as soon as possible so Dino doesn't chew our asses out again."

****

Yawer wanted to get to Bridgewater and start his search. He said to Omar, "If we get there about seven-thirty p.m., we can be done in less than an hour."

Nine

Allisa Jones sat in the small waiting room outside the emergency entrance. Justin Wallace told her, "The doctor will talk to us in about half an hour. I'm sure the surgery went okay." She felt guilty because she wasn't thinking about Baxter's surgery, just how she was going to explain all of this to the director.

Officer Tuttle joined Allisa in the waiting room and inquired about Baxter's condition. "We should hear from the team of surgeons soon," she answered.

He sat down and thought about the line of questioning that he wanted to ask. "Agent Jones, I need to ask you a couple of questions."

"This isn't the best time, Officer."

"I know, but we must act on this incident so that we can start our investigation."

The doctor came into the waiting room and asked who was with the Baxter family. Agent Jones jumped up, "I'm waiting to hear about Mr. Baxter."

"Are you family?" the doctor asked.

"Tony Baxter doesn't have any family here. I'm Allisa Jones and we work together."

"We normally want to speak to a family member."

"I can assure you that he has no family and that you can give me the details." Allisa showed the doctor her FBI identification.

"Ms. Jones, the surgery went well. His shoulder wounds were taken care of and the only complication we had was the injury to his leg."

"What kind of complication?"

"The wound was close to an artery and caused a lot of bleeding. After we sutured it we had to give him two pints of blood. It looks like his wounds should heal just fine. He will be in recovery for about an hour than we will get him into a room."

After the doctor left, Officer Tuttle resumed his line of questioning. "Agent Jones, I must ask you to either come down to the station or answer my questions now."

"Officer, I'm not leaving the hospital until I talk to Agent Baxter. As far as going to your station, this is an FBI matter and we'll deal with it. I will promise to keep you in the loop but we're going to take the lead in this investigation."

Tuttle was very aggravated and wanted to proceed but he also understood the importance of talking to the wounded agent. He too wanted to know what Agent Baxter had to say. His office called to update him on the men in Blair's apartment. He planned to not share this with Allisa Jones. While Officer Tuttle had been with Ms. Jones and Blair at The Pub, his men were completing the investigation. They had found no identification on the men who were shot and killed in Blair's apartment. They appeared to be of possible Arabic descent. The Santa Monica Police would want to run a fingerprint analysis at the morgue.

Information was also forwarded to the Los Angeles County Task Force that handled matters for the Department of Homeland Security. The head of the FBI Los Angeles Bureau, Dean Curry, had also received a copy of the report from the Homeland Security office. The Santa Monica Police were hoping to get some help in tracing the identification of the two dead men.

"I agree with you, Agent Jones, about waiting to talk to Agent Baxter. I will also share the investigation with you but I want to know what your agent has to say."

Allisa Jones reluctantly agreed but also said that she needed to make a call. Officer Tuttle waited with Justin Wallace in the E.R. waiting room. Jones walked outside and called the J. Edgar Hoover Building.

"This is Agent Jones. Is the director in?"

John Franklin Martin was the head of the FBI in Washington D. C. "Yes, he's in. I'll transfer the call for you."

"John Martin here."

"Director, this is Special Agent Jones reporting in."

"Yes, Jones what have you got?" Martin didn't waste time with small talk; he went straight to the issue.

"Well, we've made some headway in our case, Sir."

"What do you mean by headway, Agent?"

"We've searched through Mrs. Adams' apartment and didn't find any sign of the documents that we are looking for."

"That doesn't seem like headway to me. What the hell have you got?"

"Agent Tony Baxter was in the process of completing the search when two men entered the apartment."

"And?"

"Agent Baxter got into a shoot-out with the men. He was able to shoot both of them although he was wounded in the action. Both men were dead at the scene, Sir."

"Son of a bitch! That's just great! What the hell kind of headway do you think you've made, Jones? You haven't found anything, two possible leads in the investigation are now dead, and now we don't have any more than we did when you started. Agent Jones, who were these two men in Mrs. Adams' apartment?"

"We are working on that, Sir."

"Well, while you're working on that, the local police are ahead of you, Jones. Those two men are believed to possibly be Arabs and we need to know more about them."

Allisa could not believe that Officer Tuttle and the Santa Monica Police were already into the investigation and she was not in the loop. She thought she would try to redirect the conversation. "If the documents are not in California, they must be in Bridgewater."

"We haven't found anything there yet but our team is making a second check as we speak," Martin told her. "I'm not happy with your results, Jones. I suggest we send in a few more people to help you."

"Sir, I don't think I need any help."

"Well I do because there's a new wrinkle to the plot. Who are these two men that Baxter killed? If they are Arabs what are they after? Where are they from? We have to find out their identity. I've called Dean in the Los Angeles office to apprise him of the situation. I'll forward a message to him to take over the lead and you are to assist him in this matter."

"Yes, Sir."

Agent Jones was mad but understood that she didn't have anything positive to add. She did not tell the director about the local police and their involvement and that now they had the lead on the investigation. The director already knew that they had more information than she did.

She reentered the waiting room and Agent Walker said, "Baxter is being moved into room 605B. We can go up to his room in five minutes," he added.

"Officer Tuttle, I've talked to my director and he's sending more FBI agents from the Los Angeles Bureau. We will take the lead in this investigation and I will question my agent alone," Allisa said. She was still thinking about the fact that Officer Tuttle knew some key things about the men killed by her agent but hadn't said a thing. "I would like five minutes alone with Baxter and then you will have the opportunity to ask him anything you want."

"I want to be there the whole time," Officer Tuttle said.

"This is an FBI matter," Ms. Jones reiterated. She turned and began walking away.

"Bullshit!" Tuttle yelled after her. "I've called my captain and he's on his way. It happened in our jurisdiction and it is our case." They were at an impasse when the captain of the Santa Monica Police entered. Officer Tuttle saw Captain Parker and called out to him. "We're over here, Captain."

Captain Parker was a veteran of the Santa Monica Police force. He had been a Los Angeles detective for over fifteen years before taking the post of captain in Santa Monica. Captain Parker was a strong individual and would not take any crap from anyone including the FBI. He had been involved in a joint task force with the FBI on gang crime and they soon found out that he would not play second fiddle. The captain would make sure that this FBI agent knew he was not working for her.

"I'm Special Agent Jones and this is Agent Justin Wallace. Captain, I was just telling your officer that our wounded agent must be interviewed by the FBI alone. I have already talked to the director of the bureau in Washington and he's meeting with the president…"

Before she could finish her statement the captain said, "Not a problem, I just came here to get with Officer Tuttle. Bill we have some information that will help us in the case. We need to go. Agent Jones I will expect you to be available later."

Agent Jones looked confused and was caught off guard. "I've explained to your officer that we will handle this investigation."

"Agent Jones, this is our investigation, period. Don't be confused about that fact. This is Santa Monica and my turf. You are my guest. If you withhold any information I'll have your ass."

Allisa was stunned.

"Let's go, Bill," he said to Officer Tuttle.

Agent Jones just stood there wondering what had just happened.

Ten

Blair went home with Olly but she was more confused than ever. What was going on? There had been two break-ins, and now she was told that two men were killed in her apartment. The FBI was involved with the Santa Monica Police Department. Who should she trust? What should she do now? They were sitting in the living room when the phone rang. Olly answered the phone. "Blair, it's for you."

"Who is it?"

"She said it was the FBI agent you met with at The Pub."

"Agent Jones? Why should I talk to her? I think she's been lying the whole time."

"Honey, you better talk to her. She obviously knows something more and maybe now you might get some real information."

Blair doubted that the agent would disclose anything important. She felt that the only reason Ms. Jones wanted to talk to her in the first place was to get her out of the apartment. But why? *I have to know why*, Blair thought. Although she did not want to talk to Ms. Jones, she took the phone.

"This is Mrs. Adams."

"Blair, I know that you may be upset and I can explain everything."

"I'm more than upset! Remember, my husband is dead, my apartment is being used as a shooting gallery by your men, which by the way, why in the hell were they in my apartment?"

"Blair, if we can meet, I will explain everything. I will be able to help you and I have some information for you."

"This time I want to have a friend with me, Agent."

"That won't be a problem, but Blair this is critical to the FBI's investigation so I must get your reassurance that nothing I tell you will be repeated to anyone."

Blair agreed to meet with Agent Jones the next day at noon along the Pacific Coast Highway near the Santa Monica Pier. She told Allisa that there was a series of park benches by the bus stop at the entrance to the pier and no one would pay much attention to them. Agent Jones agreed and said she would be alone. Blair felt that by being outside, she would be able to talk to Agent Jones and if things got emotional she could better deal with it then being at The Pub.

"Blair, I will be meeting you with information that the FBI has and I'm not supposed to share it with you. I feel you deserve to know what it is."

Blair got off the phone and was glad that she had Olly to talk this over with. Agent Jones had given her the feeling that this may be more bad news. *How much more bad news could there be?* she thought. Olly agreed to accompany Blair to the meeting. Although it was late, the two of them sat and talked for a couple of hours before either of them was ready to go to sleep. Finally Olly told her that they should try to get some rest. They both headed off to bed. Blair's sleep was disturbed. She kept having dreams that made her question so much. She remembered the trips that Hunter had been on. The time he spent in South America and he was never able to tell her exactly where he was and what his assignment was about. She thought again about the trip to Switzerland when he got injured. The passport issue did not make sense. *Hunter, what were you doing?* She could not get those questions out of her mind. She woke up about five a.m., went to the kitchen, made a cup of tea and looked out of the window that faced the Pacific Ocean. It was a beautiful home. Sitting in the big chair looking at the moon over the ocean, Blair thought back about the trip that Hunter had taken her on in Central America. They went to Belize and she thought it was beautiful. They both loved mountain climbing and they were able to do a lot of it there. One of the strange things she remembered was that he seemed to be familiar with the area and was able to show Blair sights as if he had seen them before. She hadn't thought much about it then but now everything seemed suspicious to her.

The meeting at noon would hopefully hold some answers.

Blair wished she could have slept more but sleep was not in the cards. She could not turn her mind off to rest. Olly was fast asleep. Blair envied her and loved her. She was a great friend and Blair felt so lucky to have her. *I should call Hunter's dad,* she thought. *Three hours time difference for the East Coast. It's only a little after eight a.m. there. I'll wait another hour.*

"Blair, are you okay? Guess you can't sleep huh?" Olly mumbled.

"Not really," she answered.

"I'm going to get up and sit with you."

"Please try to go back to sleep. I'm sorry if I woke you."

Olly usually opened The Pub and was used to getting up early. "Don't be silly. I'm going to take a shower and go to The Pub then I'll be back with breakfast for both of us."

"Okay," Blair said. "Can I help with anything around here while you're gone?"

"Nope everything is good. The kids are staying with me mum this week and I have everything done around the house."

Blair continued to stare out the big window as the sun began to rise. She could see its rays coming up over the rooftops. Sunsets were the best from this view but the early morning light coming in the window to wake up the city seemed special. Blair was rarely up at this time so she really didn't get to see many sunrises. This was the California she loved. People back east always referred to California as a "nut house." "So many crazies out here," her dad would say when they visited. The Promenade always had its share of people carrying signs proclaiming the end of the world or some other future shock. On one visit a man carried a sign saying the world would end on October 21. Blair's dad would stop by him daily and count off the number of days left and laugh. On October 22 Blair took a picture of the man and emailed it to her dad. The new sign proclaimed January 15 as the end of the world. Her dad thought that was great. He called back to laugh with her about the date change on the sign. They had a special relationship like some fathers and daughters and they shared the same level of humor. He always called her his "little kid."

Olly left the house and told Blair to make sure everything

was locked. "I'll be back in a few hours," she said.

Blair looked at the clock and knew it was now nine a.m. in Bridgewater. She went to the phone and dialed Thomas Adams. The phone rang and he answered.

"Hi, I'm so glad to hear from you, Blair. How is everything going?"

"Things are really strange here. I had a call from the FBI wanting to talk to me about Hunter. When I went to meet the special agent they had another person in my apartment who ended up shooting two other men."

"What? In your apartment? Were you there? Are you sure you're okay?"

"Yes, I'm at my friend's house. I wasn't there. It's all so confusing."

"I can't believe that this isn't somehow related to the break-in at my place," Thomas told her. "What about this shooting in your apartment?"

"I'm not really sure but I have a meeting with a special agent of the FBI today at noon and hope to get some answers. I do feel that having the Santa Monica Police involved is good because I know the officer and trust him. I think he doesn't like the FBI person."

"Be careful," Thomas told her. "Is someone going with you?"

"Yes, Olly is going with me and we are meeting the agent at noon in the park. I'll be careful but I am also worried about you. Did you call about your break-in?"

"Yes. I don't know if you remember Captain Douglas, but he came over and he has his men watching my place."

"Did you tell Captain Douglas about my break-in?"

"No, I didn't think it was related at the time."

"Maybe you should tell him. You never know, especially with the FBI involved."

Being an ex-marine, Thomas had heard a lot of stories of espionage and the FBI or CIA undercover involvement that he never thought that he would actually be involved in one. What would prompt the FBI to be in his daughter-in-law's apartment? What about the two men in the shooting? Could his break-in be part of this? Now there were so many questions in his mind that were not there before.

Blair said, "I'm not sure about where I will stay. I just don't know what to do. I'm hoping to go to my apartment after meeting with the FBI to see what shape it is in."

"Don't go by yourself."

"I'll be okay. If Olly can't go with me I'll ask Blake or Ashley to go. Guess I can call Officer Tuttle and he will meet us there."

"Call me after your meeting," Thomas said.

"Okay. I'm going to ask if she knows anything about your break-in too. Seems like something is going on and I think she knows what it is."

Olly came in just as Blair was hanging up. "Are you okay?" she asked.

"I just wanted to talk to Hunter's dad. He should know about the FBI and the happenings here."

"I agree. The more information you each have the better off you'll both be. Is he doing okay?"

"I didn't tell you that he had a break-in before but now I'm wondering if it is related. I will ask Agent Jones about that."

"Maybe you should write down some questions because there are so many loose ends you might forget something. I wish I had a small tape recorder for you."

Blair's mind was in a state of total confusion. Every thought was a question. Writing some of them down made a lot of sense. "I brought some coffee and croissants from the Coffee Bean," she said.

"You are so sweet," Blair told her. "I like the idea of writing down questions to ask. Will you help me organize them?"

"Of course, I'll do anything to help. I'll go get a pen and some paper, you can get the plates."

Where do I start? Blair thought. They sat at a little table overlooking the Pacific Ocean and wrote down questions. Talking was good medicine for Blair. So much had happened that she needed someone who could listen and help her stay on track. Olly was the perfect person for that. Blair looked up to her and listened to suggestions she made. They shared so many things in common. They checked the clock. They would be meeting Agent Jones in a few hours. Time was moving slow. "I can't wait to get this over with," Blair said. "I hope that I can find out what is going on and why."

They ate their breakfast as Blair wrote down some questions that they had come up with. Blair said she was going to take the lead on questioning Agent Jones and wanted some answers. There was a determined look on her face as she studied the paper in her hands. Maybe the upcoming meeting would resolve those questions. The two women planned their meeting with Agent Jones and ate their breakfast.

Eleven

Thomas turned on some lights in the house so it would look like someone was home. He locked the front door and called Captain Douglas as instructed to let him know that he was going out. *Bill and Martha love cheesecake,* he thought. *I'll stop by and pick one up.*

****

Al Yawer told Omar that the trip would not take too long and he suggested that they park on the street behind the Adams house and walk through the woods. He told Omar the woods would offer cover for their mission. Yawer was a very organized individual who thought things out to a finite measure. He liked having Omar with him because he followed directions without improvising his own. The drive to Bridgewater in the Chevy was smooth. They traveled down Highway 13 across the Neshaminy River toward the Adams' house. "We will be at our destination in about ten minutes," Yawer said.

****

Steve Watkins told Frank Walker that they should enter the house through the woods. He said that would be the best way to stay out of sight. They parked down the street from the Adams' house and walked through the woods. Steve was making final plans when he saw Thomas Adams get in his car and leave. They noticed a local police car slowing down in front of the house and waited for it to pass. "It looks like they're coming by pretty regularly," Frank said. "The good thing is when Adams left he kept the lights on so we can go through the house pretty quick."

Steve suggested that on the last search the upstairs had been

73

gone through pretty thoroughly but they did not check the basement or garage.

Frank said, "I will take the garage."

"Okay," said Steve.

The two agents ran from their cover in the woods to the back of the Adams home. There was a door in the back of the house that Steve was able to jimmy open and he and Frank made their way into the garage. It was dark but the street light outside helped to illuminate the interior. Steve said he would head down into the basement. "Once you've finished, go back to our spot in the woods," Steve said. "I'll meet you there."

****

Omar asked, "Do you think I should take the shotgun just in case?"

"No, it would cause too much noise."

Yawer gave him a 9 mm Glock with a silencer on it. "If you see something that does not belong shoot it. We must do this quickly." The two men made their way through the woods and stopped at the edge of the tree line to case the back of the house. There were lights on in most every room. "Someone might be in there," he said. "I will go first and then once I am at the back of the house you follow." Yawer ran in a zigzag pattern across the yard to the back of the house. He noticed that the garage had a door that faced the woods and would make a good entrance. He signaled to Omar that it was clear.

Frank Walker had just finished his search of the garage and knew that Steve would not take too long in the basement. The garage produced nothing but Frank was thorough in his search. He looked through the two cabinets and made sure that everything was back in place as he had found it. He did not want to face the wrath of his chief when they got back to the bureau.

Omar ran to the back of the house and joined Yawer. A bright light appeared to be coming down the street. Both men ducked down so that they would not be seen but so they could watch the light. It was the local Bridgewater Police making a pass in front of the Adams' house. "They should be gone in a few minutes," he told Omar.

Frank saw the light from the street and crouched down behind the lawn mower. He felt that his getaway would be safe as soon as the car passed. The police car stopped in front of the Adams house and an officer got out. He grabbed his flashlight and started to walk toward the back. Due to the tire tracks found on the previous break-in, Captain Douglas told his men to make sure to walk around the back of the house on some of their trips.

The officer, Andy Emery, was new to the force. He spent four years in the U.S. Army before coming home and joining the Bridgewater Police force. He was always happy to get an assignment that may offer a chance for action. During his time in the Army he had been in Afghanistan and he was trained for action. Bridgewater was a quiet town and anything more than a traffic violation would be action for them.

Frank Walker wondered why the police car had stopped for so long. He wanted to look out the window but saw a reflection of a flashlight headed his way. He crawled along the floor toward the corner where a large workbench was built. He could crawl under it if necessary, he thought.

Yawer whispered to Omar that they should make their way around the side of the house away from the garage. It appeared that the officer was coming around to the garage side. "We can hide in the shrubs behind the kitchen," he whispered. There were three very large pine bushes that ran along the back of the house. They were about five feet tall and spread out over ten feet long. They moved near the kitchen and under the shrubs. They would be great cover for both of them. "The officer should not pose any problem," Yawer said, "but if he does shoot him."

Andy Emery was almost to the side of the garage when his radio went off. He pulled it off his shoulder and answered. It was Captain Douglas. "Yes Sir. I'm checking the yard and back of the house right now. Okay, I'll check the woods too." He returned the radio to its shoulder holster and continued around the side of the garage. He flashed his light into the garage window and then along the walk toward a back door. "No sign of anything wrong," he said to himself as he walked toward the woods. It was a clear night and the full moon made it easy to see along the edge of the tree-lined yard. Andy was a few years younger than Hunter Adams, but knew about him. He was a football legend. Everyone in Bridgewater knew the local football star who was now a war hero. Like everyone his age, Andy went to the funeral home to pay his respects. He was glad that he could help by keeping an eye on Mr. Adams' house. *Why would anyone want to break into a home after someone had just died?* he thought.

The line of trees looked clear as he walked toward the split rail fence. He turned and walked toward the back of the house shining his flashlight along the perimeter. He looked up at the moon and thought how full and bright it was. Then he shined his light near the shrubs by the kitchen. He heard a muffled sound just as he felt a sharp pain in his right shoulder. He had been shot! Andy fell to the ground clutching his shoulder. Omar crawled from under the shrub and headed toward the wounded officer.

Frank Walker came out from under the workbench when he saw the officer headed toward the woods. He watched him search the tree line and then turn around toward the house. The officer seemed to fall to the ground all of a sudden. Then Frank saw a figure headed toward the officer. Frank made his way to the garage door and caught sight of Omar in the shadow of the house. Omar had a gun extended and it appeared that he was moving in for the kill. Frank burst out of the garage and shot at the shadow going toward the officer. Omar clutched at his side and turned and shot back as he fell to the ground.

Yawer had just come out from under the shrub when he saw the garage door open. He saw Frank appear and shoot at Omar. He blasted two shots toward Frank and one hit him full in the chest. Frank fell backwards into the wall. Steve was coming up from the basement when he heard the noise from outside. He ran to see what was happening.

Yawer saw Omar go down when he was shot. He headed toward the person he had shot at who came out of the garage, and saw Frank laying against the garage wall. Yawer put another bullet in Frank's head. Blood splattered all over the garage wall as Frank lay in the pool of brain matter. The intruder was going to make sure no one would be alive to tell of this. He was heading to

Omar's side when someone came from the house and started shooting. He fell to the ground and started to crawl toward his friend.

Steve had spotted the two men in the yard. He also saw someone laying in the grass and thought it was Frank. He did not see that Frank had been shot by the back garage door.

Yawer shot back at the figure from the house. Steve was able to take cover and called to his friend to see if he was okay. There was no response. Yawer saw that Omar had been shot but seemed to be able to crawl. Neither man saw that the local police officer had turned over on his stomach and took his pistol out of its holster. Andy shot at the figures on the grass crawling toward the woods. Steve thought that it was his partner. He shot toward the woods where the two men were crawling. Andy heard where the next round of shots was coming from and he turned and shot at Steve. Now Steve was confused. Who in the hell is that laying in the grass? Why was he being shot at? Steve stayed down to think for a minute. Andy called out. "I'm Officer Andy Emery of the Bridgewater Police. Toss your gun out or I'll shoot again."

Steve called back, "Steve Watkins, United States Federal Bureau of Investigation. Stop shooting!" Steve jumped off the porch and crawled toward the wounded officer.

Andy Emery yelled, "Stop or I'll shoot. Toss me your identification." Steve saw the uniform and knew that it was a local cop. *Now where is Frank?* he thought.

Yawer dragged Omar into the woods and they made their way to the parked car. The mission failed and now they would have more problems here in Bridgewater. Steve told the officer who he was again. "I have a partner out here somewhere," Steve said.

Andy answered back, "They were shooting at someone near the garage."

While Steve headed toward the garage Andy took his radio off his shoulder and called in to Captain Douglas. "Captain this is Andy. There was some shooting at the Adams' house and I've been hit. There is also a man here who is identifying himself as an FBI Agent."

"How bad are you hit, Son?" the captain asked.

"Just shot in the shoulder. I think I got one of the other men though."

"What other men?" Captain Douglas said.

"There were two other men shooting but I'm not sure who they were."

"Where are they now?"

"Crawled into the woods," Andy answered.

"We're on our way, Andy. Hang in there."

Two squad cars were dispatched to the scene plus Captain Douglas had one car sent to the perimeter of the neighborhood. He was sure that there would be a fast car trying to get away from the scene. Steve saw Frank lying in a pool of blood. His head had been blown apart and he had a large hole in his chest. Steve was sick. What had happened here? The quiet town came alive with sirens. Locals came rushing to their doors. Must have been a bad traffic accident, most of them thought. Bridgewater had not had a murder in over thirty years and most incidents were traffic related. Two squad cars pulled up in front of Thomas Adams' home. Captain Douglas went running around the back with his gun drawn. He saw Steve standing over a body. He called out to Steve to drop his gun. Steve called back that he was FBI and was under the direction of the Philadelphia Bureau. The captain asked for his identification. He took it out and showed it to Douglas.

Three other officers ran into the woods to follow the tracks of the men who got away. They could see a trail of blood and broken tree limbs where one man must have dragged the other. Captain Douglas told them to follow it and call to the squad car that was circling the neighborhood. He went back over to help Andy. The local EMS unit arrived and headed to attend to the two men on the ground. They stopped at the back of the garage first.

Steve was on a knee and sobbing, "No hope here," as he knelt over Frank's body.

They went to take care of the officer on the ground. Andy's wound was bleeding but the bullet had gone through the shoulder. They were able to bandage him and put him on a stretcher. Andy gave his captain a recap before he was taken to the local hospital.

Douglas sat Steve Watkins down. He appeared shaken.

Steve was not responding to his line of questions. "What were you two doing here?" Captain Douglas asked.

Finally Steve turned toward him. "I have to report to my bureau chief."

"You need to answer my questions first or I will have you taken and put in jail for breaking and entering Mr. Adams' home."

"I'll answer your questions, Sir, but I have to call this in first."

Douglas agreed to let him contact his office but he sat with Steve when he called.

Dino's cell phone rang. "Steve, did you find it?" Steve didn't know where to start. Dino was probably going to blow up when he heard the news. He didn't need his two experienced agents involved in an altercation that would get the press and local police involved. Dino knew that the Washington Bureau had this mission as top priority.

"Sir, we ran into some problems."

"What kind of problems?"

"When we were coming out of the Adams' house we were ambushed by two gunmen."

Steve hesitated when Dino asked if they were okay.

"Actually, Sir," he paused, "Frank was shot, and he's dead!"

Dino was silent on the other end of the phone for it seemed like an eternity to Steve. "How did it happen?"

"Looks like he was surprised and they murdered him, Sir. They blew his head apart!"

Steve and Frank were two very experienced agents and Dino had worked with both of them for over ten years. Dino asked, "Who else is involved?"

"The local police are here and one of their men has also been shot."

"How much do they know?"

"I'm sitting with the captain of the local police," Steve said and handed his phone to Captain Douglas. "I'm Captain Douglas of the Bridgewater Police."

"Captain Douglas, my name is Dino Tuchy of the Federal

Bureau of Investigation. I'm the head of the Philadelphia Bureau and report to the director in Washington. It is very important that the local news media not be involved in this investigation."

"That may be a problem," Captain Douglas told him. "This is a small town and a shoot-out of this magnitude will cause quite a stir.

"I understand," Dino said, "but they can't know the details. I am demanding that you and your staff ensure that until I arrive no one gives the reporters any details. They can't know the FBI is involved or why we're there."

"That may be easy, Mr. Tuchy, because I don't know why the FBI is involved either, but if you want my cooperation you'll fill me in when you get here."

"Deal," said Dino.

Twelve

Olly tried to convince Blair that the meeting was probably just some information regarding the apartment shoot-out and had nothing to do with more bad news. Deep down Olly wasn't sure why the FBI agent wanted to meet with Blair and also feared the news she would bring.

Allisa Jones had been taken off the case by the FBI director, John Martin, and she was supposed to give all her information to the Los Angeles field office and the bureau chief, and now she would be expected to assist him. She did not feel that she failed; she also had no use for Dean Curry. He was a male chauvinist and made no bones about it. When she was promoted to her new position she heard from the grapevine that Dean said she had to be sleeping with someone in Washington. She was determined to solve this case even if it was in an unofficial position. She entered the agency in New York and worked in many slums, sometimes as an undercover agent.

On a cold night in Manhattan she was working a case that involved a corporate officer selling critical information to a foreign source. She had been placed as a secretary in the corporate office and was feeding the local agents the inside information that she gathered. She also found a way to get the suspect to trust her. Many of the other agents felt that she took all the glory. She never revealed to anyone how she got the information.

In the Washington assignment, she worked with some of the outlying agents. One agent was Dino Tuchy in the Philadelphia Bureau. He had her helping work on an international case of espionage. Together they were instrumental in breaking the case. This case got Allisa the attention of the new FBI director, John Franklin Martin. She was promoted to the Los Angeles Bureau and given the task of working with the Department of Homeland

Security.

She was very proud and was not going to give up on this case. She knew that she would be taking a big chance by giving Blair Adams some key information but she was used to taking chances. She took chances in New York and was not going to be stopped now.

Blair got dressed and called out to Olly in the other room, "Do you mind if I wear one of your tops with my jeans?"

"No, go ahead, honey."

"I just love your clothes." Blair had this thing about shoes like a lot of women her age. She could decide to wear almost anything in minutes except for the shoes. Today she was at a loss because she didn't have her shoes to pick from. "Can I wear one of your pairs of shoes?"

"Sure," Olly called out as she dressed in her room. She came into the room where Blair was finishing getting dressed. Blair was sitting on the floor with four pairs of shoes lined up.

"Not sure which one to choose," she said.

She could see that Blair was very nervous and tried to joke with her. "Why wear any shoes? You've got great feet." She knew that Blair hated her feet.

"Yeah, sure! I look like a bare-footed duck," Blair said.

The two women finished dressing and left the house. Blair told Olly that she wanted her to stay with her the whole time regardless of what Agent Jones would say. "I'll be with you as long as you want."

They left the house in the Suburban and headed down the Pacific Coast Highway toward the Santa Monica Pier. Blair was very quiet as they passed Wilshire Boulevard. Wilshire was the first street from San Vicente where they entered the Pacific Coast Highway from her house. Soon they would be at Santa Monica Place. Olly wanted to say something to break the ice but didn't know quite what to say. She was relieved when Blair asked her about stopping at The Pub for a bottle of water before they headed to the pier. "Sure," she said. "Do you want to get a sandwich?"

"No, just something to drink."

Olly parked the Suburban in her usual parking spot behind The Pub and both grabbed a bottle of water and headed toward the pier. It was a beautiful day with hardly a cloud in the sky. It was about 75 degrees and a gentle breeze blew off the ocean. The sky was bright blue and the palm trees moved ever so slightly in the breeze. The weather in Santa Monica was always a bit cooler than that of Los Angeles. Often there was fog that would roll in early in the morning but the sun would burn it off, and the gentle breeze that came off the Pacific Ocean was always welcome. They crossed the Pacific Coast Highway at Santa Monica Boulevard and walked toward the pier. Blair could see a woman sitting on one of the park benches that she had suggested as a meeting place. It did not look like Agent Jones but as they moved closer Allisa got up from her spot and waved to them. Both women were surprised to see that it was, indeed, Special Agent Jones. She was wearing jeans and a sweater. Her hair was light auburn with blond streaks and hung shoulder length. The only other time they met her she looked older then with her hair pulled back off her face. They all looked at each other with a bit of a surprised look on their face.

"Agent Jones," Blair said.

"Glad you agreed to meet me Blair." All three women sat on the park bench and Agent Jones began to talk. "Blair, I have been working with the FBI for a long time and we in the bureau often use people outside of our organization to help us in some of the cases we have. I would like to offer you and your friend the chance to help the FBI."

Blair looked at her. "I'm confused; I really don't know what you're ever talking about. I want to know about Hunter and the information you have regarding the break-in at my apartment."

"I'm going to get to that, but first I want to have you involved in more than just giving you information. I'm offering you the opportunity to work with me."

"I'm not sure; what do you want me to do?"

"I am going to tell you everything we know about this case. If I don't find the answers here I will continue by going to Bridgewater and talking to Hunter's dad. The answer is somewhere and I have to find it." Blair felt her heart beating a thousand times a minute. She could hardly breathe let alone answer this request. What did Bridgewater have to do with this? The agent knew so much it startled her.

"If you decide to come with me to Bridgewater, you could be of great help. Hunter's dad will know that we are on a mission and he will cooperate with us if he knows anything. I'll pay for everything if you decide to come along and I will be with you the whole time."

"First I want to know more about my husband and why my apartment has been broken into."

"I said I will tell you, but first I need to know if you'll work with me to solve this. I want you to know that I need your help in this investigation. If I give you the information you need, do you think you would be willing to do this?"

"Yes, if it gives me the answers that I need to go on," she said.

"Blair, I'm going to detail the case we are working on. It will give you the answers you are looking for and you just may give me the answers that we need to solve this case. Your husband was working for the FBI in Iraq. He was a special agent and had been one for many years."

Blair almost blacked out at this revelation. She was too stunned to say anything. Olly started to say something but Jones gave her a signal to be quiet as she continued.

"Hunter was recruited while he was going to school at the University of Mississippi. It was rumored that there was a cult of men who were storing weapons outside of Tupelo. Your husband was injured but still on the football team. This would be the perfect cover. He would be able to get into places we would never get into. He was an Ole Miss football player and that was the key we needed. It took some time to convince him that he could do this. He worried about you and how this might affect your relationship."

She almost cried out when she heard this news. She had tears in her eyes and her friend held onto her.

"Blair, please don't be mad because he didn't tell you about his work. He couldn't because it may have put you in danger. You can see already what danger has come your way now. We found out that there was a local chapter of separatists that planned to blow up the court house in Tupelo. They wanted to kill two prominent politicians who had helped to end racial segregation in the Mississippi schools. Hunter was able to get introduced into the group and earned their trust. He needed to be able to assimilate into their organization while keeping the façade of playing football and being a student. He was responsible for us breaking the group up and we were able to arrest most of the leaders. He was also able to keep his identity intact without being found out as the informant. Because of his success and the importance that he saw in this work, he agreed to continue full time with the FBI."

Blair sat on the edge of the park bench as Allisa Jones continued the story. "We had him join the Mississippi National Guard as a cover. He was transferred to the United States Army Special Forces. He had missions to South and Central America and was one of the most highly regarded agents we ever had. The war in Afghanistan and Iraq offered him many opportunities."

This information left both Blair and Olly silent.

"We have many agents like Hunter stationed with the armed forces helping the FBI and Homeland Security protect the interests of the United States. The U.S forces have their mission but our mission is broader. We plan the future; the military plans for the present. We have to make sure that our country is safe today and tomorrow. We have people in key places. Our government knows that the Middle East and the possible oil crisis that comes with our involvement there will affect our future as well as most of the rest of the world."

Blair was not a fan of the United States' stand in Iraq and often felt that we had overstayed our presence. She also was not a fan of the current administration. Blair had become more politically involved with Hunter in the military. She was an avid reader of political articles and books. She often was outspoken about her views and very knowledgeable when discussing them. "Agent Jones, I can hardly believe that Hunter was with the FBI, but I have had so many questions lately about events in the past and maybe this answers some of them. If he was with the FBI some of these things make sense. But why, if he was undercover, is everyone breaking into my apartment? Is this also why Hunter's dad had his house broken into?"

"Yes, the break-ins must be linked to this. I am telling you things that our agency has kept secret and not all the agents involved know the whole story. You have to understand that I could get fired and face jail time for telling you this."

She was grateful to Agent Jones and finally felt she could be trusted. "I am willing to help you but I'm not sure what I could do."

"Before you get too involved you better think this out," Olly warned. "You're not trained for this."

"Blair, your friend is right. However you probably have information that many people are looking for and don't even know that you have it," Agent Jones said. "The break-ins are due to them seeking that information."

"I don't know what you mean, Ms. Jones."

"Think about it! Had your husband sent you anything and told you to keep it until he gets home? Maybe you received a letter with a map or information regarding one of his missions."

"I don't have anything like that," Blair said. "What would this information be about?"

"The information I have is that on one of his last missions he was in charge of a search party that may have found important documents in a castle that belonged to Saddam Hussein. This material would be critical to our efforts. The president wants to have this information, that's how important it is."

Blair was thinking when her cell phone rang. She looked at the screen to see who it was and saw it was Hunter's dad. *I'll call him back later*, she thought. "I'm still not sure, Agent Jones. I need some time to think this out. Olly might be right. I don't know anything about this type of investigative work. Can I have some time before I give you my final answer?"

"Blair, I'm not trying to rush you but by tomorrow I may have to leave here to continue the investigation. You have to decide by tonight, even if you only decide to go through all your things to see if you have something that seems suspicious. I want your help and you must keep your promise not to tell anyone what I have told you."

Both women agreed to keep the information secret. Blair said she would call Agent Jones by seven p.m. with her decision. Allisa handed her a note. "My cell phone number is 555-678-2315.

It isn't on my card that I gave you earlier."

Blair felt grateful but more confused than ever. "Olly, I'm not sure what to do."

"I can't tell you what to do Blair, but I will support any decision you make."

The two women left the pier and walked together back toward The Pub. Agent Jones was hoping that she may have triggered some thoughts in Blair's mind that would have her search through items that Hunter had sent. If nothing else, this would eliminate the need for searching the apartment a third time. She was sure that with the revelation about Hunter, Blair would be willing to share information with her. In any case she was going to continue with the investigation.

Thirteen

The two friends walked quietly back to the car. Then Blair said, "I'm so angry that I didn't see this before. How could I not know that Hunter was involved with the FBI?"

"Blair, he was in the Army and operating undercover. He couldn't tell you. Agent Jones told you he worried about your safety. Let's stop in at The Pub and have some lunch. We could talk about this until you feel comfortable with your decision."

"That sounds good. I need to call Hunter's dad back; I'll wait until we get to The Pub."

The noise on the street along the Promenade was always loud. There were people standing on corners playing guitars or other musical instruments. There was the occasional preacher barking out his message to those passing by. They crossed Second Avenue and headed toward Santa Monica Boulevard. When they got to Santa Monica and Second and headed up toward Third, a man was carrying a sign that read: "The end of the world is at hand." Blair looked at Olly and said, "He might be right."

The temperature had gone up about five degrees since they first sat down at the pier with Agent Jones. Blair said, "I need a cold drink." Walking to The Pub they decided to sit at an outside table. Olly went inside and came out with two bottles of water then left Blair to go to the market. Ashley was working that day and walked outside to say hello. She hugged Blair and asked, "How are you doing?"

"I'm still in a state of shock. The first break-in was one thing, but the second time was more than I can handle. I'm not sure I can ever move back after men had been killed there."

"Olly filled me in about the shoot-out. Have they found out who those men were yet?"

Blair wasn't sure how to answer that. "I really don't know.

Officer Tuttle hasn't gotten back to me. I spent the night at Olly's and he might not have known where I was."

"I saw him here a little while ago," Ashley said.

"Was he looking for me?" Blair asked.

"Yes, and I told him that you had stayed with her last night. Manuel said that she had come by to open up and she said you were still at her house. What can I do to help you?" Ashley asked.

"You've done so much already. I'm okay."

Blair decided that this was a good time to return the call to Thomas Adams. She dialed his home number and the phone rang but there wasn't any answer. She left him a message. "Hi, this is Blair. Sorry I missed you, but if you get a chance, call me back. Hope everything is okay."

The sun was high over the top of the buildings on the corner and Blair was glad that there was an awning over the outside tables. She was watching the people on the corner waiting for a bus. The usual array of kooks stood in line with the normal work force. She couldn't help but chuckle when she saw a man wearing shorts and a woman's bra standing in the line. *This is my California*, she thought to herself. Just then her cell phone rang.

"Hello Blair, it's Blake. How are you doing?"

She hadn't talked to him in a while and wanted to update him on so much. She also remembered the promise to Agent Jones and was being a bit cautious with what she said. She knew that he had an early class and probably just got out of it. They had a great relationship and Blake had been there from the first day that she moved into her apartment.

"Blake, it appears that the FBI knows more than they told me and I want to try to get Agent Jones to trust me with some of that information."

"Be careful, Blair. The FBI is not to be fooled with. Do you want me along for protection?"

Blair laughed. She thought that must have been the first time she laughed aloud in a long time. "What kind of protection do you think you can offer?" This caused both of them to laugh. Blake was one of the nicest people she knew and he was not someone you would think of for protection.

"Well I guess protection was a bad choice of words," Blake said. They both laughed again. "I could at least go with you when you meet with her if you wanted."

"I appreciate the offer and once I know more I might ask for your help." She felt guilty not telling Blake what she had already found out. He would understand she told herself because there is so much more she needed to know. She promised to call him when he got home from school. Today was his late night class and he would not be back until after ten.

Ashley came out with Blair's lunch and Manuel also came out to see his prized creation and make sure she was happy with it. "You're the best, Manuel," she said.

"You too, senora."

She always loved working her shift at The Pub when he was cooking. He would make sure all the customers who were regulars had a little special touch to their order.

"Can I get you anything else?"

"No, this is perfect. I hope to be back working in a few days," she answered. As she started eating her salad her thoughts took her in many directions. *What's next? Maybe I should call Hunter's dad again before I decide on what to do.* She enjoyed the time eating alone on the patio of The Pub. It was almost as if nothing had happened.

"Hello." The voice was from the street; it startled her. It was Officer Tuttle. "Sorry I didn't mean to scare you," he said.

"I was just in a dream world. Sit down, Officer."

"I don't want to disturb your lunch," he said, "but I have some important information for you."

"Please join me. I'm done anyway." She wiped her chin. "Manuel makes these salads so big I can never eat the whole thing."

He sat across from her and took his hat off. "We have been working on the identification of the men who were in your apartment. Our office seemed to hit a roadblock with every move until Captain Parker got a call from the FBI office in Los Angeles." Blair almost dropped her fork. "Well, it appears that we will be working on this investigation with their office and the bureau chief, a Mr. Dean Curry. He called back and gave us their

90

identification. Not exactly sure why they were in your apartment but both men are Iraqi nationals. Their ID did not help but it was through a fingerprint analysis that their true identification was discovered."

Blair didn't know exactly what to say but the look on her face must have said a lot.

"Are you okay?" Officer Tuttle asked.

"Yes, I just get more confused with every piece of this puzzle."

"I know," he said. "We're pretty confused too. Captain Parker has gone to the FBI's Los Angeles bureau office to meet with Dean Curry. I wanted to find you to let you know what we've found out."

"Do you know what these men were looking for?" Blair asked.

"No, maybe that's why the FBI agreed to meet with Captain Parker today. I think they have an idea of what's going on but won't tell anyone. We have part of the puzzle and they have the other part. They're normally not willing to share information. If you find out anything, Blair, please let us know and I will try to keep you informed."

"I just have a few questions, Officer. When you say they were Iraqi nationals, just what do you mean?"

"That's one of the crazy things. It appears that one of them may be on the Army's list of Saddam supporters."

"You mean the men who were pictured on the terrorist deck of cards that the Army put out?"

"Yes, it appears that one of them may be a close confidant of Saddam."

"This really doesn't make any sense. Thanks for giving me the information."

Officer Tuttle got up from the table and again asked one more time if she was okay before he left.

"Yes, I'm doing as well as can be expected. Thanks for asking." This new information helped her make up her mind. *I will call agent Jones and help her.* She figured that she needed to know more about what was going on. Blair also wanted to make sure she protected Hunter's name.

Olly returned from the market and Blair filled her in on what Officer Tuttle had to say. She also told her of the decision to help Agent Jones. "I just have to make sure that the information they think Hunter had gets to the right people. I know he was always very loyal to the Army and our country and I don't want anything bad said about him."

Olly understood. "I don't blame you. I'm just worried that this might be too dangerous for someone not trained in this sort of thing."

"Agent Jones said she would make sure that I was safe. I'm going to give her a call." Blair dialed Jones' cell phone number. Agent Jones answered and seemed pleased that she called her so soon.

"Blair, I'm glad that you called."

"Agent Jones, I know a little more about this situation and want to help if I can. I also want you to level with me before I commit to assisting you."

"What kind of information are you talking about?"

"About the details about the men in my apartment. When we met you didn't say anything about them. Have you found out anything else?" Blair felt that Officer Tuttle gave her a lot of the details freely and had no reason to hold back the truth. She wanted to see what Agent Jones would tell her.

"Blair, I'll level with you. Like I told you before, the FBI director wasn't too pleased with my performance on the search of your apartment. The shooting caused him to take the case away from me and put it in the hands of Dean Curry and the L.A. office. I have the opportunity to solve this case with your help and clear both your husband and myself."

"That doesn't answer my question about the men in my apartment. Why should I be concerned about clearing you?"

"Because I'm the one person who can get you the answers you want. The two men found dead in your apartment were both Iraqi nationals and one of them has been on the Homeland Security watch list. How he got into this country we're not sure. His first name was Ahmad and he had recently been under investigation by the U.S. Army and held at the Abu Ghraib Prison in Baghdad.

They're still investigating the identification of the second man." Blair listened as Allisa continued. "Blair, I told you everything that I know. I told Dean Curry that you have been very cooperative in the investigation. I'm sure he will want to talk to you, but unless I get more information I can't help you with your other questions. I feel that you have some information that you haven't shared with me. This may be information that you don't even realize you have."

"The only information that I had was that the two men were Iraqi. I found this out just minutes ago from Officer Tuttle. I don't know anything else."

Allisa didn't like it that Tuttle knew so much. "I still want your help, Blair."

"I want to help you Agent Jones."

"We'll be a good team, Blair. I'm packing for the trip to Philadelphia. Come with me and together we can get some answers."

"I'm not sure of what value I would be but I will come along."

"Pack lightly; we'll be on the move a lot until we find out the answer to this mystery. We'll fly out of Los Angeles this evening. I'll take care of everything."

"I'll meet you at the airport. What airline are we leaving on?"

"I have a contact with United. I'll pay for everything. Meet me at the United ticket counter at eight thirty. We'll probably be on the red eye."

Blair felt Agent Jones had leveled with her and she was hopeful about the prospect of working on this mystery, versus just being part of it. She told Olly her plans and said she would stay in touch. "Tell Ashley and Blake that I had to go to Philadelphia to see Hunter's dad; they'll understand and won't ask too many questions." She left the table at The Pub and headed down the Promenade toward her apartment. Olly wanted to do something but just stood and watched and hoped that this was a good move.

Ashley came back out and asked, "Where's Blair?"

"She's going back to Philly," Olly said. "Guess Hunter's

dad needed her. She just felt she came home too soon."

"I understand," Ashley said, "especially with the break-in and everything else. I forgot to remind her about the package she left here yesterday. I put it upstairs in the office for her."

"She'll be back soon and we can give it to her then. It's probably nothing important." Olly was busy thinking about the danger Blair was putting herself in.

Fourteen

Al Yawer helped Omar to his feet after they crawled into the woods. "Can you make it back to the car?" Omar just nodded and it was obvious he was in a lot of pain. It was too dark to tell exactly where he had been hit and how serious. Shots were still coming from the yard of Thomas Adams' home and Yawer knew that they had to move quickly. Although it was night, the moon's rays filtered through some of the trees on the clearing ahead. The shadows shielded the two fugitives from the back of the Adams' house. The woods were thick with large maple trees that helped hide both of them but the sound of sirens rang out in the night. Omar was wet from crawling into the woods. He could not tell what was blood and what was wet from the previous rains. They had to get to their car and get there soon. Sirens seemed to surround them as they made their way through the thickest part of the tree line. The car was still a block away and Omar slumped as they came out of the woods. Yawer lifted him over his shoulder. He would have to carry him the rest of the way. Omar was close to comatose. Yawer could not leave him there.

Back in the yard, Captain Douglas stood over Andy as the paramedics helped him onto a stretcher. "You did real good, kid. Did you see the men who went into the woods?"

Andy was pretty clear about the events but said he only saw the man who identified himself as an FBI Agent. "I know that when I got to the area by the split rail fence the bullets came from under the large shrub behind the house. I was knocked down by one of the shots and lost it for a minute or so. There were many shots after that along the back of the house. Not all of the shots seemed to be coming at me," he said.

The captain got on his radio and called to the two cars that he had circling the neighborhood. "Do you see anything suspicious?" he asked.

"No Sir, but we are moving to Blue Bird Street right behind the woods and Mr. Adams' house."

"Fan out and make sure you cover every inch."

Steve asked Captain Douglas how he could help. "You and I need to head into the woods to see if those men are still hiding. You also need to fill me in on what in the hell is going on here." Steve wasn't exactly sure himself. The objective seemed so easy. Get into the Adams' house, search it one more time and get out. Where had it gone wrong? Steve told Captain Douglas that his bureau chief, Dino Tuchy, would fill him in on the details. The only thing he could tell Captain Douglas was that he and his partner were ambushed on the way out of the Adams' house. The moon gave the two men entering the woods a clear view of the exterior of the tree line ahead. They decided that the safest move was to stick together and fan out when they got half way through. Neither man knew what they were dealing with nor if there were more fugitives in the woods waiting for the original two who were escaping.

Yawer had Omar over his right shoulder and moved inside the tree line for cover. The plan to leave the car a few blocks away was a good plan but now it made for a hard retreat. Omar had passed out and Yawer was carrying dead weight. He wanted to get to their car and escape the sirens that seemed to be getting closer. The car was in sight and he felt a bit of relief. He got Omar into the back seat when a squad car with a bright light came toward them. He jumped over the front seat and started the car. He had the element of surprise on his side. With the lights off he gunned the engine and headed right at the squad car. Yawer rammed the squad car, spinning it around as he headed down Blue Bird Street. He knew that the retreat out of town would not be easy. He planned to eliminate some of the men chasing them. The police car was lodged against a parked truck and was badly damaged. Captain Douglas heard a loud crash as he and Steve Watkins made their way into the woods. "Sounds like it's over to our right," he said. Steve agreed. They moved in the direction of the crash they had heard.

Yawer, still speeding, headed down Blue Bird Street and took the first left. He heard more sirens headed his way. The chase was on. He kept the headlights off on his car so that he could not be seen from a distance. Scouting the neighborhood beforehand had helped. He knew that Blue Bird Street did not go through to the highway. He also knew that there were many dead end streets in the area and did not want to get trapped in one of them. Yawer turned down Cannon Street and sped up. Just when he turned to look back, a car from out of nowhere came out of a driveway. He swerved to miss it.

Captain Douglas and Steve made their way out of the woods and saw two officers standing next to a badly damaged cop car. "What the hell happened?"

"Someone driving without their headlights on hit us," they said.

"Shit, would you turn your lights on if you were trying to get away?" He called out on his radio to the other squad car. They said they were in pursuit of a dark compact vehicle that was headed west on Cannon. "Get a good description for us. I'll get the state police on the horn and have them join the chase. They may be driving with their headlights off so be aware." He called to the local office of the state police and filled them in. They said they would cover Highway 13 in both directions. That was the only way out of town. Sounded like a good plan. Captain Douglas told Steve, "We should get back to the squad car to join the chase."

Steve said, "I'll wait here for my chief. I can't leave Frank lying here all alone." He was still feeling the pain of losing his partner.

"Okay, you and Mr. Tuchy meet me at our headquarters in Bridgewater."

"I'll give him the message."

Douglas got into his squad car and took a shortcut to Cannon Street. He came to a car still in the middle of the street. He got out and asked the two people standing near the car if they were okay. Billy Bridges and his wife were shaken but said they were fine. They told the captain that a dark car, they thought it looked like a Chevy, came down the street without headlights on and

97

almost t-boned their car. The captain did not alert them to the fact that these were men being pursued. He took their information and headed back to his squad car. He got on his radio and alerted both his men and the state police that they were probably looking for a dark midsized Chevy, possibly a Malibu. He also said that the passenger's side had been hit when it collided with the squad car.

Yawer kept driving through the neighborhood and looked for a spot to hide their car. He knew that by now the local police would have a description of the Chevy and that the damage to the car would give them away. There was a large field a few blocks away. The headlights were still off when he turned right on Apple Lane. He saw a perfect spot and pulled the Chevy over the curb and into the tree-covered cove. They needed a new getaway vehicle. He drove into the brush and was able to cover the back of the vehicle from the street view. The woods were very thick in that area but Yawer found a clearing allowing him to pull close to two hundred yards off the street. He crawled into the back to check on Omar. He had been bleeding very badly. Yawer tried to listen for a heartbeat but there was none. Omar was dead! He knew he must hide the body so the police wouldn't find it. Omar knew that this was a dangerous mission and Allah would be pleased that he gave his life for this cause.

Yawer left the vehicle in the woods as he started a search for another way out of town. He saw some lights from the corner and slowly walked toward them. It was a party store and a group of teens had gathered in front. He just walked by and ventured down the street. He could come back to get Omar's body once he found new transportation. The group of teens had been playing loud music and never looked up as Yawer passed by. He looked at the street signs as he turned the corner. He was now at the intersection of Apple Lane and Pine. He headed north on Pine and saw a line of cars parked along the side of the street. As he approached it became evident that someone was having a party in the neighborhood. He scanned the line of cars and a group of motorcycles caught his eye. That would be the perfect getaway vehicle. Yawer pushed a Harley away from the group and toward the end of the line of cars. He was able to start it and headed around the corner of Pine back down Apple Lane. The group of teens was still standing outside the party store. They looked up when they saw a red Harley pass by. They did not seem to take notice of the person riding it.

Yawer pulled the Harley into the woods next to the Chevy. He was able to get his gear out of the Chevy and put it into the side saddle bags on the Harley. He would have to leave Omar. He pulled Omar out of the back seat and dragged his body deeper into the wooded area. Yawer found a ditch, probably created by heavy spring rains or melting snow. It was about three or four feet deep. He laid Omar's body in the ditch and covered it with branches and dead leaves. Once Omar's body was covered he returned to the car and wiped it down. He did not want any evidence left behind. He put the documents that they had brought with them on the bike. He wanted to make sure that the maps were not left in the car.

Yawer pushed the Harley out of the woods and started it. He headed down Apple Lane and knew that he had to get out of town before the Harley came up missing. The streets would lead him to Highway 13 and back to Mansfield Square. He felt there wouldn't be a problem now that he found a new form of transportation.

Captain Douglas circled the streets of the neighborhood. He sensed that the fugitives were still close by and that they would be looking for an escape route. He passed a group of teens standing in front of a party store. Captain Douglas stopped and asked the group if they saw a dark Chevy go by. They said that they did not. "Did you see anyone driving really fast or without their headlights on?" No, was the answer from the teens. Douglas headed down Apple Lane and turned onto Pine. *Wow, cars everywhere,* he thought. *This would be a good place to hide the Chevy; no one would notice it among this line of vehicles.* The Captain drove down Pine slowly looking at every vehicle. He did not see any sign of the Chevy or any other vehicle that matched that description. With suspected damage to the driver's side it would be easy to spot. The cars were lined up and down the street. There weren't any empty spots; nothing seemed out of the ordinary. There were about four motorcycles in the middle of the line of cars.

Yawer turned off of Apple Lane and onto Main Street. That

would lead him to Highway 13 and his escape route. He saw a state police car headed his way. The first test was about to happen. Yawer had the helmet on that was on the seat of the Harley and hoped that he would not cause any additional attention. The police car went by and Yawer kept his head down. He was driving at a normal speed so as to not cause any additional attention. Highway 13 was ahead and he would head north toward Mansfield Square. He did not feel that he should alert El Jaafi and Abdulla until he was safely out of Bridgewater.

There was a line of traffic on Highway 13 after he made his turn. The police had set-up a roadblock. They were stopping every vehicle. Yawer knew that they would be looking for two men in a car but he did not want to take any chances. He watched as the cars proceeded slowly to the checkpoint. It appeared that the police were searching the cars and trucks. Two officers were checking from each side. It also looked like the drivers were producing some sort of papers to be inspected. Yawer had to get out of this line.

The captain called to his squad cars to see where they were and if they had found anything. They had circled the area twice and had heard from the state police that the roadblocks had been set up on Highway 13 in both directions. Captain Douglas told them that they should continue to concentrate on the local area and the state police would handle the highway. He headed back toward Mr. Adams' house to see, if by any chance, the fugitives headed back to the scene of the crime.

Yawer pulled the bike off to the side of the road. He got off the bike hoping to make it appear that he had engine trouble. The vehicle behind him slowed down and the driver asked if he could help. "No thanks," he said, "just seems to have a miss and I don't want to get stranded. Do you know what is going on up ahead?"

"No, I'm just headed to New York." He waved goodbye and wished Yawer good luck with the bike. Yawer continued to act as if he was having problems with the bike as other cars passed by and he pushed the motorcycle further off the road. When he was sure that he was far enough off the side of the road, he got back on and ducked into the woods. The ride through the woods would be easy as long as he did not make too much noise. When he felt he was near the roadblock, he turned the bike off and pushed it for about thirty feet. This was not an easy task. The Harley was very heavy and the ground was soft in spots. He was able to get past where he felt the police were and restarted the bike. He continued riding through the woods until he was about half a mile past the roadblock. Yawer returned to the highway and headed north toward Mansfield Square.

Steve Watkins called Dino Tuchy to find out how close his boss was to Bridgewater. "We're just about to get off of Highway 13," Dino said. "It took a little longer because the state police had a roadblock set up on the highway."

Steve said, "It might be best to meet at the Adams' house. The local and state police are checking the area for the men that got away and we can check the house one more time if you want."

Dino agreed. "We should contact Captain Douglas but not until I have one more look around."

Douglas circled the Adams' house but there was no sign of the fugitive. *I have to try to contact Thomas*, he thought. *Maybe we should set-up a 24 hour watch here just in case they return.* He figured that after a few hours of searching for the men who got away in the woods he would redirect a team to the Adams' home. He continued down the street searching the next few blocks.

Yawer was an experienced motorcyclist and the road up Highway 13 was a smooth trip. Many times at home he would ride a bike from village to village. He thought the best route would be to head toward West Bristol and cross the Delaware River at the Burlington-Bristol Toll Bridge. That would be less traveled than the bridge on Highway 276. He would be in New Jersey after crossing the Delaware River and would contact El Jaafi to update him on what had happened. His escape was critical.

Fifteen

Dino Tuchy had been with the bureau for over twenty-five years and was one of its most decorated field agents. He was given the Philadelphia assignment after he helped break up a case where a man was trying to sell state secrets. He was a tough boss and Steve knew that all hell would be raised when he arrived. Dino had been divorced for a long time, a by-product of the job. Many agents knew that the job caused marital problems. It was once rumored that Dino had an affair with another agent but no one knew for sure.

Steve Watkins was still dealing with the sudden loss of his long-time partner, Frank Walker. How would he explain that to Dino? Frank Walker was single and had been living in an apartment near the downtown area of Philadelphia that had seen a lot of renovation. Steve was glad that he didn't have to tell a wife and children that their husband and dad had been killed on the job. Steve had been to Frank's place a few times when he and his wife would head to a concert or ballgame. Frank was a quiet guy who liked to play golf and ride his Harley on weekends. He was well liked by everyone. Steve and Frank had been partners; however, because Frank was single they did not socialize often. Although many of their assignments were investigative work, the reality of danger was always there. When it did happen, it was always a shock, and Steve was in shock.

Steve moved his car in front of the Adams' house and waited for Dino to arrive. After about ten minutes the black Chevy Suburban pulled up. Steve got out of his car to greet Dino. He had brought another agent, Jon David, with him.

Steve was surprised when Dino put his hand on his shoulder and offered his concern over Frank's death. "Are you okay, Steve?"

"I'm not really sure. So much has happened so fast that it hasn't quite registered yet."

"I know it's hard to lose anyone," Dino told him, "especially your partner."

Steve almost broke down and struggled to hold it together. He felt that they needed to solve this and get the men who killed his partner.

"Fill me in," Dino said.

"Frank and I made our way onto the property with no problem. We saw that the local police were passing by and watching the house from the street so I decided to go through the house and Frank was searching the garage. We would be in and out in less than fifteen minutes. I'm not exactly sure what happened but I was in the house when I heard a couple of shots. They were muffled like a silencer was used. I came out on the back porch and there were some shots being fired from a man on the lawn toward the woods. I thought it was Frank shooting until the same person shot at me. It took a few seconds to realize that it was a local cop. I found Frank at the back door of the garage. They murdered him, Boss." Tears welled up in Steve's eyes.

Dino felt sorry for Steve. He had never lost a partner and didn't quite know what to say. He thought it would be best to keep Steve thinking about the case. "Did you complete your search?"

Steve cleared his throat. "I was about done but I don't know what Frank accomplished."

"You and Jon go back into the house and I'll call the local captain to tell him that we'll meet him here. It will give you both a few minutes to complete the search." The two agents headed toward the Adams' home as Dino called Captain Douglas.

The captain's phone rang. He thought that there were more calls to his phone and radio in the last couple of hours than in the last two years. "Captain, this is Bureau Chief Dino Tuchy of the FBI. I'm almost to the Adams' house and would like to meet you there."

"I'm just completing the trip around the neighborhood. I passed by the Adams' home a few minutes ago and all seemed quiet. I will be there to meet you in about ten minutes."

103

Dino thought he would move to the front porch of the Adams' house so that he could alert his men when the local police arrived. Steve had told him that a second EMS unit had taken Frank's body to the Bridgewater Hospital. Dino knocked on the door and Steve came to see what was up. He told them to complete the search quickly then look around the yard for clues to the shoot-out.

Captain Douglas soon pulled up to the Adams' home and saw two cars parked in front. He did not see anyone in the cars so he pulled behind them and got out of his squad car. Dino called out to the captain.

"We're up here."

Captain Douglas walked toward the porch. "Where are your men?"

"I told them to check out back where my agent was killed. Steve is still shook up and I need him to focus on the situation."

Douglas thought that was a normal move although no one really knew what was normal for the FBI. Douglas was about to find out. Dino was quick to point out to him that the FBI would be taking the lead in the investigation but would keep the local police involved.

"I need to know what's going on," the captain said. "We have one of our citizen's homes being involved in multiple break-ins and now a shoot-out."

Dino agreed to give him a heads-up. Captain Douglas said, "I still have to find Thomas Adams and let him know what has happened."

Dino suggested that his men and Captain Douglas should search through the Adams' home together to make sure that there wasn't any problem before Mr. Adams arrived. "My men should be done searching the yard and the back of the garage."

"Sorry for your loss," Captain Douglas said.

The two men walked around the garage to the back of the house to find the two FBI agents. By this time they had been through the home and were on the back porch. "We need you two to accompany us through the Adams' home," Dino said. Steve looked a little confused knowing that they just finished going through the house a minute ago. "I want to make sure everything is okay inside and Captain Douglas should be with us," he said. It was obvious to his men that Dino was making it seem that they were going to share everything with the local police. Steve knew if they found something in their search it would not be detailed to the local guys.

Douglas said, "I'll lead the way."

"Sure," said Dino.

They entered the home through the back door of the garage. It was still open from the earlier break-in. Captain Douglas had not asked why the FBI was there in the first place but Dino knew that it would come up. The garage led to the kitchen door where all four men entered the house. They turned on the kitchen light and everything looked in place. Douglas turned to Dino and asked the question. "Why are you here and what is the FBI so interested in a break-in here in Bridgewater?"

Dino looked back at him. "First we should complete the search of the home."

Captain Douglas said, "I need to know what is going on, and I want to know now."

"I can't tell you the whole story until I talk to my director in Washington," Dino said. "But before the night is out I will fill you in. I will also need to know what you and Mr. Adams have to offer to the story."

The captain shook his head knowing that getting information from the feds was like pulling teeth. "We will see about that. Let's all split up and check the rooms."

"Good idea. We're just making sure that there isn't someone still here or they haven't left any evidence behind."

The four men walked through the kitchen and Dino suggested they not touch anything so the crime lab could do a fingerprint analysis. Captain Douglas said that they would have to have the state police do that because he did not have that capability.

Dino turned back toward him. "I ordered a crime lab team to Bridgewater and they should be here any minute."

Captain Douglas knew now that the FBI wasn't going to let the local police handle much of the investigation.

105

The house seemed neat and did not appear that anything was out of place. The captain told Dino that in the first break-in there were tables and lamps overturned and papers tossed around. "Looked like someone was looking for something," he said. "We thought it was kids because Mr. Adams' son had a pretty big baseball card collection and a lot of trophies from his high school days.."

"Did you find anything missing?"

"Mr. Adams said he checked and everything seemed to be here. That is what made me suspicious because the baseball cards were never touched and kids would have taken them."

"I agree," Dino said. "Seems like you had that detail covered."

"We still don't know who broke in," Captain Douglas said, "but maybe your crime lab guys will be able to give us some answers."

"You know I will give you a copy of their report," Dino answered.

The search through the house produced nothing other than to confirm that it was empty and nothing had been disturbed. All four men walked out to the front porch and Dino said he wanted to wait for the crime lab team to arrive. Captain Douglas called out to his squad cars on the radio to see where they were in their search.

"Captain we've gone up and down every street and cannot find anything suspicious." He then called the local hospital to see how Andy was doing.

Dino turned to Steve, "Making it look like kids in the first break-in was a good idea but you should have taken something that kids would have wanted like a television or a few baseball cards."

Steve said, "We didn't want to take anything due to the loss of Mr. Adams' son; it would only cause him more grief."

"We would get them back to him," Dino said.

"I guess, but we thought it was best at the time to do it the way Frank and I planned." Dino knew that Steve was still hurting so he dropped the line of questions and walked over to Captain Douglas. "Our crime lab techs will be here soon. Do you want to wait with us for them or should we meet you back at your office."

"I still have fugitives on the loose in my town," Captain

Douglas said. "Until that is resolved I will be in on the search for them."

"I'll call you and we can set up a meeting place," Dino suggested.

Captain Douglas reminded him that Mr. Adams did not know about the second incident at his home and may come back at any minute. "I will keep a lookout for him," Dino said.

"Mr. Adams' brother lives just outside of Bridgewater near Croydon. I'm going to send a man over to his brother's house to see if Thomas is there."

"Good idea," Dino said. "Call me if you need our help."

The captain walked to his squad car and when he got inside he called the state police to see if their roadblocks had come up with anything. The vehicle searches both north and south on Highway 13 had not brought any results. They decided that they would keep their position until midnight. He informed the state police that the FBI had sent a team headed by a Dino Tuchy to Bridgewater. The state police had the same reaction that the local police did. Why the FBI? What was going on and what was the FBI not telling them?

Captain Douglas called to Croydon to get the local police to see if Mr. Adams was at his brother's home. He talked to an officer and did not want to cause any more concern than necessary. "We have a small problem here in Bridgewater and one of our citizens may be visiting his brother's home just outside of Croydon. If you could send a car out to check on him and ask him to call me, I would appreciate it. His brother is Bill Adams; he lives off Highway 13 on Columbia Drive." The Croydon officer said they would be happy to help and they would send a squad car over to the Adams' home on Columbia right away. They knew who Bill Adams was and where he lived. Captain Douglas gave the officer his cell phone number. "If he's not at his brother's house let me know." The officer agreed to call Captain Douglas once they visited the Adams' home.

******

Yawer headed up Highway 13 through Croydon when he spotted a local police car headed toward him. He made sure that he was doing the speed limit and tried not to look suspicious. The car passed him by and he breathed a sigh of relief. He would soon be at West Bristol and out of Pennsylvania. The officer turned to look at the red Harley as it passed. *Wow, that's the first Harley Dyna I've ever seen.* Being a motorcycle enthusiast he had seen one in a recent bike magazine. *I'd love to drive one*, he thought.

****

Dino sat on the porch of the Adams' home and he and Jon talked about the best way to keep critical information from the local police. "They have to know that it's something big but what should we tell them?" Jon asked.

"We'll let them know that there is the possibility of a group of anti-war activists that is causing a disturbance at the homes of military personnel who have been killed in Iraq. We could say it has happened in other cities and the FBI wants to make sure that we can protect our citizens from them."

"Great idea," Jon said. "It may cover both break-ins and this incident. We'll have to tell them that this is the first sign of violence and that is why they hadn't heard about it."

The search for the men continued both through Bridgewater and on Highway 13 in and out of town. The two squad cars continued to drive around the neighborhoods near the Adams home. When they came in contact with local citizens they said they were looking for kids that may have broken into a home. They did not want to cause concern especially since they hadn't found the men that caused all the shooting.

As he drove back down Apple Lane, Captain Douglas got a call from his office. "Captain we just got a call from the Dietlins. Seems they were having a graduation party and someone stole a motorcycle parked in front of their house."

He was only a block away from there. He turned down Pine Street to where he had seen a line of cars and four motorcycles parked on an earlier search of the neighborhood. Mr. Dietlin came out and said one of the men attending his son's graduation party

108

had his Harley taken. Captain Douglas wanted to get a full description of the bike.

Mr. Dietlin continued, "The owner said it was a new Harley Davidson Dyna. There were only a few of them made," the man said. "The bike is worth over $20,000."

Captain Douglas now knew that the fugitives must have ditched their car in favor of the Harley. He went back to his squad car and immediately called the state police to alert them to look for a red Harley with one or two men aboard. He doubled back around the corner and saw the group of teens that he had questioned earlier.

"Have any of you seen a Harley come by in the past hour?"

"Yes," said Perry. "It was headed down Apple Lane toward Highway 13."

"How many people were riding on it?"

"One. It looked just like the one that Billy Jamison owns."

"What color was the Harley?"

"Red."

Captain Douglas called back to the state police. "We need to send information north and south to be on the lookout for a new red Harley with one rider. Seems to be a special bike," he told them. Captain Douglas felt that the man must be out of town on the highway by now. He wasn't going to share the information with the FBI yet at least not until he knew more about why they were involved. An APB was sent out by the state police and would go to every police officer in the state so that they could be on the lookout for the red Harley. Captain Douglas called to his men to let them know about the new information. He also said they needed to search the wooded areas by foot because they must have ditched the dark Chevy. This would be no easy task. Bridgewater, like many small towns, was heavily covered with trees and parks. That was part of its small town charm.

The search began with all the local officers in Bridgewater searching the woods. Because of the location of the missing Harley, they decided that they should start the search around that area. They were told to tell anyone who asked that a fox was spotted and could be rabid. People should report it to the main

109

police office if they spotted it. Captain Douglas knew if the story got out that they had shootings and fugitives on the loose it would cause a panic. The fox story would make sense, especially in the spring. Because there were so many wooded lots around Bridgewater the local residents would often see foxes, rabbits and beavers building their habitats.

The cell phone rang and Captain Douglas answered. "Glad you called Thomas. I sent the local Croydon police to make sure you were okay. Thought you might be at Bill's house but I wanted to make certain you're safe."

Thomas said he was sorry that he didn't inform Captain Douglas that he would be going out for the whole night. "I plan to spend the night here and return home in the morning," he told the captain.

"Probably a good idea. When you get back to town call me because I would like to go over a few things with you. It's not urgent but I just want to make sure you're kept in the loop."

Thomas figured that there must be some new information regarding his break-in. Thomas hung up and told Bill and Martha that Captain Douglas just wanted to make sure he was okay.

"Nice to have the authorities looking out for you," his brother Bill said.

The Croydon officer went back to his car and headed back on his normal route, but as he headed out his dispatcher radioed him. He got the information that an APB had been put out to be on the lookout for a red Harley with one rider possibly going north or south on Highway 13. It had to be the red Harley he saw before on Highway 13 when he was headed to Bill Adams' house. The officer got on the radio and informed the state police that he spotted one rider going north on Highway 13 in a red Harley Dyna about fifteen minutes ago. When the news came in, the state police ordered all patrol cars to travel north of Croydon and be on the lookout for the biker. They asked the officer how he knew what kind of bike it was.

"I love Harleys and the Dyna was featured in an article this month in a biker magazine."

The chase was on and so much lay in the balance. No one really knew how critical this information would be.

110

Sixteen

Blair got out of the airport limo. She used the service whenever she was going out of town. She paid the driver the eleven dollars and grabbed her bag and headed across the street to the LAX terminal. She looked at her watch: nine p.m. *I can't believe I'm early*. Agent Jones told her that they had the red eye flight to Philadelphia and that they should meet at the United ticket counter around ten p.m. She thought that she should call Olly and let her know that everything was okay. She grabbed her cell phone and dialed the number.

"I'm at LAX and everything is going good," she told her. "I will call you when we get to Philly." Olly was still uncertain that this was a good idea, but when Blair made up her mind there was no changing it. "I feel bad that I didn't talk to Blake and Ashley," she said. "They have been so great to me."

"I told them that Hunter's dad was having some problems and you needed to help him. They understood and said they wished they could help more."

Olly made her promise that she would call every day.

"You know that I will," Blair said.

"You probably should call your parents."

"I haven't told them about the first break-in let alone all the other things. Maybe I'll wait to see what happens in the next few days. I talked to my mom yesterday just to let her know that I was okay; I don't want to get them upset about the problems here. You know, I've talked to them every day but until I know what's going on for sure, I don't want to have them come out here."

Blair walked to the United Airlines ticket counter and saw Agent Jones by the ticket booth talking to a gate agent.

"Hi," Blair said.

"I'm glad that you're here a little early. This is Steven. He

111

works for United Airlines; we went to school together in New York."

Blair said hello and seemed unsure as to why they were talking to a gate agent instead of going to the ticket counter.

"Steven said he'll get us on the next flight to Philadelphia so we can make our meeting at headquarters." Blair was even more confused, but went along with the conversation.

"You know the meeting is very important," Blair added.

"Yeah, you're right about that," she answered. When Steven walked away she filled her in. "We're flying standby as government agents. I showed him my security clearance and I have a set for you." Blair looked at the packet that Allisa handed her and saw it had a picture and a description of her with the FBI logo on it. Her name was inscribed across the documents with the FBI seal in the lower right corner; it looked very official.

"Blair, you're an FBI agent according to these documents. Just be cool and no one will suspect."

Blair thought this would be like rehearsing for a play. "I can do this, no problem Allisa. I just don't know how you got all this and so quick."

"I'm FBI, that's what we do. I have my contacts and your picture was on file from your Screen Actors Guild card. I've had a lot of time from our noon meeting to plan this."

"What if I said I wasn't going to go with you?"

"Then I would burn these and go myself. But I knew that you needed to have answers and felt pretty sure you'd be here. It looks like you packed very light. How did you get all your things into one large duffle bag?"

"It's something Hunter showed me. He traveled so much and always said he traveled light. You just roll all your clothes like a newspaper and set them in your travel bag like logs. That way you can pack double the amount of clothes. You didn't tell me what we would need so I brought a suit and some casual things. The tough part was shoes. I just love my shoes."

Steven came back and said everything was set. The plane had plenty of open seats and he would get them on before takeoff. He asked to see Blair's documents and after checking them out he said they looked fine. He told them to meet back at Gate 17 about thirty minutes before takeoff and he would escort them onto the plane. He gave them both a boarding pass for security check-in.

Allisa kissed him on the cheek. "We'll have to get together when I get back" she said.

"Sure thing" Steven answered.

"Let's get a coffee and talk," Allisa told Blair. They walked to the security check-in and handed their boarding passes and driver's licenses to the officer checking documents. Their bags came off the scanner and they collected them and headed for the coffee shop. Blair had more questions but knew that now was not the time to ask; this was the time to listen. Maybe Allisa would give her answers to some of her questions. She was committed to the trip and anyway she was an FBI agent now.

Allisa got them two coffees and asked if Blair was hungry.

"Not really, I haven't been able to eat much for weeks but I had a large salad earlier and that should hold me for a long time."

"We're going to be on the move so you will need your strength."

"I'll be okay," Blair said. It was obvious to Allisa that Blair was in good shape. Blair always watched what she ate and exercised a lot. Hiking and jogging were two of her favorite things, but the past few weeks had taken its toll on her. With the news of Hunter's death and the ordeal of the funeral she had lost a few pounds. Her mom made sure that she was getting some food and taking vitamins but this had been a tough time.

"Blair, I'm going to need your help on this mission. The FBI thinks that I blew it at your apartment. When Baxter got shot and those two intruders were killed, they took me off your case. I plan to use my contacts in Philadelphia to get the information we need to solve this."

"I hope you have some good contacts," Blair told her.

"Well, I have a real good old friend who is the head of the Philadelphia Bureau and I have alerted him to our arrival. He will help me because he is on the same case. This will either make both of our careers or kill mine for good."

"What do you mean he's on the same case?"

"The bureau figured that either the information we were

113

looking for was with you or with Hunter's dad. He has been working to find the information in Bridgewater, if it exists there."

"Does that mean that the FBI was involved in the break-in at his dad's place?"

"Yes," Allisa answered, "but they didn't find anything."

"I'm not about to help do anything that will hurt his dad," Blair told her.

"I don't want that either. We'll work together and solve this."

"You mean like the two that broke into my apartment."

"Yes, that's exactly what I mean."

"Okay, but I have to know what's going on to be effective."

"In due time." They drank their coffee and waited until their flight's departure.

Blair knew that Allisa had given her some of this same information before, but this time she filled in a lot of the blanks. Now she knew the FBI was working on a case that included Hunter's dad's house as well as hers. She also knew that the documents must be extremely important. *I wonder what is in them* she thought. *Hunter, you must have uncovered something big.*

"We should walk to Gate 17." It was at the end of the United concourse.

"Where in New York did you meet Steven?" Blair wanted to know more about her.

"He went to the same college I did. We were in a couple of classes together and guess we went out a few times."

"He seems to have a thing for you."

"Blair, I admire you. You and Hunter seemed to have the real thing going. I've never had that luck. I researched both of you before we met and I found out that you were very loyal to him. I know he was gone a lot and that must have been hard. I also know that you had an offer to do a show on Australian TV but turned it down because he was coming home from Afghanistan. You're a very special person."

Blair was embarrassed and uncomfortable that Allisa knew so much about her and Hunter. "I kind of wish you didn't know all of that, but guess that it's just part of your job."

"That's exactly right. Until I got to know you, it was just a job. Now that I know you, I think we could be real good friends."

Blair was starting to like Allisa and kind of identified with her. She felt that once this was over, they might be friends. The flight to Philadelphia from LAX was going to be a long one. "I'm going to stop and get a magazine. Allisa, do you want something?"

"No thanks, I brought some material that I have to go over before we get there."

"Can I help with it?" Blair asked.

"I planned to give you some information to read so that you will be up to speed on the investigation. Nothing that I give you is classified but it is background information that should help. I hope you don't get mad but I had to black out some of the info that I would get in trouble for if you saw it."

"I guess that I understand."

They sat down at the departure gate and she said, "I want to wait until we're in the air to give this to you. Can't be too safe," she said. Blair picked up her magazine and started to look through it. Allisa peeked at a page that Blair seemed to be looking at for a while and laughed.

"I should have guessed…shoes!"

"Yes, aren't they great looking? I could wear them with so many different outfits." They looked at each other and both started laughing at the same time.

"I told you, I just love shoes," Blair added.

"I guess so," and they continued to smile. Other passengers seemed to wonder what was so funny. Both women just winked at each other.

The flight started to load and Steven came out to talk to Allisa and Blair. "I have a couple of seats in the back for you. I figured that you needed some space away from the other passengers. I'm so glad that we got to see each other again, Allisa."

"Steven, you know that I often think about the times we had in college. It was a lot of fun."

Steven walked back to the check-in desk and talked to the two women checking everyone in. They looked toward the two agents and nodded. "I'll wait here until you're both on the flight," he came back and told them.

They grabbed their bags and headed for the check-in desk. Allisa again gave Steven a kiss on the cheek. "I'll call you when I get back," she said. The plane was about sixty percent full and almost no one was in the back few rows. The two women settled in and left an empty seat between them.

"It's a five-hour flight so we can catch a few Zs," Allisa said.

"I've been on this too many times in the last few weeks."

"Yeah, guess I didn't think about that. Are you okay?"

"Yes. I'm looking forward to solving this and can't wait to see the other information you have."

"Once we're airborne I'll give you the packet to look over; that should help you."

A voice came on overhead reminding everyone to put their bags either in the overhead compartments or under a seat; they would be taking off soon. She looked at Allisa and said, "Thanks for including me."

"I probably couldn't do this without your help." The two were quickly becoming friends. The attendant came down the aisle to demonstrate the use of the oxygen mask and continued with the explanation of the safety features of the 747. Blair told her that she had thought about becoming a flight attendant for a while after moving to California.

"Why didn't you do it?"

"Hunter wanted me to be home where he could get hold of me if necessary. I think he didn't like the fact that I would always be in different cities."

"It would be interesting for a while I guess," Allisa said.

"Yes, but then I got a role in a play that lasted for six months and I never thought about it again."

The plane took off with a quick lift to its flying altitude of twenty-five-thousand feet. Blair looked out of her window and the shore seemed to disappear in seconds. The only thing you could make out was a string of lights that lined the coast. Blair took a deep breath and wiped a tear from her eye. She had just been on the flight from Philadelphia a few days earlier and now she was headed back. So much had happened that it was hard to figure out what was the right thing to do.

"Are you sure that you're okay?" Allisa asked.

"Yes, I'm fine, just thinking about all that has happened in such a short time." She sat there quietly.

Allisa waited before she said, "You've gone through a lot and it's understandable that you would be upset. It is also evident that you're a strong person. I don't know many twenty-three-year-old women who would have been able to handle all of this."

"Thanks; I'll be fine. Now let me have some of the information that you've been holding."

Allisa knew that she made a good choice asking Blair to come along. She also knew that she would need Blair to get Hunter's dad to feel comfortable and help with the search in Bridgewater. If she had any chance of solving this mystery, she needed help. Allisa didn't know Thomas Adams but having his daughter-in-law along would be a key to getting his cooperation. Both women settled in to read the details of the ongoing case. Allisa knew that when they landed Dino Tuchy would be there to pick them up. He would not send one of his men; he couldn't afford to have any of them finding out that they were involved, and especially that he was helping her with a case. She looked forward to seeing him. Dino was special. She also knew that he would flip out when he saw Blair. Allisa could handle Dino; she was sure of that.

Seventeen

The crime lab technicians arrived at the Adams' home in Bridgewater. Dino wanted his agent, Jon David, to stay with them as they went through the house. "Jon we need to know more about these men who killed Frank." Dino liked Jon. He was new to their group but had performed very well on other cases. Jon was methodical. He would make sure any information would be recorded and get it to Dino. He was a good investigator. It wasn't clear if either fugitive had actually entered the house but they must be sure. It was also an opportunity to clean the house of any fingerprints of the two FBI agents.

With his men in place, Dino would follow up with a call to Captain Douglas to meet with him and see what the local police had uncovered. The FBI would not share critical information with the local or state police but giving them some details might help Dino get key information. Captain Douglas answered and said he would have to call right back. Dino looked at his phone with a puzzled expression.

"What's wrong, Boss?" Jon asked.

"He hung up on me!"

Both men looked at each other and raised their eyebrows.

"I'll give him a few minutes and call back," Dino said.

Captain Douglas was driving toward the checkpoint on Highway 13 north of the city. He wanted to tell the state police captain in person about the red Harley and one rider headed north past Croydon. He knew that the APB would get through to all their officers, but the captain of the state police was a friend of his and Douglas felt he owed him a personal update. He arrived at the roadblock and saw Captain Campbell talking to his men.

"Hi Ron," Captain Douglas said.

"Bob, I'm surprised to see you here."

118

"I have an update for you. We found out a few minutes ago that one of the suspects is riding a red Harley headed north and may have just passed Croydon." Both men walked off to the side of the road to talk about their next move.

"I saw the APB," Campbell said.

"I also sent the information to all the local authorities."

"I should get it out to the Jersey state police," Campbell suggested. "With so many opportunities to cross state lines we need all the help possible to find him."

Captain Douglas told Ron that he had his men searching the wooded area of Bridgewater for the missing dark Chevy and the other man involved in the break-in and shooting.

"Do you need our help, Bob?"

"That would be great, Ron. We have two groups combing the woods starting from the Adams' house and fanning out north and east. If your men could cover the area south and west we'll be sure that everything is searched in as short a time as possible."

"We're on it, Bob." Captain Campbell got on his radio to his men. He told them to move into Bridgewater to start a search on foot south of the Adams' home through the wooded area for the Chevy and possibly one of the fugitives. Any search should come under the direction of Captain Douglas of the Bridgewater Police. He would coordinate the search team to cover as much ground as possible. The weather forecast was for a possible thunder storm and they needed to get some answers before it started to rain.

Douglas heard his phone and thought about not answering but he picked it up.

"Captain Douglas, this is Dino Tuchy. Is everything okay?"

"We've had more information just in and I was trying to coordinate it with the state police."

"What kind of new information?"

"It appears that the two fugitives may have separated and one of them could be on a motorcycle headed north out of town." Douglas knew that he had to give the FBI something but was not going to give them all the details, not at least until he found out what the FBI was doing in his town in the first place. Dino suggested a meeting as soon as possible. Douglas said that he was in the field helping his team search for the other missing fugitive.

"I'll meet you and we can help," Dino offered.

Although he didn't want their involvement, Captain Douglas had no choice. "You can meet me at the corner of Apple Lane and Pine," Douglas told him. "It is just a few blocks from where you are now. Do you need directions?"

"No, we have a local map." Dino went to get Steve Watkins and reminded Jon to stay with the crime lab team until he called. Dino and Steve got into Dino's car and headed toward Apple Lane. The town was small but due to so many dead end streets, a few blocks seemed to take a long time. Dino looked at the street map that Steve had and saw that they were just a few blocks over from Apple. The street was heavily wooded but they saw a light at the end of the block and headed in that direction. There was a small store on the corner of Apple and Pine, and they saw two police cars parked in front of it. It appeared that it was closed but Captain Douglas was standing with two young men in front. Dino pulled his Suburban up to the corner and started walking toward the men. Captain Douglas turned and walked up to Dino and asked him not to tell anyone that they were with the FBI. "We don't need a panic in our little town," he explained.

Dino agreed. "We'll stand off to the side and wait until you're done talking to them." When Captain Douglas walked back to the two men in front of the store, Dino turned to Steve and said, "This actually works best for us. The last thing we need is the director finding out that we're working with the local or state police." Steve understood. He and Dino knew that John Martin was not a forgiving person and getting involvement from local or state police was always a "no" in the FBI's book.

Captain Douglas completed his conversation and walked over to where Dino and Steve stood. "We got a report from one of our citizens that a red Harley had been taken from in front of his house. They were having a party and just found it missing. It appears that the Harley may have been used as a getaway vehicle from Bridgewater. We have an APB out for the Harley and the rider. We know that there were at least two fugitives and feel that one of them may still be hiding out in Bridgewater. Perry White, who I was just talking to, told me that he saw a red Harley pass by with only one rider. I have all my men searching the wooded areas around town. The state police are also combing the area."

"Well this does add to the mystery," Dino said. "Our techs are processing the scene at the Adams' home and should have some information soon. I'll get on the phone to our Newark office so that they can alert their men; that should cover the area north and east of here."

"That's a good idea. We've already sent the information to the Jersey state guys."

Dino walked over to his car and started making a call. Steve Watkins was surprised that Dino was going to call another FBI office to inform them of the situation. Dino held the phone and looked at Steve. Douglas had moved toward his men on the corner. "I'm not calling anyone," he told Steve, "I just want the dumb shits here to think I'm calling for more help." Dino had no use for local or state police and just working with them pissed him off. He also wasn't going to get anyone else involved in his mission. John Martin gave Dino the mission in Bridgewater and he wasn't going to seek help from another office. Dino wanted to solve this and he knew his team was competent and they didn't need help. The two agents walked back toward the front of the party store and waited for Captain Douglas to come over to them.

"I called our Newark office and they will start searching on their side of the river."

"I would like to know what the FBI has to do with this."

Dino said, "We have had a rash of anti-war activists who are causing a disturbance at the homes of soldiers who have come back from Iraq and now at some of the homes that have had soldiers killed in Iraq. We thought they are pretty much just causing concerns for the families of these soldiers, but this is the first sign of any physical break-in or violence. The director wants to make sure we help local authorities keep peace in their communities."

Captain Douglas seemed surprised that Dino gave him that information and understood the concern. He was also smart enough to know that this wasn't the whole story. He told Dino that his men would cooperate in any way necessary.

"Let us help you with your search."

The captain said, "We'll start right here on Apple Lane. I have two groups of men that have moved west down toward Pine and the state police have two groups that are moving south through the woods."

Dino said, "Let's head north from here." The search through the wooded area of Bridgewater could take hours. Dino looked at his watch. He told Steve, "I have an early meeting at the Philadelphia airport and will stay around here until about midnight. Steve, I want you to head the group in Bridgewater."

"Sure," Steve said, "anything you want, Boss." They continued walking into the wooded area behind the party store and followed Captain Douglas and his men. "I don't think they'll find anything," Dino said, "but let's humor them."

The captain told his men that if they made a discovery to wait and call for reinforcements. "There may be a fugitive in hiding and we don't need anyone else hurt."

They understood; everyone respected the captain. He had been the head of the Bridgewater Police force for over twenty years. Once a highly decorated war hero from Viet Nam, he came back home to Bridgewater. He rose through the ranks of the police department and was soon named captain. Although Bridgewater did not have much in the way of crime, his men would often be called upon to help the state police. He had been offered an important position with the Philadelphia Police Department but turned it down. He loved his town and protecting the people he knew. His best friend from high school was Ron Campbell. Ron was also in Viet Nam and when he came back he joined the state police. Both men made a good team whenever they worked on the same case.

The search through the wooded area wasn't bringing any results except mosquito bites. Dino suggested that he and Steve should fan out a little further down Apple Lane so that they could cover the area quicker. Captain Douglas agreed but asked them to follow the same rule he told his men: "This is my town and I'm responsible."

"Sure," Dino said. "I'll fall back if we find something."

The local police seemed to be combing the area pretty

quickly. With the state police in on the search it would be a shorter task. Dino and Steve walked slowly through the woods. "Steve, we need to make sure that if we come up with something we get a good look around before we phone it in. I don't need these local guys finding our man and screwing it up."

Steve added, "Maybe if we do find something we shouldn't tell them."

"That would be great if I thought we would get away with it."

The wooded area off of Apple Lane behind the small party store was very thick. Dino knew that there was no way to hide a car back there which is why he suggested fanning out further down the street. With all the large pine trees and their branches so close to the ground it was hard enough just to walk through the woods. The area further down the street had more hardwood trees and it appeared that there was a trail through there. It looked like either kids or snowmobiles had made a path deep into the woods. Dino and Steve came to the path and followed it for over two hundred yards. There was no sign of anything. He called to Captain Douglas to see if their search had come up with anything concrete.

"Nothing so far, how about you two?"

"Nothing here either. I think Steve and I are going to double back a little further down the street." Dino hung up and saw Steve sitting on a large rock. "Hey buddy, everything okay?" he asked.

"You know when all the shooting started; I thought that Frank was in the middle of the yard shooting toward the woods. I know that I saw a couple of figures escaping and then the individual in the yard started shooting at me."

"I know that Steve, you already told us."

"Yes, but now I remember that one of the two figures moving toward the woods looked like he was being dragged."

"You think he was shot?"

"Yes, maybe that's why only one person was seen on that Harley."

"Glad you remembered more, Steve. That may help us." Dino knew that Steve was still hurting about the loss of his partner.

123

He wanted him to keep busy and any information that he remembered could be vital.

"Should we tell Captain Douglas?"

"No, I don't want to give him any more information than I have to. We'll be able to go on the premise that only one fugitive is on the loose and the other is probably hiding here in Bridgewater or dead. They already think one guy got away on the Harley."

Both men moved slowly along the wooded trail and looked carefully into the brush and along the tree line. Then it appeared, a car lodged in a clump of small shrubs and covered by tree branches that hid it from the street. It was easier to see it coming out of the wooded area than it was entering the woods. Dino tapped Steve and signaled for him to stop. They both crouched down and moved slowly toward the car. It was a dark Chevy that was about ten feet ahead. Dino motioned to be quiet and that they should circle the vehicle. Both men moved around the car so to make sure no one else was around. They stooped down about five feet away and Dino drew a plan in the dirt. Steve watched as he drew a diagram of the car and angles that they should approach. He wanted to keep the finding quiet until they were sure what they had found. Steve knew that Dino was happy that they were the ones who found the car. They moved closer following the plan. No one seemed to be in the car. They didn't want to use their flashlights in case someone was lying in the back seat.

With the information that Steve had just remembered, there may be an injured fugitive in the car, so they approached slowly. When Steve got closer he used his flashlight to shine on the undercarriage of the car. No one was underneath. Dino was on the left side of the car as Steve approached from the right. Dino knew that this was the missing car because of the damage to the side. Anyone in the car would be watching only in one direction after the flashlight was used, they thought. He could get a lot closer and have Steve hold his ground. He was next to the driver's front door and he signaled to Steve with his flashlight. He let it shine under the car back toward Steve so that the direction of the light did not give his position away. Both men held their position for about five minutes. Dino pressed the driver's door handle and felt it release. He stayed low as he opened the door. No movement came from inside the car. He signaled for Steve to move in. Steve moved the last five feet slowly and crept toward the right rear door. He reached for the door handle and pulled it open. Both men had their guns drawn as they waited to be met by the missing fugitive.

The car was empty. Dino looked at Steve and they quickly searched the interior with their lights. There was nothing inside the car. Dino looked for the trunk release and found it under the dash. He motioned to Steve to move toward the back of the vehicle so he could be in position when the trunk popped open. Steve slid toward the rear of the car. The trunk came open and he pointed his gun into the trunk. A light came on in the trunk but it was empty. Both men moved back to check the interior. The rear seat was soaked in blood. It looked like the person or persons in the back seat had bled on the seat and the floor. They now knew why only one person was seen riding the Harley. "We must have gotten one of them," Steve said. "With this much blood, one of them has to be dead." Steve felt better that at least they got one of the fugitives. But now where was he?

"We should close the doors and trunk," Dino said. "We can tell Captain Douglas that we found the car but haven't moved in to examine it."

"Good plan," Steve agreed. "They'll think that we want to help and are following their plan."

"Before we call it in let's search the area for a possible body."

Dino left Steve to close the car and wipe the doors down while he moved toward the passenger side to see if there was a trail of blood that would help his search. No trail was found on the ground. They could use bloodhounds he thought. He would call it in to Captain Douglas and even offer his crime lab technicians to check the interior when they finished at the Adams' house.

Douglas heard his cell phone ring. "Damn Feds!" He could not get away from their interference.

"Captain Douglas, this is Dino. We've found the getaway car hidden in the woods further east off Apple Lane. Steve and I are about fifteen feet away from it and there doesn't look like any movement in the car."

"Don't touch anything, we're on the way," was the answer.

"We'll let them have their fun," Dino said. "Dumb shits really thought we're going to wait for them." They continued to look through the wooded area for a body. They were sure that the individual in the back seat could not have survived after losing that much blood. They figured that it would take at least ten minutes before Captain Douglas and some of his men would make it to their position.

Dino's cell phone rang. He saw it was the captain. He was requesting specific directions. He said they would move away from the car further and shine their flashlights so that it would be easier to find them. This was also a great cover for the search for a possible body. Bob Douglas headed toward the flashlights in the woods.

"We're over here," they called out.

"Glad that you called us so we could search the car together."

Dino almost felt guilty but knew that his mission was much more important than helping the local police. Douglas suggested that they approach from the driver's side while he and his men took the passenger's side.

"You're sure this is the car?"

"Yes, the door is badly damaged and it fits the description." Dino no longer felt guilty with that question. *Damn local shits. Like there would be more than one abandoned car fitting that description in the woods.* The two teams moved in and all five men held their guns in position in case there was a fugitive aboard. Captain Douglas called out to the car.

"This is the police, toss out your weapons and we won't shoot."

The two agents almost laughed out loud. "I told you, dumb shits," Dino whispered.

No answer came from the car. The Captain signaled that they should all move in. The five men were less than five feet from the car and were searching with their flashlights as they approached. No movement came from in or around the car. Douglas was the first to pull open the right front door. There was nothing inside. They all moved in and opened the doors. Douglas pointed out the pool of blood on the back seat and floor. "Andy must have gotten one of them. Let's open the trunk and check it out." They opened the trunk but found it empty. "Someone must be badly wounded," Captain Douglas announced. "Let's fan out and search the area."

Ron Campbell and his state police team were called by Captain Douglas to let them know that the car had been found. Ron told him that his team would head in that direction and help search for the wounded man. Dino told him that his lab techs could process the car once they finished at the Adams' home.

"Thanks," the Captain said.

Dino was pleased that he had the local police thinking that he was working with them. He hoped that he and Steve would find the missing fugitive. The search could take a long time. He looked up at the sky just as a hard rain started to fall. The men tried to take cover under some of the larger trees. This was not going to make the search any easier. Any trail would soon be washed away. The rain was heavy and it started to lightning and thunder.

"We need to get out of the woods," the captain said. "This storm is going to be short but could be dangerous." They all agreed and headed toward the store on the corner. Bob Douglas placed an orange cone on the street so that it would be easy for them to find the spot where they came out. The rain was now falling at a very heavy rate and the ground that was already soft could not absorb the water. "We can go back in when this slows down," Captain Douglas said. He called to his other teams that they should get shovels and boots for everyone. "This is going to be a long night."

Dino checked his watch. It was close to eleven and he knew that he had to be at the Philadelphia airport early the next day. "Steve, I want you to get with Jon and see how the search at the Adams' home has gone. You both should stay with the local police and see if you can search some of the area on your own. Call me if you find anything."

Steve was glad that Dino was still confident enough to leave him in charge. He was afraid that Dino would have been mad at him for the mess at the Adams' home earlier. "You can count on me, Boss."

"I need to get back to Philadelphia and the office before my morning meeting."

Dino knew that Allisa was coming in on the red eye from Los Angeles and her plane would arrive around eight a.m. Eastern Standard Time. Dino had not seen Allisa for a couple of years but the thought of her being back in Philadelphia started to stir old memories.

Eighteen

The night was dark and the sky had grown heavy with clouds. The ride up Highway 13 along the Delaware River was smooth and without incident except for the earlier roadblock that Yawer had evaded. He passed one police car before Croydon but had not seen anything since. West Bristol was just a few miles ahead and he planned to cross the Burlington Bristol Toll Bridge. Once across the Delaware River he could head back toward Mansfield Square and El Jaafi. His search of the Adams' home had not accomplished anything. Not only did they not get into the house but now the local police had shot and killed Omar and would be on his trail soon. He knew that the Harley would have been reported stolen by now and that an APB would be out on it. He hoped to get across into New Jersey and on Highway 130 headed toward Mansfield Square before having to look for another getaway vehicle. He saw the sign for the toll bridge ahead. The town of Springside was on the other side of the bridge and he would head north on Highway 130. He saw rain drops on his helmet shield and could see that the road was starting to look shiny from the rain. It began to thunder and he knew the heavier rain would be coming soon. He turned right onto the bridge and pulled in the automated lane.

He tossed a variety of coins in the catch basin and after it opened he proceeded across the bridge. The other lane was operated by a Connor, a young bridge employee who occupied his time watching a Phillies ballgame. The rain started to come down harder as Yawer turned north on Highway 130. He hoped that he could make it up the highway before having to change rides. The Harley was so impressive of a ride and he felt that he could go anywhere with it. It would allow him to outmaneuver a car if it came to a chase. He could only hope no one noticed it missing yet.

Back down the road a state trooper vehicle pulled up to the toll booth at the bridge. Connor slid open his booth door while still watching the ballgame and held his hand out for the toll.

"Hey kid, have you seen a red Harley cross?" The voice came from the car at the toll entrance.

Connor looked up and asked, "What did you say?"

"Have you seen a red Harley come through here?"

The rain had been coming down harder and Connor had kept his window in the booth closed. He would open it if a car was coming but he had not seen any cars for over an hour. Connor was surprised to see that it was a trooper asking questions. "No Sir," he said.

"How many people have crossed in the past hour?"

"There haven't been any cars through here in over an hour."

"Are you sure that none of the people crossing were on a motorcycle?"

"I haven't noticed one," Connor answered.

The trooper proceeded across the bridge and called back to his commander. He reported that there was nothing at the Burlington Bristol Bridge. "Maybe he's headed for Levittown and the crossing at Highway 276," was the response. He would go back across and head up the highway further north. The state police captain headquartered in Trenton dispatched four cars to head to all the bridge crossings along the Delaware River. There were three crossings north of Croydon, Pennsylvania, into New Jersey. They would stake each one out and send a car along I-295 south. The red Harley would be easy to spot this time of night. Not much traffic would be on the road; at least not until after the Phillies' game. The captain of the state police knew that with the Braves in town a lot of people would be coming back across from Philadelphia after the game. Southern Jersey was Phillies' country and many of the locals had moved across the Delaware River but kept their hopes of a Phillies' World Series win alive.

****

The rain started to fall harder and the sky came alive with

lightning and thunder. Yawer slowed down and looked for a spot to get under cover. Mansfield Square was only about thirty minutes north of Springside. He kept an eye out for any police vehicles in the area. He hoped that he could somehow ditch the Harley for another ride. If only he had a way of getting another ride and keeping the Harley. The thought of it being the perfect getaway ride stayed in his mind. He found a gas station near Springside that was closed. The overhang was perfect cover from the rainstorm. He got his cell phone out and called back to El Jaafi in Mansfield Square. It was close to midnight when the cell phone rang. El Jaafi looked to see who the caller was. They had purchased one-time-use cell phones in New York so that no one could trace any calls or who was using the phones. El Jaafi had used a stolen credit card to make the purchase. No trace would be found. The caller was Yawer but he had expected to hear from him earlier. "I am on my way back," he told El Jaafi.

"كيف انتقل البحث؟"? he asked about the search.

"Not good; we had some problems. The local police had the place staked out and we were sure that we could handle the officer we saw. In fact Omar shot him and we thought that we could get into the house but two or three more police were in the house and ambushed us. We did get one of them but Omar was badly wounded as we tried to escape into the woods and did not make it. Our brother is dead!"

"He did not die in vain, praise Allah," Jaafi said. "Where are you now?"

"I just crossed into New Jersey and am heading toward Mansfield Square. I have another ride and had to ditch the car. I took care of everything. I hid the car and I buried Omar's body in a ditch. They will not find it for quite a while. I took the license plate off the car and all our belongings out of it. I have Omar's identification with me."

"How did you get out of Bridgewater?"

"I have a Harley that I'm riding but will look for another ride before I get to Mansfield Square."

"We should go back to New York and regroup," Jaafi said. "I will get our things together here and you should just head to the safe house in the Bronx. We cannot fail in our mission. We can travel to California if necessary and let everything calm down here."

El Jaafi planned on checking them out of both rooms and making sure nothing was left behind. They would clean off all possible fingerprints as they left the motel. Yawer was hoping to join El Jaafi but knew that this was a better plan. Why endanger the whole group as he tried to escape. Right now they were just looking for one other person. At least El Jaafi and Abdulla could continue with the mission if necessary. The rain seemed to slow down and he could get back on the highway. It was no longer necessary to try to get to Mansfield Square. Yawer looked at his map before getting on the road.

The best route to New York would be I-95 toward Newark. He had many options to cross over into New York from I-95. It would make sense to stay off the main roads until he had a new ride. He moved the motorcycle onto the local road that would lead back to Highway 130. As he rode through town he searched for a new ride. He passed a farmhouse that seemed to have a lot of pickup trucks out in front. Everything was dark and he stopped to make sure no one was around. It appeared that it was a working farm and the vehicles were parked until the next work day. He searched through them and found most of them had keys either in the ignition or lying on the seats. He wanted to take one of the trucks but also did not want to ditch the Harley right there. The Harley was very heavy and Yawer struggled to hoist it into the back of the pickup. He found one of the trucks near a mound and was able to get the Harley in the bed from that angle. Once the motorcycle was aboard, he closed the tailgate and started the truck. He headed to Highway 130 and would take some back roads to the interstate.

El Jaafi and Abdulla gathered their items and cleaned out the rooms. They loaded everything into the second vehicle that they had rented under a false name and proceeded to make sure everything was out of the second room. They would call the house in the Bronx to inform them that they were on their way back. The Days Inn lobby seemed to have a lot of action at night. The Air Force staff staying there from McGuire Air Force Base was watching a late ballgame in the bar just off the lobby. El Jaafi decided not to go into the lobby and he and Abdulla slowly pulled out of the lot and headed toward the interstate. Traffic would not be an issue this time of night.

Yawer was pleased that he was able to get the Harley into the pickup truck. He thought that he would keep it because there would not be any checkpoints until he reached the toll bridges into New York. The Harley would allow him a second escape vehicle if necessary. Most of the toll booths had automated lanes and he could pass through them without being noticed. He planned to cross at the Verrazano Narrows Bridge and take Highway 278 all the way back to the safe house. It was still raining but had slowed down and he would be at the safe house in about three or four hours. He knew that El Jaafi would call ahead to inform the rest of the group what had happened.

The night was very quiet as Yawer pulled the pickup through town. The ride would be safe as long as he did not bring attention to himself. He looked at the gas needle and it read about a quarter of a tank. Damn, he knew that was not enough to get to New York. He'd have to stop and get fuel. The best place would be along the interstate where there were plenty of nondescript rest stops with fuel and food. He would not even have to get off the highway. The ride to the interstate from Springside was short. He had to enter off Highway 295 north because there wasn't an entrance at Springside. Yawer could jump on the New Jersey Turnpike before Mansfield Square.

The pickup was a late model Chevy 1500 series Silverado. Yawer was headed toward I-95 when he saw a state trooper headed south on the other side of the highway. He made sure that he was doing the speed limit and kept one eye on the fuel gauge. The trooper passed his vehicle and kept heading south. He felt some relief as he saw the sign for I-95. He wanted to call El Jaafi once he got the truck fueled to let him know where he was and that he was able to get a new ride. When he entered I-95 north he looked in his rearview mirror and saw another state trooper behind him. The hair on the back of his neck rose. He again checked his speed and kept an eye on the fuel gauge. Yawer came to the first of the tollbooths and saw that the only lane open was an attended lane. He would have to get a ticket for the toll charges on the turnpike. He kept his head down and took the ticket from the attendant. He entered the turnpike and headed north.

The state trooper was two vehicles behind the pickup. When the officer got to the toll booth he asked the attendant if there had been a red Harley that had passed through the booth that evening.

"The only one I saw was in the back of a pickup."

"When?" the officer asked.

The attendant pointed to the Chevy Silverado that was just disappearing onto the highway.

"Thanks," the officer said.

The call came into the state police headquarters at twelve thirty-one a.m. It was from Trooper Greg Jones. "I have a late model Chevy Silverado dark blue, headed north on the Jersey Turnpike with a red Harley in the truck's bed."

The response was hurried but clear, "Follow the vehicle but do not give your position away. We will send backup. Don't try to apprehend him." The trooper was a long-time member of the New Jersey State Police force. He followed the pickup leaving about three or four vehicles between them. There was an exit at Crosswicks about eight miles ahead.

The captain of the Trenton State Police called to Campbell to inform him that they may have found the fugitive headed north on the New Jersey Turnpike in a late model Chevy Silverado and that he had a red Harley in the back of the truck. They were not sure if it was their man but it was the only lead they had. Captain Campbell thanked them and asked to be kept in the loop.

Ron called Captain Douglas. "Bob, the New Jersey Police have a trail on a man driving a pickup on the turnpike. He has a red Harley in the bed of the pickup."

"Thanks Ron; I hope it's our guy."

"I'll keep you informed. How is the search for the missing fugitive going?"

"We had to fall back because the rain was almost blinding, but it has slowed down and we are going back in the woods soon."

"If you need my men a little longer, just let me know."

"I think we can handle it from here but I will keep you up to date on our search. Thanks, Ron, for all your help."

"That's what friends are for."

The Silverado kept going north on the interstate and Officer Jones stayed a good distance behind. His goal was to keep tabs on the vehicle but not to cause the driver any special concern. He knew that there would be backup coming soon and his job was just surveillance. He kept in radio contact with the main post and they informed him that there would be backup at Crosswicks. If the Silverado stays on the interstate, we will continue to follow him with both of you, he was told. The Crosswicks exit was one mile ahead and the Silverado made no move toward the right exit lane. The driver of the Silverado was doing the speed limit and did not seem to be aware of being followed.

A sign ahead said that there was a rest area with gas station and food in two miles. The officer saw that the second patrol car entered at Crosswicks and fell in behind him. He radioed back to the post to inform them that both cars were now following the possible suspect. The main post said that they were putting stakeouts at the next three exits and the upcoming rest area. This could be a long night they all thought. The Silverado driver put his right turn signal on and moved into the right lane. It appeared that he was getting off at the rest area. Officer Jones got on his radio. "I have our suspect exiting the interstate and entering the rest area three miles north of Crosswicks."

The answer came back to follow the car but keep a distance. "We have a car stationed in the rest area at the gas station." They thought that with a squad car already parked it would not seem out of place.

Yawer looked down at the fuel gauge and was happy to see the gas station. He figured that he could fill the truck and grab something to eat. He pulled up to the left fuel island and got out. He noticed that a squad car was parked in front of the station but it appeared to be empty. Yawer ran the credit card through the pump and began to fill his vehicle. While he was doing this he looked around to see if anything appeared unusual. The only thing he saw was that one squad car with no one inside. Using the automated pump to pay for the gas would allow him a quick getaway if necessary. He was putting the pump handle back when he saw a second police car along the side of the restaurant. That car had one occupant behind the wheel. Yawer decided to get back into the truck. He did not want to make any sudden moves but slowly pulled out of the gas station while he watched the car on the side of the restaurant.

He drove slowly like he was going to reenter the interstate when he saw the squad car pull out and head in the same direction. He turned back and saw an officer come out of the gas station and head toward the parked squad car. That officer was on his radio. He circled the lot and pulled the Silverado between two eighteen wheelers. He walked around the back of the pickup, pulled the tailgate open and started to pull the Harley out of the back. The driver of the semi next to him saw what he was doing and asked if he could help.

"Yes, thank you." They got the bike out and Yawer tossed a backpack on it and took off toward the wooded area behind the restaurant. The truck driver just stood there wondering what had just happened. Both state police squad cars took off and headed in the direction of the Harley that was now closing in on the wooded area. Yawer jumped the curb and was now on the walking path heading into the dense woods. The Harley sped into the wooded area just off the parking lot. The squad cars could not follow him. Officer Jones called to the post to inform them about what had happened.

"Shit," came back the answer. "He made us and now we'll have a hell of a chase on our hands."

Nineteen

The flight was long and Blair was able to sleep for a couple of hours. She woke up and saw that Allisa was reading some documents. "Are you ever going to tell me what the FBI is searching for?"

"I told you, we know that Hunter found some key information and never turned it in. It wasn't found in his things in Iraq. We thought that somehow he may have sent it to either you or his father."

"I understand that, but what's in this key information?"

"Blair, really I don't know; just that they feel it's critical to our operation in Iraq. The orders for the search came from the director in Washington." Blair settled back and asked what time it was.

"We should be landing in about an hour," Allisa answered.

"Guess I should go freshen up; I must look a wreck." Blair headed to the bathroom that was just two rows behind their seats. When she got in there she looked into the mirror. *Hunter, I need you to help me. Make sure I'm doing the right thing.* She washed her face and thought she needed some makeup. She knew that they would be picked up by someone that Allisa had arranged to meet them at the Philadelphia airport.

The pilot came on the speaker requesting everyone to return to their seats. They would be landing at the Philadelphia airport in twenty-five minutes. Blair returned to her seat and asked Allisa, "Who is going to pick us up?"

"I have a friend in the Philadelphia Bureau. His name is Dino Tuchy. He'll pick us up and take us to a hotel. We can settle in and get caught up on the investigation there." Allisa was concerned that she had not told Dino about bringing Blair and she hoped that he wouldn't flip out. This was the best way in her mind to gain the confidence of Hunter's dad and move the investigation along as fast as possible. With her failures in Santa Monica, Allisa had to do something positive or she was going to be relegated to a desk job.

The plane made its approach into the Philadelphia airport and Blair recalled that she had just left there a few days ago. So much had happened in such a short time. She was hoping that coming with Allisa was the right thing to do. She knew that she had to get answers to all her questions. They were soon on the ground and both women reached up into the overhead compartment for their baggage. They both had carry-on luggage so that getting out of the airport to meet their ride would not take too much time. Allisa reminded her not to talk about the operation to anyone. "Blair, it is important that we stay out of the limelight as much as possible. Once we get to our hotel I'll get two rooms so that I won't put you in any danger."

"Guess that makes sense. What do I say to the person who is picking us up?"

"I'll do all the talking; he doesn't know that I brought you yet."

"Is that going to be a problem?"

"He may freak out at first but I know it's the only way to solve this and I can protect you this way."

"You really think someone will try to hurt me, don't you?"

"I'm really not sure, but I just don't want to take that chance".

They exited the plane and headed toward the main terminal. Blair was pulling her duffle bag along.

"That looks pretty easy to manage."

"I got it at a flea market in Santa Monica."

They continued along the concourse and the walk was very quiet because their flight must have been the first one to arrive at the terminal. It was a little after eight a.m. and most everyone in the airport was departing for their trip, not arriving.

Allisa moved toward the curb when they got outside. She seemed to be sure what type of car she was looking for and waved to a vehicle approaching. He pulled up a few feet past the women and a nice looking man about forty-five got out.

"You always look beautiful, kid," Dino Tuchy said, wrapping his large arms around Allisa and hugged her.

"Don't joke around," she replied.

He was surprised by her statement.

She gripped his right arm and smiled, "You know that I will always have a special place in my life for you Dino. I want to introduce you to a friend I brought along. Dino, this is Mrs. Blair Adams."

Dino looked puzzled and didn't quite know what to say.

"I know that bringing Blair with me is a surprise but she wants to help us find the information we need".

"Jesus Christ, are you crazy?"

Blair didn't know exactly what to say or do. A police officer came over and told them that the vehicle had to be moved now. Dino flashed his credentials. "Look, buddy, this is important." The officer just nodded and strolled down the line of vehicles. Allisa opened the back of the Suburban and tossed in their bags.

"Let's get going. We can talk on the way to the hotel." They all got into the truck. Allisa jumped in the front with Dino and Blair got in the backseat. The Suburban had so many gadgets on the dash that Blair didn't know what most of them were for.

"Wow, I've never seen so many different types of radios in a car before."

"Government vehicle, Mrs. Adams. We have to make sure that we have various types of communication equipment to do our job." He glanced over at Allisa and hoped that she had a good reason for bringing the main person they were investigating in California with her. When she gave him a stern look, her eyes could bore a hole in his brain.

"I'm sorry for your loss, Mrs. Adams," Dino said.

"Thanks, it has been very difficult especially with all that has happened since".

"Dino, I told Mrs. Adams, I mean Blair, that I want two rooms for us at the hotel so that she would not be in any extra danger. Let's put her room under a false name."

Dino had a puzzled look on his face before he answered,

139

"Yes, yes, that's exactly what I would have done." Dino realized that he needed to change the reservation he had made for Allisa right away. Dino got his phone and made a call to change the reservation. He made sure the person understood that they now needed two rooms and neither room would be listed under Blair's or Allisa's names. The drive from the Philadelphia airport to the hotel was about twenty-five minutes. As they drove Allisa brought Dino up to speed on all the details of the California investigation. She seemed to leave out a few, but Blair felt it was because she was in the vehicle. Dino said he would go over the information that he had once they were in the hotel. Blair sensed some tension between them and figured that it was because Allisa did not tell Dino that she was bringing her along. They pulled up to a Marriott hotel on Cottman Avenue. Blair noticed a large mall across from the hotel.

"This looks like a very nice area," she said.

"I thought it would be better to put you out here because there are stores and places to eat nearby," Allisa said. "I'm not sure how long we'll be here and I know since we don't have a car the location seemed to be a good one." This was the new trendy area in Philadelphia. A group of businessmen had opened a few chic bars and shops that seemed to catch on with the locals. It had a New York sort of flair. They parked in front and Allisa turned to Blair. "Let me go in with Dino and get our keys."

"Sure, whatever you say."

The two agents got out of the Suburban and walked toward the lobby of the Marriott. Dino stopped near a small sitting area that was currently empty.

"Now, are you going to tell me what in the hell you were thinking by bringing her here?"

"We had a lot of trouble in California and I had to give her some information about the investigation. With her here she can't tell it to anyone else and she seems to be willing to help us with Hunter's dad."

"Son of a bitch! This could backfire on all of us. How much does she know?"

Allisa was surprised that he waited this long before blowing up. "I had to tell her that Hunter was in the FBI and that he had some critical documents that we haven't found; that we were thinking that maybe he sent them to either her or his dad. I didn't tell her much of anything else."

"Hell, she knows as much as we do!"

She touched Dino's hand and looked at him. "I hoped by getting separate rooms we could spend some time together."

"Allisa, you know that I've never forgotten the times we've been together. I missed you a lot." The two smiled at each other and laughed. "Better get back out to your guest," Dino said.

He helped them get their luggage out. "I thought I would leave you two here to unpack and get some rest before I come back for you later. I will be back here for both of you about three. I have some unfinished things that I was working on."

Allisa said that they were going to rest first and they would meet Dino in the lobby. They grabbed their bags and headed for the lobby. Dino got in the Suburban and drove away.

"I hope that he'll let us help in the investigation here."

"Blair, he's like all guys, if it wasn't his idea it isn't a good idea. I convinced him that having you here was the only way we would be able to get the information we need as quickly as possible."

"I'm glad that I came."

"Bet you're tired."

"Maybe a little. I need to call Olly to let her know that I'm okay. I promised to call her."

"You're lucky to have so many special friends." They got on the elevator and Allisa pressed the buttons for both the seventh and the ninth floors. "You're on seven, Room 716 and I'm in Room 925. I'll make sure that you are not in any danger and keeping us apart will help protect you. Other FBI agents may find out that I'm here but they won't know that I brought you along. Dino won't tell anyone and he knows that I promised to protect you."

"I appreciate that." Blair got off on the seventh floor and asked, "Should I call your room later."

"I'm kind of tired. How about if I call your room around two? Get some rest Blair; we will be very busy later on." Blair got off on the seventh floor and Allisa rode the elevator up to nine. She opened the door to her room and looked around. *Nice room,* she thought. It had a king size bed and two very comfortable looking chairs with a small table in front of the window. There was a desk with a chair in the far corner. She put her bag on the end of the bed and sat down. Her feet were tired and she slipped her shoes off. The phone on the night stand next to the bed rang.

"Hi, how is the room?"

"Real nice!"

"Did you get Mrs. Adams off to her room?"

"Yes, I told her that I would give her a ring about two. I'm sure she is tired and needs some time alone."

"Do you need time alone, or can I come up?"

"I'd love to see you. Come on up." Minutes later there was a knock on her door. She looked out the peep hole to see who it was. "That was quick, where did you park?"

"I parked in back of the hotel. You don't know how happy I am to see you again. It has been a long time since we've been together".

"Yes, a couple of years. I'm glad to see you too. You know how much I appreciate your help. Unless I can recover and find some critical information here my career is over."

Dino put his hand on her shoulder. He looked into her eyes and moved closer to her. "I would do anything to help you. You mean a lot to me. I haven't forgotten the times we had together."

She put her hand on the side of Dino's face and touched him softly. "When I left here for California and my new assignment I was excited to get the promotion, but leaving you was really hard." Dino moved closer and kissed her on the cheek, then the lips. They embraced and held each other as he slipped his hand around her back and pulled her tight against him. They fell back on the bed and his hands moved to her thighs. She leaned back and her head rested on the bed as he moved his hands to her waist. She had a strong, lean body. Dino moved his hands back to her face.

"I will do whatever necessary to help you with this investigation. We have had some problems here that I need to fill you in on."

She let out a heavy sigh, "Not now Dino, not now."

142

He moved his hands along her side and kissed her gently. Dino slipped his fingers across her blouse and unbuttoned the top two buttons. His hands caressed her breasts. Allisa opened her mouth but nothing came out. She pulled Dino down to kiss him. They undressed each other as they kissed. The luggage tumbled to the floor. She rolled on top of him. She kissed him all over and they found comfort in each other as though they had never been apart. It had been a long time since she had made love to anyone.

She was a career FBI Agent and that always seemed to come first. When she was assigned to his team, some of the other agents thought that she was having an affair. Most of the men felt she was getting some of the easier assignments. When she was given an undercover spot and helped Dino solve a major case her career took off.

They laid on the bed for over an hour. He wanted to tell her how much he missed her and wished she would come back to him but he knew that was not what she wanted. Solving this investigation now was critical to her. He wanted to help her save her career. Maybe someday they would be back together. Right now, this moment was to be savored. She looked over at the clock and suggested they should compare cases.

"I agree, plus I need to make a call and fill you in on everything here."

"Yes, that's a good idea." Allisa was happy to be back in Dino's arms and working with him. She hoped that their lovemaking would not get in the way of this case. She watched as he sat on the edge of her bed and called one of his men.

"Boss, this thing has really gone to hell on us!" Steve told him. "We thought the New Jersey State police had our guy on the interstate headed north when he entered a gas station. He ditched the truck that they tailed him in and got back on the Harley."

"How in the hell did he have time to do all that!"

"He had the Harley in the back of the truck and pulled it out with help from a trucker who just happened by. He took off into the woods behind the buildings and they have a manhunt on for him now."

"Did anyone question the trucker who helped him?"

"Yes, it seems that he was getting out of his semi when he saw a man struggling with the Harley. He said he asked if the guy needed help and they pulled the bike out of the bed of the truck. Then the guy just took off."

"Shit, how could all that happen so fast?"

"The trucker really didn't give us much of a description."

"I need to update the director. He's going to go nuts."

Allisa sat up and asked what had happened. Dino brought her up to speed on the action at the Adams' home in Bridgewater and now the chase for the fugitives. They knew that they had to get moving now. "I have to get back up there," he said.

"Let me call Blair's room and tell her that you called and we need to get moving in fifteen minutes."

"You really want to bring her along?"

"We can leave her at the Adams' home with Hunter's dad if necessary but I think she's the key to the documents."

"Okay, give me a few minutes to get dressed; I'll meet you downstairs." Dino left her room and headed for his Suburban. He had to call John Martin and update him on the situation. This was a call he didn't want to make unless he had positive news.

He dialed the director's office. "Hi Diane, is he in?" John Martin's secretary would send the call through to the director's cell phone regardless of where he was. He had told her as soon as Dino calls to put him through.

"This is Martin."

"Sir, I have an update for you. After the incident at the Adams' house last night, we found the fugitives' car in the woods. It appears that one of them stole a Harley and headed north on the interstate through New Jersey."

"This damn thing is growing like a cancer. Who else is involved now?"

"The New Jersey State Police were trailing him."

"So they know that we're chasing this man."

"Yes Sir, but no one knows why. I gave the local police a cover story and they bought it. They had a tail on our guy but lost him at the rest area north of Crosswicks. They don't know exactly what is going on, just that he was one of some men who were involved in the incident at the Adams' home."

"Shit, this is really getting to be a mess, Dino. Not only do we have fugitives on the loose but you lost one of our men in the process."

"I'm sorry, Sir, but I've contacted all of our agents in the area to be on the lookout for him."

"Dino, I will talk to the president and the Homeland Security chief about putting out a Code Red Terror Alert. We can say that an informant gave us information regarding a possible terrorist cell on the East Coast."

"I will keep you informed, Boss."

"Don't screw this up or your ass will be in South Dakota protecting the monuments."

"Yes Sir, you can count on me."

"That's what I'm doing but don't prove me wrong. The director of Homeland Security is up to pace on this. I need to report some kind of success."

"Yes, Sir, we're on it." Dino knew that many of the high ranking officials in Washington tried to keep things from the president. The theory was to tell him only when you were successful. John Martin added, "I just got some weird news from California that Dean Curry doesn't know where Mrs. Adams is. He has tried to contact her at home and at her work, but no one seems to know her whereabouts. He has men stationed at her apartment and place of work. She might be involved in this thing."

Dino knew that he had even more problems. Allisa was counting on him to help her. Mrs. Adams was here and he didn't want too many people knowing that. Now John Martin was putting him on notice that he will be held responsible for the fugitives' capture. *Why me?* he thought. This should have been a simple search and report back to the director. Now it was a chase though a couple of states for a fugitive who may or may not be involved in the original case. Dino knew in Washington there were no winners or losers, just survivors.

He wondered if the two men that were shot in Mrs. Adams' apartment by Agent Baxter had any relationship to the man they were now chasing. He also remembered that Allisa said that one of the men had been identified as an Iraqi national. This thing may be bigger than any of them knew. He pulled the Suburban to the entrance of the hotel and waited outside for them. It was close to noon and he had to get back to Bridgewater. Dino also needed to call the Trenton FBI office to get them involved. As he waited in his car he was wondering how cold it was in South Dakota this time of the year.

Twenty

Thomas Adams thanked his brother, Bill and his wife, Martha, for the evening and the overnight stay. "I need to get back," he told Bill. "It's almost noon and I think the visit was good for me. I have to call Bob Douglas and see what he wanted from me. Maybe they may have a lead in the break-in at my house." Thomas got in his car and headed toward Bridgewater. The night before there had been a heavy rainstorm and spots along Highway 13 had water standing over the road. He drove slowly along the highway and watched as a road crew did some repairs on the way. *Must have had a couple inches of rain,* he thought. He passed a state police car that seemed to be driving slowly toward Croydon. Maybe there had been a report of an accident. The sun was bright as he headed home. Rain seemed to bring life to many of the trees and flowers. The ride from Croydon to Bridgewater was always enjoyable. The road followed the river and you would often see boaters and people fishing along the river banks. He dialed Captain Douglas as he got closer to Bridgewater. "Bob, this is Thomas Adams. I'm headed home and you said to call before I got there."

"Glad you called, Thomas. I will meet you at your house in a few minutes." Thomas wondered what had happened that Bob needed to talk to him in person. Maybe it was the new neighborhood kids who broke in and they wanted to apologize. *It's probably nothing serious,* he thought. At least everything was put back and no real damage occurred.

Thomas pulled down his street and saw the captain's car in his driveway. There was another car in the street that he didn't recognize.

"Thomas, this is Steve Watkins from the Federal Bureau of Investigation. He and I want to go over a few things with you."

"What's going on, why is the FBI involved?"

147

"We'll explain everything. Can we go inside?"

"Sure, has something else happened?"

The captain covered the second break-in and the shoot-out in his yard. Thomas was so stunned that he just sat there listening. He never asked any questions. Steve Watkins told him a story about a group that was causing trouble for families of soldiers who had been in Iraq. He explained that the FBI had heard about the break-in and just wanted to make sure that Thomas' family had not been harassed by this group. With the shootout, now it was more serious.

"We will be involved from here on out," Steve Watkins told Thomas. "My chief will be here in a little while and he can give you more details. His name is Dino Tuchy."

Thomas didn't know what to think. He asked if anything had happened in his house.

"We had our crime lab people go through your house to see if anything had been disturbed or if any fingerprints were found. We didn't find anything," Steve Watkins told him.

"How about the men who got shot," he asked.

Captain Douglas said that Andy Emery, the officer, was in the local hospital. Thomas said he knows Andy, that he's a nice young man and hopes that he will recover quickly. Douglas said that Andy's girlfriend had called and said the surgery went well and Andy would be in the hospital for only a couple of days. Unfortunately, the FBI agent who had been shot had died at the scene.

"I'm sorry to hear that," he said."

"Thomas, I will be with you and my men will be here 24/7 to make sure you're okay. I'm not going to let anything happen to one of our citizens and a good friend of mine."

"Thanks, Bob, that does make me feel better."

Steve Watkins asked to be excused for a minute. "I have to check in with our agent who's at the rest area north of Crosswicks." Jon David was working with the state police team and they had mobilized their local force to search the wooded area. They knew that Groveville was due north and that the fugitive could make his way to State Route 524. They had stationed a squad car at each end of the road in case he came out of the woods and headed that way. The fugitive had a head start before they could get their men into position. The search had begun in the dark and they felt that he couldn't travel too far, even on the Harley.

"You'd have to be one hell of a bike rider to pull that off," their captain had said.

Jon answered his cell phone, "Jon, this is Steve, how's it going?"

"They have the area covered and brought in some motorcycles that have headed into the woods. It's so muddy that I don't see how anyone could get very far."

"Did you search the abandoned truck?"

"Yes, and we found some papers that Dino is going to want to see."

"I hope it helps, he didn't seem too happy when I talked to him a few minutes ago."

"This may be a little confusing, but it looks like it may lead to a group headquarters in New York, somewhere in the Bronx."

"Wow, that's great news. I'm going to call the boss and tell him. I bet he'll get the director to mobilize the New York unit." Steve looked at his watch and saw that it was about one p.m. *I should call Dino now and not wait,* he thought.

The phone rang and Dino saw it was Steve calling. "I'm on my way Steve, what have you got?"

"Jon's been working with the state guys and has found some papers in the abandoned truck. He found a map. We're thinking it may lead to a house in New York. Could be where they're hiding."

"Good work!" Dino thought, *finally something positive.* "I want to report this to the director but I would like to see the documents first. Have Jon fax them to me." Steve went back into the house.

"Captain Douglas, do you have a fax machine in your office?"

"Yes I do."

"I need to get some information faxed to me right away."

"I don't mean to butt in but I have a fax machine here," Thomas said.

149

Steve called Jon and gave him the fax number to the Adams' house. "Chief is going to want to see as much of that information as you can fax to us." Steve stood by the fax machine as the pieces of paper started to come through. He looked at each one and saw what Jon was talking about. There was a map that had a circle drawn around the exit off Interstate 87 and Third Avenue in New York. It was just a few blocks from Yankee Stadium. Steve wasn't sure if it was the location of a possible safe house or signifying Yankee Stadium as a target. Steve put the documents in the order that Jon had faxed them. There were seven pages in total.

Dino called Steve to see if he had gotten the documents yet.

"I have them all right here, Sir. Mr. Adams let us use his fax machine."

"We will be there in a few minutes, Steve. You need to tell Mr. Adams that I have his daughter-in-law with me. Don't get him too excited, but explain that we wanted to make sure both of them are safe and having them together was the best way to accomplish it. You also have to tell him, for her safety, no one should know that she's with us."

"Holy shit Boss, you pulled that one off without any of us knowing."

"Yes, guess I just thought it was the best move for now." Dino figured that since he would get blamed for Mrs. Adams being along, he might as well take credit for the idea. He also didn't want Thomas to have a heart attack when Blair walked in. He told Allisa and Blair that they'd arrive at the Adams' home in a few minutes and they would enter from the rear. He didn't want anyone else to know that they were with him. He would handle Steve and knew that he could count on him keeping it quiet. Blair was happy that she would see Hunter's dad and hoped that they could have some time together. She also wondered what role she would play in this adventure. Dino pulled into the Adams driveway and three passengers got out of the vehicle and walked around the back of the house.

Blair stopped at the back of the garage and asked, "What happened here? Is Thomas okay? Is there something you're not telling me?" She was close to tears.

"It's okay, Thomas is fine and in the house. We had an

incident here last night and I lost one of my men."

She took a few deep breaths. "Sorry," she said. She walked through the garage with Dino and Allisa. Thomas came into the kitchen and when he saw Blair they hugged. They both had tears in their eyes. "I'm so glad that you're okay," they both said at the same time.

Blair was so glad to see Thomas. He was such a nice man and she knew that he would be lonely after losing Hunter. Thomas thought that she was the best thing that had happened to his son. She brought him closer to his family. Girls have a way of bringing sons back home.

Dino asked them all to go into the living room. "Blair, we need you and Thomas to think back to the last things you may have gotten from your husband and your son. It is critical that we know if he sent you anything that may help us."

Thomas said that he had talked to Hunter several times but he didn't send anything to him. Blair sat on the couch next to Thomas and did not answer. They thought that she had a funny expression on her face. Dino looked at her again and asked if she had received anything from Hunter in the past few weeks.

"I haven't opened anything from him in close to a month," she said. She turned to Thomas and apologized for the surprise visit.

"Don't be sorry, I'm just happy to see you."

Captain Douglas seemed puzzled as he listened to the questions that Dino asked. "Could Hunter have sent them something important?"

"We think that may be the case. We also think there is a group causing problems for our soldiers who have returned from Iraq." Dino had to toss that in to cover his earlier statements. "Captain, I want to leave both Mr. Adams and Blair here. Can I ask your people to help keep an eye on them? I want to make sure they're safe."

"I've already ordered a 24/7 watch and will be involved myself to help protect Mr. Adams and his daughter-in-law."

Steve and Dino went out onto the porch; Dino wanted to look at the fax that Jon had sent. "Steve, I don't want you to say anything about Blair or Agent Jones being here to anyone. It is for our benefit that they've come along."

"I don't know anything, Boss."

Allisa came outside to see what they had found from the search of the abandoned truck.

"I want to be involved in this," she told them.

"Don't worry; we will need everyone on the case that we can get." They all looked over the fax and the map that Jon had found in the truck. It showed an area circled near Yankee Stadium. What did that mean? They were not sure if it detailed where there was a safe house, or was Yankee Stadium a target?

Allisa turned to them, "I know the area. I went to NYU and lived in a loft near Yankee Stadium. It will make sense if I was to go there with you."

She could be of great value to the investigation, or maybe his downfall. He also knew that the director would have his ass if he found out.

"Let me think about the best way to proceed." He wanted to report something positive to the director as soon as possible. "I'm going to report the map that we found to the director and let him suggest the next step. We can make our plans once we know the direction he will want to take." He walked off the front porch and made the call. His mind went back to the director's last statement about guarding the monuments in South Dakota.

****

It was just past one in the afternoon when the phone call went through. "Director, this is Dino, I have an update and some good news."

"About time you got something for me."

"We found some documents the fugitive left behind that may lead us to something really big."

"How much bigger do you want this thing to get Dino? Do you need help with the case?"

Dino just knew that he had to get the director off his back. "Sir, we have terrorists on the loose and now we have a map that shows the location of their possible location and next target."

"Tell me again, where did you get this map? And what about this location?"

Dino slowed down and calmly told him. "The map we found along with other papers was left in the abandoned truck. They belonged to the escaped fugitive. It has a circle around the area that Yankee Stadium is in."

"Oh shit! We don't need this now. After the events of 9/11, New York can't handle another bombing. Hold on a minute," he said. Martin came back in a few seconds. "I just checked and the Red Sox are in New York tonight and after last year this series has been sold out for months. There will be 60,000 plus people at the game. I will need to mobilize our units to put special precautions in place around the stadium."

"How do you want my team to proceed?" Dino asked.

"You need to continue to try to find the fugitives that got away. Also, we need to know what this has got to do with the Adams' situation. I want you to fax me a copy of the map and any other documents you have."

"Sir, I would like to be involved in New York."

"Dino, first you need to get your men on the fugitive search. I will call you later to possibly get you involved with the Yankee Stadium thing."

"Thank you, Sir." Dino was now hoping that Mount Rushmore could find someone else to guard it. He walked back toward Allisa and Steve. "We need to get the fugitive captured and maybe we can head to New York. The Yankee Stadium thing could be our ticket." He reminded Steve, "I don't want anyone to know that we have two guests from California here. I want you to take Allisa with you to the search the site at Crosswicks. You can introduce her as Special Agent Mary Kathleen. You both take control of the situation and report to me as soon as possible."

Allisa was happy that she would be included. Maybe if they could get the fugitive they would get the information to help solve her case.

****

153

Blair asked Captain Douglas if it was okay for her and Thomas to go into the kitchen. He said, "No problem," and she asked if he was hungry. He said, "No thanks, but I bet you are."

Thomas just looked at her and walked to the kitchen as she opened the fridge. She looked inside and he asked, "What would you like to eat? I haven't been to the store in a few days."

"This is important but I don't want anyone else to know about it. We can pretend that we're making lunch." He was confused but went along with her. "None of this makes sense. I'm not sure why the FBI is involved but I may have what they are looking for."

"What do you mean?"

"It just dawned on me. I got a package from Iraq a couple of days ago. I didn't open it because that was the day I was going to meet the FBI agent. I was so shook up about the break-in at my place and then Allisa called. I forgot all about it until a few minutes ago."

"Who was it from?"

"When I picked it up at the post office the return address was Hunter's. I was on my way to The Pub to meet Agent Jones. I just left it downstairs at The Pub and that's when I found out that there was a second break-in at my apartment. I've been so upset I forgot all about it. When Mr. Tuchy started asking his questions it triggered my memory."

"We should tell the FBI," Thomas said.

"No," said Blair. "I want to know what's going on first. What if this is bad for Hunter? I want to know what's in the package. We can't tell anyone."

"Not even the lady that came with you?"

"No, not her or anyone until we know more about the contents."

Thomas understood and agreed with her.

"I have to get back to Santa Monica and get the package."

"You could call and have someone open it for you."

"No, there have been too many people hurt already and I don't want any of my friends involved. I have to do this myself."

Thomas remembered that Hunter told him once that when Blair made up her mind there was no stopping her.

"With all the police protection, how do you plan on getting back to Santa Monica without them knowing?"

"That's what we have to figure out."

Captain Douglas walked into the kitchen and asked what they were going to make. "Guess I could have something after all," he said.

Blair looked surprised to see him and started pulling out some packages that Thomas had in the meat keeper. "Looks like we have some lunchmeat so I'll make us some sandwiches," she said. "Do you have any bread?"

"There's a package in the refrigerator."

Blair made them all lunch all the while thinking how` to find a way to get back home. She could not call any of her friends and put them at risk, besides, what could be in the package that has caused all this? If she was to get back home she would need help. Allisa came in with Steve and said that they were going to head up to Crosswicks but should be back around dinner time. Dino had already left for Crosswicks to have a meeting with the state police.

Steve said, "This investigation needs to be resolved because there is another case that needs our attention."

The three listened and said fine. "We're just going to have lunch. Can we make something for you?"

"No, we'll grab something on the way."

Blair didn't want to hurt Allisa but it was important that she be the first one to open the package. Maybe it wasn't anything but she had to know. She told Thomas and Captain Douglas that lunch was ready. They sat at Thomas' table and the captain expressed how sorry he was that all of this had happened.

"I know that you both have had a great deal of grief with the loss of Hunter and this on top of it is almost too much for anyone to handle."

They sat and ate without much being said. Once she had picked up the dishes she told the captain that she was tired and was going to lie down for a while. Thomas walked with her to one of the spare bedrooms and Blair told him that she would try to make some plans and would let him know what she was going to do.

"Be careful." He was worried that she was taking on too

much.

It was close to ten a.m. back in Santa Monica when Olly's phone rang. "Blair, I'm so glad to hear from you. Is everything okay?"

"Yes, I said I would call once we got here and would let you know what was going on. It appears the FBI is on the lookout for some men that may be involved in the break-in at my place and his dad's place."

"That doesn't make sense."

"I know, but that's what they're telling us. Thomas and I agree that I need to head back to Santa Monica."

"Why do you need to come back here?"

"I'll explain once I figure out how to get out of here. There are some things that just don't make any sense. I can't tell anyone what my plans are except you."

"You know I will do anything you want me to. There have been a couple of FBI agents asking about you. We've all said that we don't know where you are. They seem to be worried that you've been kidnapped or are in hiding. We know that they have a man stationed outside of your apartment building and one at The Pub."

"Olly, somehow I will get back there as soon as possible. I will need your help, and continue to tell everyone that you don't know where I am."

"Okay, but you need to be careful. You're not prepared for this."

"I'll be fine. I've learned a lot from the bureau folks already and I can put it to good use."

She sat on the bed and planned her escape back to Santa Monica. She knew that she would have trouble shaking Allisa but maybe they will be moving on to the other case. Knowing that they have men stationed at her apartment and The Pub would make this even more difficult. She might have to get another friend involved because they are probably watching Olly too. She also knew that the local police were watching Thomas' house so just getting out of there would be a problem. She had to think up a good plan and get back to Santa Monica to see what was in that package.

Twenty-One

Jon went back to the state police mini-post that had been set up at the rest area. He told the state police chief that his bureau chief and a couple of agents were on their way to Crosswicks. He also wanted to gather any other details that Dino may want to know. Jon had just been promoted to the Philadelphia bureau and wanted to make sure that he could fill Dino in without getting him angry. He had heard from the other agents that Dino had a temper. He didn't want to look bad in front of his new boss. He learned that the state police had covered most of the areas that the fugitive could escape from; that included the wooded area around Groveville and State Route 524. He also knew that the Trenton FBI office had their men mobilized and were covering the interstates that led north to New York.

Brad Ferguson was the New Jersey State Police chief headquartered in Trenton. He gave Jon a local area map that had the main routes marked so that Jon knew where the troopers were positioned. Brad hated working with the FBI on the task force because of the way they treated local cops. Jon seemed different. He asked questions and listened to the answers. He took advice from Brad on the search and was appreciative for the documents that Brad turned over to him. Jon had a feeling that Brad would not like Dino.

Dino arrived at the Crosswicks rest area and Jon brought him up to date on the search. He wanted to review the papers again that Jon found at the scene in the abandoned pickup truck. He told Jon that Steve Watkins and Mary Kathleen, another agent who was bought in, would be arriving soon. Dino wanted to cement the false identification of Allisa. He could not take a chance on someone slipping up and calling her by her real name. He wanted to gather all the information possible before talking to the state police chief.

157

He did not want to deal with any local authorities unless they understood that he was in charge. They walked to the abandoned pickup and Dino asked who had searched through the truck.

"The two local state police officers who were trailing the fugitive were the only ones in the truck besides me," Jon said.

"I want our crime lab guys to go through this and report back to me. Get those two local state cops to give us their fingerprints so that the crime lab can rule those out."

"They're still here and the crime lab is on their way, Boss."

Dino was pleased with Jon's progress on the case. They walked toward the wooded area and saw the motorcycle tracks. He understood that the local state police had also sent in three other motorcycle riders to see if they could locate where the fugitive was headed. *How far could you get in all this mud?* he thought. He saw that Steve and Allisa were arriving at the rest area. He wanted to make sure that she was introduced as Mary Kathleen, special agent from Washington. He waved to them as they came walking over. The four agents were talking when the state police chief came over to cover his team's strategy.

"I'm Brad Ferguson, New Jersey Police. Our team has made some progress through the wooded area but it's so muddy that it's been difficult."

Dino put his hand out and greeted Brad. "Dino Tuchy, Philadelphia Federal Bureau of Investigation, and these are my agents, Jon David, Steve Watkins and Mary Kathleen."

"We have been working with Mr. David and I have an update that just came in. The fugitive's motorcycle tracks were followed through the wooded area that leads toward State Route 524. Mr. David has that marked on his map. We lost the tracks near a small stream that ran through the woods. We have gone up and down the stream but the tracks do not reappear."

"How far into the woods are these tracks?"

"They stopped about three and a half miles into the wooded area."

"Where are your men now?"

"They have split up and one is headed south along the stream and the other two have headed north. Our other teams are stationed along the state route so that if he comes out of the wooded area they will be in position to track him."

Dino thought for a minute and put his hand on Brad's shoulder. "Your people are doing a good job. I want to be kept informed on their progress. I have agents from Trenton also in position along major routes in case he was to make it past your men." Dino knew that this posture signaled that he was in charge. That was the initial impression he wanted to make on the chief.

Brad understood what Dino was doing. But he had some questions that needed to be answered so he played along.

"Thanks, I know I have a solid team. Who is this guy we're all chasing anyway?"

"I can't divulge that just yet."

"It would help if we had more details."

"Once I have clearance from the director in Washington I'll pass the information along."

Brad Ferguson walked away from the meeting shaking his head. Just as he figured: most local and state police thought the FBI people were crap. He felt that Jon might be different but his bureau chief was not. They never shared what they knew and always wanted you to give them all the information you had. If the case was ever solved they always took the credit. He had told Dino that he would keep them informed but he felt that his men were more than capable of tracking this guy. Brad felt that he gave Dino everything that he knew but Dino never answered his question.

****

Captain Douglas told Thomas, "My men will be making constant passes around the house. Thomas, we will be here to protect you and your daughter-in-law. I have to leave but I will be back in an hour or so. If you need anything just call my cell phone number.

Bob, I appreciate everything that you're doing for us. I know you have other things to attend to so just take your time. We will be fine." He was hoping that when the captain left he and Blair could plan her attempt to get out of the house and back to Santa Monica.

The two men walked outside to the captain's car. "Thomas, I'll be back. Do you need anything before I leave?"

"Before you get back, Bob, maybe I could get one of your people to go with me to the store."

"Sure, that won't be a problem; just let me know when you're ready."

Thomas was looking for as many different opportunities that they could use to accomplish Blair's plans. He wasn't too sure what she had in mind but knew that it would not be easy getting out of his house, let alone making her way to the airport. Once he was back inside he walked down the hall and stood outside the bedroom door. He quietly asked, "Blair, are you awake?"

"Yes, you can come in."

He opened the door and saw that she had changed.

"You look so different."

She had put on some jeans and an old sweatshirt of Hunter's. She had tied her hair back and had on boots. "I need to make myself look as different as possible without causing too much attention."

He told her that Captain Douglas had left for a while but would be back. He also informed her that there would be local police cars passing by to keep a watch on the house.

"Okay, let's think about this," she said.

****

Dino wanted to make sure that everything possible had been covered at the rest area. He also had to update John Martin but needed more positive news. He called to the bureau chief in Trenton to give him the latest information. He told him that John Martin wanted all the information to be filtered back through him and that he would contact the director with the data. He was an authority freak. Everyone who worked with him knew that. They also knew he was one of the best people to handle this type of situation. He told Steve that he and Jon needed to stay at the rest area and to call him as soon as they had any news. He would take Allisa with him and head toward Trenton and coordinate the search from the other side of the wooded area. "We might get a couple of motorcycles and have some of our men enter the woods and follow that stream from the northern end."

Dino did not want to leave Allisa at the rest area for fear of someone recognizing her. He knew the false name was just buying time. He also knew that if John Martin had any idea that she was with him he would be on the next flight for South Dakota.

****

Thomas called Bob Douglas and said that he would like to go to the store now.

"I'll have one of my men come by and get you," Bob said. "Is Blair going with you?"

"No, she's really tired and will stay here."

"We'll continue to cover your house while you are at the store. Tell her that she doesn't have to worry."

"Thanks again, Bob, for everything you're doing for us." He felt guilty that he was lying to his friend but knew that Blair was probably right. They had to know what was in the package that the FBI was determined to find. He told Blair that he was going to the store.

She said that should help with her plan. "I may still be here when you return, but if I'm gone, I will leave a note in the top dresser drawer for you. Once you read it make sure that you tear it up."

"Blair, please be careful. Remember there are other men that want that package too."

"I don't have a choice. I have to see if there is anything in that package back home, and if so, I have to protect Hunter."

He wished he could be that strong. Blair was a determined person. "Blair, what if I called my brother, Bill, to help us?"

"What do you have in mind?"

"Bill could drive down and meet you on the street behind my house. You could sneak through the yard into the woods and come out on the next street. He could take you to the airport."

Blair thought for a minute. "Are you sure he would do it?"

"Bill would do anything I ask. He has been a great help

with the funeral and everything. I can explain it to him and I'm sure he will help."

"That's a great idea. Let's call him," she said.

Thomas called Bill and went over the situation. Bill said that he would do whatever they wanted if it would help. How could all of this have happened? It was hard to believe that so much had transpired since Hunter's funeral and now, here were more problems for his brother and Blair.

The rendezvous was set up on Blue Bird Street. Thomas felt that if the police thought that Blair had gone to bed for the evening, she would have eight to ten hours before anyone suspected that she was gone. This might give her the time she needed to get to Santa Monica before they started to look for her. Blair agreed that this was a good plan. She called the airlines to check on flights to Los Angeles. There were two flights that left Philadelphia that evening. One was at ten forty-six and the other was at eleven twenty-three p.m. With the time difference she would be in L.A. before midnight Pacific Time. That would be good. She could have someone meet her. She still had to devise a plan to get the package from The Pub. It would be open until two a.m. but with the FBI watching The Pub she would need help. The exit from Thomas' house was set. Thomas decided to go to the store and Blair said she was going to change back. "I'll hang on to the disguise for later."

****

Dino and Allisa walked to his Suburban. "You'll need to be in the background as much as possible," he told her. "I will make sure that you are involved and anything that helps you will be yours."

Allisa knew that Dino would keep his promise. She also knew that he was taking a great chance having her along with him. "Dino, I can never tell you how much this means to me."

"Maybe we'll get lucky and catch this guy. But if the shit hits the fan I will have to get you the hell out of there."

"I understand," she said.

****

Yawer felt like he had walked through the shallow stream for miles. When he came to an area of the stream that had some dead tree limbs in the water he pushed the Harley out of the stream onto a large tree limb and onto a path that seemed to be hard enough to ride on. He was soaked but still on the move. Finding the stream in the woods helped to cover his tracks and would buy him time to escape. The Harley was heavy but he was able to maneuver it through the water and wooded area. He covered the tracks by pulling the large limb out of the water. He wasn't sure what direction he was going in. He still had some maps in the saddle bags on the bike and now that the rain had stopped he could check them out. He wanted to get out of the woods and into an area where he could change his mode of transportation. He was sure that people would be tracking him. When he looked at the map he could see that Trenton was due north and that he should be close to Yardville. If he could make it out of the woods he could get to Highway 130 north and maybe steal a new ride.

It would be light soon and he had to make his way out of the woods and get as far from there as possible. He knew that he had a head start on anyone who was tracking him through the woods. He also knew the police cars that chased him at the rest area would mobilize men on the roads that surrounded the area. The area was very dense, and because it was nighttime, he was able to ride the Harley deep into the brush. Once out of the deep woods he saw a clearing and rode the bike to the edge of what appeared to be a gravel road. He turned right and headed north on the road. It was still dark but he could see a few farmhouses as he rode past them. He slowed down when he saw a large barn with the doors open. He rode into the barn and thought that it would serve as a good place to clean up. Once he got into the barn he found some work clothes hanging up. He quickly changed and buried his dirty clothes in a hay pile. He walked around the inside of the barn and looked out the back and saw some late model trucks parked. He had to keep moving. He got his items out of the Harley's side bags and pushed the Harley into a hay pile. He was able to cover it with a few bales of hay and hoped it would not be found for a few hours, then he hot-wired a truck and pulled out from around the back of the barn onto the gravel road that led to a blacktop road about a half mile past the farmhouse. Yawer turned right and was glad to see that he had over three quarters of a tank of gas in the truck. He stayed on the blacktop until he came to a sign that said Groveville one mile. He headed toward Groveville and figured that Highway 130 was straight ahead.

Yawer found his way to Highway 130 and kept heading north. He hoped to get up the road before he would have to change vehicles again. He figured that he would have at least a two-hour head start with the pickup truck before it was reported as missing.

****

The state police were still far behind. Brad Ferguson had mobilized his men and cars as soon as possible but the suspect had a big head start. He also found it difficult to get help from the local police in Groveville. They had only two cars and because it was nighttime only one man was on duty. The FBI had said that they would cover escape routes that lead to the interstate. There were not enough men and too much territory to cover.

****

Thomas called his brother Bill back and explained the plan. Bill said that he could leave his house in Croydon and be on Blue Bird Street to meet Blair whatever time she wanted. Thomas told him that Blair wanted to get to the Philadelphia airport by nine so that she could catch one of the two departures for Los Angeles. Bill offered to fly to L.A. with her if she wanted him to. Both Thomas and Blair were very appreciative but said that it would be best if Blair traveled alone.

The plan was set. Blair would make an excuse to go to bed early and sneak out to meet Bill for the ride to the airport. It was about a forty-five minute ride from Thomas' house to the airport. Blair wanted Thomas to make sure that he made excuses for her as late into the next day as possible. She said she might try to return

164

to Philadelphia before anyone knew she was gone. Thomas doubted that the plan would work that well. He said, "You have two flights of four to five hours plus having to get the package from The Pub."

"I know but I have the time difference on my side. Traveling at night gives me an additional advantage. If I get to L.A. by midnight and can get the package in a couple of hours, I can do it. The flight back would put me here about noon tomorrow."

"Blair, you have to get everything to go perfectly for that to work out."

"So far nothing has worked out for us. Maybe this time it will." Blair and Thomas went back into the living room. Thomas was getting ready to go to the store.

"Blair, don't do anything silly while I'm gone."

"I won't; I'll be right here waiting for you."

Thomas noticed a squad car pulling in his drive. "I need to go now. I will be back in about thirty minutes. I really don't have much in the fridge. Is there anything you need or want?"

"Pick up something for dinner. I made a small list of groceries. I can make dinner for anyone who's here. It will be a good diversion."

"Sure, sounds good."

"Could you also pick up some English breakfast tea?"

"You bet, is that all?"

"Once we get our hands on that package, then I'll be ready for food."

"Agreed," Thomas said.

****

Dino told Allisa that they should head back to Thomas' house. "You could get some rest and I'll pick you up later. I would also like you to question Blair and Thomas one more time to see if something might trigger a memory that would help us. I got the feeling that she's not telling us everything."

"Dino, I'm convinced that she doesn't know anything. I

tried in California but she just doesn't know what we want. Remember, I still want to be involved. I'm not going to stay out of sight at the Adams' house."

"I promise that I will come back for you later. I'm thinking maybe around eight. There will be more progress here by then and we still have a fugitive or fugitive's body in Bridgewater to find."

The two drove back to the Adams' home. Allisa knocked at the front door when they arrived. Blair went to the door and looked out the small glass window to see who it was.

"I didn't know when you were coming back."

"I need to rest some and Dino thought it would be better if we continued our search later this evening."

Blair stepped outside and waved to Dino. She wanted to make sure she was seen as often as possible.

"Where's Thomas?"

"He went to the grocery store with one of the local Bridgewater police officers. They have a car down the street watching the house while he's gone."

"Dino pointed it out when we drove up. I waved to them to let them know that I was coming back." The two sat in the living room.

"Do you want anything?" Blair asked.

"No, I'm just happy to sit for a while and rest. While we were gone, did you or Thomas remember anything that might help us?"

"No, we've just been talking about Hunter and really don't have any ideas that would help. This is all so confusing that we're just trying to catch up ourselves."

"That's understandable. If you do have anything, no matter how small you might think it is, just let me know. Blair, you know I will do everything to help you and solve this puzzle."

"I know that. I promise to tell you anything that might help." Blair felt a little guilty not telling her what she remembered but until she knew what the package held, there was no sense in telling anyone. It might be nothing but Blair had to know.

Allisa said, "I'm going to catch a little nap. Blair, if I fall asleep, please wake me in two hours."

"Not a problem," Blair answered. "Use the bedroom on the

right. It's a guest room and all ready for you."

"Thanks, I guess I'm more tired than I thought. What room are you using?"

"I'm using Hunter's old room."

Allisa didn't want to say anything else for fear that Blair would break down. She went into the guest room and shut the door.

The front door of the house opened and Thomas walked in with the officer behind him.

"Can I help you with those bags?" Blair said as she headed to help. "Did you buy the whole store?"

"I just followed your list. You have to remember, I haven't shopped for a group in a long time."

"Is there anything else I can do for you Mr. Adams?" the officer asked.

"No thanks, Jeff, you've been a big help."

"Allisa is here and I said she could sleep in the guest room."

"When did she come back?"

"Just a few minutes after you left for the store." He carried the bags into the kitchen and Blair started to put the groceries away with him.

"Thanks for the breakfast tea. I enjoy tea more than coffee except for an occasional latte." They talked quietly as they put the remainder of the groceries away. "Do you think I should tell Allisa about my plan?" Blair asked.

"I really don't trust any of them, Blair. They have an agenda that is different from ours. We just want to make sure nothing bad is said about Hunter. They want something and we don't know what it is."

"You're right; I needed your perspective. I wonder what they think he found."

"It must be big, Blair, or the FBI would not be involved."

Blair knew that Thomas was right. She again wondered why the FBI was involved. If Hunter was one of their agents they must think he did something wrong. She wanted to trust Allisa but didn't trust the other agents. What to do next was her dilemma.

Twenty-Two

Bill Adams pulled down Blue Bird Street and turned off his headlights. He had some reservations about Thomas' and Blair's plan but he would do anything to help them. He had met Blair two years ago when she and Hunter had come to Thomas' house for Christmas. His first impression was that she was a very beautiful girl but probably just another California type. He judged her looks, not her. He was surprised when he talked to her about current issues regarding the war in Iraq. She was very informed and had some valid reasons for her position. Blair was against the war although she supported Hunter's position. She had her own opinion on the involvement of the United States in the war.

Bill realized that Blair was a strong person and that she had a great influence on both Hunter and Thomas. He understood that because she had him sitting on Blue Bird Street waiting to help her escape back to Los Angeles for some reason he was not privileged to know. He had many questions and he hoped that Blair could fill him in on the trip to the Philadelphia airport. It was a little before eight p.m. and he was in position earlier than he should have been, but he wanted to be there in case the plans changed and he was needed sooner. He dialed Thomas on his cell to let him know that he was there and to reconfirm the plans.

When the phone rang, Thomas almost jumped out of his skin. He was getting more nervous as the time got closer to nine. Allisa was still sleeping in the extra bedroom and Blair was making dinner. Thomas picked the phone up and was happy to hear Bill's voice.

"I just wanted to call and let you know that I'm where you said I should be."

"Plans are still the same. We may have a little variance in the time because we have company here."

"Thomas, are you both sure everything is okay?"

"I promise. She will fill you in when she sees you. I'll ring your cell phone once when Blair leaves the house. You will know that she is on the way."

The woods behind the Adams' house were very dense and at night they could be hard to go through. The woods had seen a lot of action with the night of the shoot-out in the yard and the chase of the suspects with the FBI in pursuit. They were becoming heavily traveled.

Allisa came out of the bedroom. "I guess I really needed that rest. What time is it?"

Thomas looked at his watch and said, "It's ten minutes until eight."

"Wow, I can't believe that I slept so long. Where is Blair?"

"She's making dinner."

Allisa walked into the kitchen and saw that Blair was busy setting the table. She had made a roast with all the fixings.

"This is a great looking dinner! I wish you'd asked me to help."

"You needed the rest. I got to sleep when we got here. I hope you're hungry."

"I can't remember the last time I ate."

"I made a large meal because I didn't know if Dino or some of the other men would be here. Do you know what their plans are?"

Blair was fishing for information. She had her plans but would be somewhat flexible depending on who else was at Thomas' house.

"Dino said that he would pick me up about eight p.m.," Allisa said. "Blair, I need to tell you something. I cannot let you be in the dark about everything. Washington thinks that Hunter found some information that may lead to a discovery involving a lot of money. They also now think that Hunter was going to sell this information."

Blair stopped setting the table. "When did you find this out?"

"Dino told me before he dropped me off. He said that John

169

Martin, the FBI director, told him about it yesterday. They think that is why you or Hunter's dad may have had the information sent to you."

Blair was shocked. She sat down and was very quiet.

"Blair, I'm telling you this because you have taken a chance on coming here with me. I also think that you have been very honest with me. I am betting that Hunter just didn't have time to get the information to his superiors before he was killed."

It was very quiet in the kitchen for what seemed like an eternity.

"Blair, please talk to me."

Blair took a deep breath. "I don't know what to say."

"This is the first time we have been alone since I found this out and I had to tell you. I hope you can understand that I trust you and hope you trust me."

Blair wanted to think before she said anything. "I do trust you but I don't trust the other FBI people."

"I understand and don't blame you. You've been through so much and now this."

"I'm going need to have some time alone to figure some of this out. Would you help me?"

"I don't know what you mean."

"After dinner I would like to go somewhere and check some things out. I might be able to give you some help once I have been able to complete this."

It all sounded pretty suspicious, but Allisa asked, "What kind of time do you need?"

"A lot, but I've come up with an idea. I will say that I'm going to bed. Can you could cover for me until tomorrow?"

"Wow, all the way until tomorrow. What time?"

"Maybe close to noon."

"That's a lot of time. Where are you going? You promise that you won't leave me holding the bag here."

"Allisa, I think you are being very honest with me. Right now, I trust you with this information. I promise that I will not leave you holding the bag; however, I'd rather not say where I am going yet."

"If I did this, I could cover for you by saying that you're

sick in the morning."

"That would work."

"They're going to want to see you."

"I'm pretty sure I will have some answers by late afternoon tomorrow but I can't do this without your help."

"This is an awkward position but you trusted me by coming along and I have to trust you on this. I'm not sure we can pull this off but I'm willing to give it a try. Just where are you going?"

"I have to get out of the house for a while."

"How are you going to get out of the house?"

"I have a plan."

"We have a lot in common. You're my kind of agent."

Blair laughed. "Yeah, a real FBI agent."

"Remember Blair, you have all those credentials, use them if needed."

Blair forgot that Allisa gave her a full set of FBI credentials. That could be her key to getting on the flights she needed without a reservation.

"Dinner's ready," Blair said.

"Boy, everything looks great. You made so much," Thomas said.

"I didn't know how many people would be here, plus left over roast makes for great sandwiches." Blair was a good cook, although her schedule at The Pub did not leave her much time for cooking.

The doorbell rang. Thomas went to the door; it was Dino, Steve and Jon. "Come on in," Thomas said. "You must have smelled dinner."

"We don't want to interrupt; we just came to get Allisa," Dino answered.

"Blair made enough for a small army. You should all come in and eat with us." Dino looked at the others and said it sounded good. He wanted to make sure that Thomas and Blair felt that they were being friends and friends usually ate together.

Allisa and Blair came out of the kitchen. "Dinner's on the table," Blair said. This would work out great for her plan. Everyone would see her late and no one would wonder where she

171

was. With Allisa helping to cover for her the next morning, she could follow her planned trip to LA and get back to Thomas' house with the package.

"Great looking dinner," Dino said. Being single he often ate fast food or frozen dinners. "This looks like a feast." They all sat down at the dining room table.

"You really went all out for this," Dino said.

Steve and Jon were happy that Dino agreed to let them join the dinner party. It was nice having a good meal after the last few hours of fast food while sitting in their cars searching for the fugitives. Everyone started to pass the food and Blair was happy that they seemed to be enjoying everything. The dinner conversation was about the escaped fugitive and the search for him. Blair seemed to ask a lot of questions and Steve and Jon were free with information. Allisa knew what she was doing. Feed them and ask questions. Seemed innocent enough and now she realized that Blair was cunning and very good at finding out information she was after. Dino cautioned Blair and Thomas that the investigation was still in progress and nothing should be repeated outside of the room. Steve started to tell them about the connection with a possible terror cell in New York when Dino stopped him.

"Steve, we don't need to bore them with details, let's just eat and enjoy the meal that Blair made." Everyone was eating and the talking continued to focus on the investigation.

Blair looked at the clock on the wall and saw that it was eight thirty-five. She hoped to get to Bill's car and off to the airport by nine. She glanced at Allisa and gave her a look. "Boy am I full. I could use a nap after a meal like that."

"Blair, why don't you let us clean up? After all, you did all the work preparing this great meal."

Thomas knew that the time was getting close for Blair to leave. "Yeah, Allisa and I can clean up. You go and rest," he added.

"Guess I'm just a little tired from the trip and all. I hope everyone had enough. Don't forget the pie in the fridge."

Dino and Steve got up and thanked Blair for the dinner. Jon wiped his face and said he would help Allisa pick up. "I was the youngest of six and was always stuck in the kitchen with my mom," Jon said. "I can help her and then we can get going."

Blair said goodnight to everyone and hugged Thomas. She went off to her room and Allisa and Jon helped Thomas gather the dinner dishes.

Dino said, "Once you're done we need to get going. He hoped that the meeting with the New Jersey and New York state police would have some updated information for him.

Blair pulled the disguise out that she had hidden under the bed in her room. She heard the front door close and looked out the bedroom window to see that Jon and Steve were getting into the back seat of Dino's Suburban. Dino and Allisa were getting into the front seat.

Blair headed down the hall toward the back door. It was a few minutes past nine.

"Be careful," Thomas said.

"I will. Should I call you when I get to Santa Monica?"

"It might look too suspicious because of the time of night when you get there. Instead just call me once you found what you are looking for."

Blair hugged him and headed out the back door. He dialed Bill as planned and let it ring one time. He went to the front porch and stood outside watching to see if the local police patrol car was there. He didn't see anything. Blair ran from the back of the house into the wooded area. She found the brush thick and some low lying branches almost knocked her to the ground. She made her way through the woods to Blue Bird Street. She waited at the edge of the woods to make sure that Bill's car was in sight before she ran out toward him. Bill was glad to see her and pushed the passenger front door open so that she could jump in. She ducked down and winked at Bill.

"We make a good Bonnie and Clyde."

"This is a bit more excitement than I normally have," he said, "but I'm at your service."

"I want to go to the Philadelphia airport."

"That's what Thomas said you wanted to do. I'll get you there as quickly as I can."

Blair sat on the floor until Bill got on the interstate. They

173

headed toward the airport and Blair put her disguise on. She pulled her blond hair back and put on the boots and sweat clothes. "I need to make sure that I don't look like the image that the FBI would be looking for in case they find out that I'm gone." She also knew that they were looking for her in Los Angeles so she had to be doubly careful. She called the airport and asked for the United flight information. They confirmed that there was a flight leaving for LAX at ten forty-six and that there were seats still available on that flight.

Bill told her that they would make it to the airport in less than forty minutes. She would have to hurry but she could make that flight. If necessary she would use the FBI documents that Allisa made for her. Bill pulled up in front of the Philadelphia airport and looked for the United Airlines sign. Blair said, "I really appreciate your help. Thomas will call to let you know if I'll need to be picked up."

"Be careful," he said. "I'm not quite sure what you're doing but if you need my help just call me."

"Thank you for everything. I'll explain it all to you once I get back." Blair jumped out of the car and jogged down the terminal toward the United desk. "I need to get on your next flight to LAX," she told the woman behind the desk.

"We have one that leaves at ten forty-six but you will have to hurry."

Blair gave the attendant her credit card and the FBI identification fell out on the counter. "Sorry, I didn't know that you were with the FBI. I will issue you a gate pass and call the gate to let them know that you are on the way."

"Thank you," Blair said. She turned and headed through the terminal toward the departure gate. The United gates were the closest to the main terminal and she was able to make it there in about ten minutes. The longest part was getting through security. She walked up to the gate and handed her boarding pass to the gate agent.

"Headed to L.A. in a hurry tonight?"

"My fault. I should have been on an earlier flight but the meetings lasted longer than expected."

"You can grab a seat in the back. We are not full and most

everyone wants to sit closer to the front."

Blair thanked him and boarded the plane. She could relax for the four-hour flight and plan how to get the package. Once she was aboard she called Olly to let her know what flight she was on and when she would arrive.

"I'll pick you up."

"That's probably not a good idea. If they're watching The Pub they may be watching you too. No, I'll grab the local hotel shuttle to the Holiday Inn on Colorado and Second Street. We can meet there and make our plans to get what I'm looking for."

"Just be careful."

"I'm on the plane and okay. I'll see you in a few hours." She leaned back and took a deep breath. *I need a plan for getting back after I get the package,* she thought. *What if the FBI was right? What if Hunter did send me some information that I shouldn't have? Only time will tell.*

A voice came on overhead and said that they would be departing in a few minutes. He then said, "I want to recognize a special person on the plane and ask everyone to acknowledge Captain Dennis Montgomery. He's just flown in from Iraq and is headed to Los Angeles." The people on the plane applauded and Blair watched as a soldier sitting about four rows ahead of her waved. The pilot added, "Captain Montgomery was part of the Special Forces that were stationed in Baghdad." Blair became very nervous. Hunter was stationed in that same group. This was a strange coincidence, or was it? Blair was on her way to discover what the package held. Now she wondered who this soldier was and why was he going to Los Angeles. Blair could not remember the name of Hunter's commander although he had mentioned him a few times. Brian had also mentioned their commander, but what was his name? Blair slouched in her seat and was glad that she was in the back of the plane. She had hoped to catch some sleep on the flight. She asked the flight attendant for a pillow and blanket. She leaned toward the window and covered her shoulder and part of her face with the blanket.

Blair drifted off as the 747 banked toward the west and climbed to a cruising altitude of twenty-eight thousand feet.

Captain Montgomery had been looking at some papers that he had on his lap. As he read them he was looking at some pictures of Hunter Adams and his wife. Little did the captain know that Blair Adams was just four rows behind him on the same flight.

Twenty-Three

John Martin had just finished his phone call to Dino. He gave him an update on the situation in New York. "I've brought our task force up to date on your information regarding the situation in New York. Of course no one is sure what we have yet but we're sure that this could be significant. Dino, once we catch this guy on the motorcycle I'll want you to head to New York to help with rounding up this possible cell. I feel that they're somehow related.

Dino was pleased that the director was placing this responsibility on him.

"I'm going to call Don, our bureau chief in Manhattan, to let him know what we have so far."

Dino was hoping that he could get the situation handled in Bridgewater as quickly as possible.

Don was the top FBI bureau chief. He had been instrumental in the aftermath of the 9/11 Twin Tower disaster. He was also a good friend of John Martin. He once worked as John's chief inspector early in their careers. John Martin knew that he could trust Don to handle the situation and work with Dino on it. Not all the bureau chiefs worked well together, but Don was an exception.

It was after midnight when Dino pulled into Thomas Adams' driveway and got out of the Suburban. Allisa said that she would stay at the Adams' home with Thomas and Blair. Dino thought that was a good idea. He figured that she could keep an eye on them. It was late and she said that Thomas had given her a key. "I'll call you tomorrow about nine and we can touch base with Blair and Thomas one more time."

"Can we make it a little later? I was thinking that if I could eat breakfast with them alone maybe I would have more luck getting some questions answered."

"That's a good idea. She trusts you and maybe you can get the answer we need. I still think she knows something she isn't telling us. What if I show up about noon?"

"I like that plan," Allisa said. She opened the door and said goodnight.

He watched from the Suburban and told Jon that he should stay behind and keep an eye on the Adams' house. "You can use Steve's car; it's still parked in the driveway. Just keep an eye on the house and make sure no one comes in or goes anywhere." Steve offered to do it but Dino said, "We should stay together. I want to make one more pass at the rest area and the abandoned truck."

Allisa knew that she had bought Blair all the time she could. Blair said that she needed until the afternoon and at least this would get her close to noon. She hoped that her trust in letting Blair leave the Adams' house would not backfire. She had no idea where Blair was going but it must be big. When Dino and Steve drove off, Dino's cell phone rang.

"Dino, John Martin here. I just got confirmation that our special envoy is on his way from Iraq to Santa Monica. It will take some time to get him from Iraq but I will keep you apprised of his progress. We think that he might be able to get some information from Blair or be able to snoop around because of his relationship with Hunter."

"Thanks for keeping me in the loop, Sir."

"You're my main man on this one; don't let me down."

Dino knew that everyone still thought that Blair was in Santa Monica. Only he and Allisa were aware that Blair was with them. He turned to Steve, "We have to close this thing up here so I can get up to the Big Apple. This is our career opportunity. If it all works out, Steve, you know that I will take you with me."

Steve was happy that Dino still trusted him. After Frank was killed and the search of the Adams' home had not gone well, Steve was concerned that Dino wouldn't trust him with any important assignments. "Thanks Dino, I will do anything to help." Steve sat a little taller in his seat as they drove toward the rest area.

****

The night was cool and Yawer was still driving north on Highway 130. He decided to stay on that road because it ran parallel to I-95 and was less traveled than the interstate. He looked at his map and saw that the he would meet Highway 1 at North Brunswick. He could stay on that all the way until Elizabeth and then cross over into New York on Highway 278 and the Narrows. Yawer wanted to get to a larger city before he changed rides again. It would be less suspicious if a stolen vehicle gets reported in a big city versus in a small town. He planned to contact Jaafi when he was a little closer to the Bronx. Yawer remembered back to when his parents were killed in fighting along the Iranian border. Being alone and on the run in the woods and now trying to get back to the safe house sent his mind spinning back to that time. El Jaafi was like his brother. Jaafi taught him the art of fighting and how to flee to safety when needed. He was smart and he had learned much from him. When Jaafi was in trouble and captured by Iranian guerrillas it was Yawer to his rescue. He wanted to prove his value to his mentor. He was cunning and making his way to New York.

****

The New Jersey State police were still looking for a single rider on a red Harley. They had cars patrolling the interstate and sent some cars to check out various sections of Highway 130. Brad Ferguson had contacted Captain Campbell of the Pennsylvania State Police to advise him of their progress. Campbell kept his friend, Bob Douglas in Bridgewater, aware in case the fugitive doubled back.

****

The night and a new ride were the best allies that Yawer could have. He wished that he didn't have to escape from the state troopers at the rest area because he was sure that he had left some documents in the pickup truck, but what?

El Jaafi and Abdulla informed the group in the safe house about the situation in Bridgewater. They didn't detail their mission, but wanted to make sure they had an escape route if necessary. El Jaafi remembered the September 11 incident when he had to flee the area and stay hidden for weeks until he was able to return home. He knew that Yawer would make it back to the house in the Bronx. He had trained Yawer from the time they found him laying on the bodies of his parents. The war between Iran and Iraq took its toll on many families that lived in small villages along the border. Yawer's family was one of them.

The safe house was a refuge for the group of men who had been planning to disrupt American lives. They had initially planned to plant bombs during the annual Times Square New Year's Eve event that always drew a million people and was seen around the world, but security was so heavy that the plan did not come off. They were now hoping to accomplish a disaster that would be carried worldwide. A splinter group that was headquartered in London had just successfully created havoc by placing bombs in the London subway system. El Jaafi and Abdulla would have liked to have helped in this endeavor but they had a mission to complete.

****

Jon circled the Adams' house and saw the local police cruiser pass him by. The cruiser slowed down and he was sure that it was the same car that had just passed him on Blue Bird Street. *Guess he's wondering who I am, especially this time of night,* he thought. He kept driving and turned on Apple Lane and figured that he should drive out of the area for a little while. He saw a donut shop that appeared open on the corner of Apple and Green Streets. Jon thought a cup of coffee and a donut would help him stay awake. He was sure the donut would not be a match for the pumpkin pie that Blair had made but he needed something, so he pulled into the parking lot. He was placing his order when a voice behind him said, "Put your hands up." Jon started to turn around and a voice said, "Don't move or I'll shoot." He believed the voice because it sounded a little shaky. *Never mess with a shaky person holding a gun,* he thought. He could see that the reflection in the counter glass was that of a local police officer.

"I'm with the FBI," Jon said.

The donut shop clerk ducked down on the floor behind the counter.

"Put your hands on the counter and spread your legs," the officer said.

Jon did as instructed but again identified himself.

"I know that your people are in our town but I must make sure you're who you claim to be." The officer patted Jon down and felt his gun in the shoulder holster. The officer took the gun out of the holster as Jon kept his hands on the counter. He then told Jon to turn around.

"Let's see some identification."

Jon felt embarrassed that he hadn't been paying attention to whether someone was following him. Now he had to show his identification to a local cop. He took his right hand and reached into his breast pocket.

"Stop right there. I'll get that for you." The officer patted Jon's pocket and reached in and pulled out an FBI badge. He looked at it and lowered his gun. "I'm sorry but I've seen you passing the Adams' home a couple of times and I wasn't sure what you were up to."

"Just doing my job."

The officer handed the badge back to Jon and apologized. Both men laughed. Maybe they were just both a little nervous and now feeling relaxed.

"Can I buy you a coffee and donut?" Jon asked.

They realized that the young clerk was still on the floor behind the counter. "You can get up now, everything is okay."

The clerk looked up from the floor and said it was just his second day and he was sure it was a holdup. He hadn't heard the conversation between the two lawmen and was scared to death.

"How about two cups of coffee, young man," Jon said.

"What was that all about?" The clerk asked as he dusted off his pants.

"We are just looking for someone and mistook each other for him."

"Is it dangerous for me to be here late at night?"

"We never have any trouble in town," Jerry McCarthy, the

local officer answered. Tom got the men two cups of coffee and a couple of donuts. The men took their coffee and sat at a small table near the large window at the front of the shop.

"Since we're both doing the same thing, let's work out a pattern so we're not chasing each other instead of watching the house."

Jon knew this was a good idea although Dino would not want him to work with local authorities. "How about if I just position my car down the street and you could do the surveillance of the neighborhood," he suggested.

"I've been driving past the house about once every fifteen minutes on my route. I've also been circling the back side where the fugitives had hidden their car."

"Here is my cell number. If you see anything and need assistance just call me," Jon said.

"Thanks, that's a good idea," Jerry answered. Both men headed out of the coffee shop and back to their cars.

Jon had been with the state police at the Crosswicks rest area and was good at working with other local authorities. He was originally a police officer in Philadelphia before joining the FBI. He had been placed on a joint task force working with the Feds and impressed them. The offer to work for the bureau was a dream opportunity. Jon's wife Cindy didn't like the hours. He would often be gone on assignment for days without being able to contact her. This was often a normal situation for both federal and local officers. It was hard to have a stable home life.

****

Allisa decided to go to the bedroom. She knew that Blair would not be back for hours and wanted it to look normal in case someone was watching. She sat on the edge of the bed and hoped that Blair was telling her the truth. She had put a lot of trust in her, but knew that Blair had put a lot of trust in her. She wondered where she'd gone. Allisa set the alarm for seven and figured that she would ask Thomas in the morning if he knew what Blair was up to. She wondered if Thomas was even aware that she had left. *Maybe I'll just play it by ear*, she thought. Sleep was something that she hadn't had much of lately. She lay back on the bed and fell into a deep sleep in minutes.

****

Dino and Steve headed toward the rest area in Crosswicks. The state police had a car stationed by the pickup truck and had closed off that area of the parking lot. They finished lifting fingerprints from the truck and would have the results by early morning. Dino wanted to go through the truck one more time himself. He had left Jon at the scene when it all happened and felt that Jon did a great job faxing Steve copies of the documents that were found. What about this thing in New York with the area in the Bronx circled? Could this be linked to their original assignment? What did this have to do with the Adams' house in Bridgewater? He had questions and he wouldn't stop until he had answers. That's in part what broke up Dino's first marriage. He was engrossed in his work. Many officers and bureau members had been divorced because of the job.

The two men got out of the Suburban and approached the officer left to guard the pickup. "We would like to take one more look around," Dino said as he displayed his badge. The officer obliged and handed Dino the keys to the truck.

Dino was surprised that they had the keys to the truck. "He didn't take the keys?"

"No," Steve said. "He got the bike out of the back with help from the man parked next to him and took off. When they searched the truck they found the keys still in the ignition."

"Do we know anything about the man who helped him get the bike out?"

"He was just a truck driver thinking that he was lending a hand. The state guys questioned him and got all his information in case they wanted to talk to him again." They searched the truck and the truck bed for any bit of information that would help their case. Dino knew the crime lab guys would pick up every small item in case it helped to detail who the fugitive was, but Dino had to see it for himself.

183

"Do you know when the report will come in from the crime lab?"

Steve looked at Dino and shrugged his shoulders. "They said we should have something in the morning."

"If we could find out who this guy is we might be able to get a jump on him. His identity might lead us to where he's going."

Steve knew that Dino was grasping for straws. He hoped the crime lab would give his boss some answers. They went back to their Suburban and the officer said that his chief wanted to know if any identification had been found.

"We hope to have something by morning," Steve answered. Nothing was learned from this secondary search but Steve was going to follow any lead that Dino felt was important. They would head back to Bridgewater without any more information. The ride back was quiet. Both men were exhausted.

Twenty-Four

The trip back to Los Angeles was the red-eye flight. Most of the passengers would normally fall asleep the whole time and the flight attendant's service would be minimal. Blair closed her eyes and kept the small blanket over the corner of her face in case Captain Montgomery walked by. She didn't know who he was, but the significance of him being in the same group as Hunter bothered her. So much had happened that she didn't trust anything to just coincidence.

Flying east to west always took a little longer because of head winds. The pilot did not make any announcements because most of the passengers were sleeping. The three attendants would take turns walking down the aisle to check on passengers and see if anyone needed something. As one of the attendants approached, Blair signaled to her.

"I've got a question. Do you know anything about the soldier that the captain introduced when we were taking off?"

"I didn't talk to him but one of the girls said that he got on early in Philadelphia. He said he was from Georgia and had just left Baghdad yesterday morning."

"I wonder why he's going to Los Angeles if he is from Georgia."

"I'm not sure, but maybe his family has moved out there."

Blair was now even more concerned about the soldier. Why is he on this plane and how did it work out that he is on her flight? Did Allisa know where she was going and was he sent to watch her? No, that didn't make any sense if he just came in from Baghdad. She wished she knew more but figured that she needed to catch a few hours of sleep before landing in Los Angeles.

"Don't say that I asked about him," she told the attendant.

"I won't," she said. "He is cute!"

Blair left it at that figuring the flight attendant was thinking she was interested because he was a young, good looking soldier. She leaned toward the window and closed her eyes. Tomorrow would be a long day and she needed to get back to Philadelphia as soon as she got the package. If things bogged down she had Allisa's cell phone number to let her know what was going on.

****

Olly looked at her watch and figured that Blair would arrive in about three hours. The time difference would put her in L.A. about eleven-thirty p.m. Pacific Time. She looked out the front of The Pub and saw the man she felt was watching the place. He had been sitting at a table in front of Hooters for the last couple of hours. He wasn't acting like a normal tourist who would eat and check out the girls for a while then leave. He was drinking something other than alcohol, maybe coke or tea and had not ordered any food. *He must be on a one-man stake out. I'll keep an eye on him and hope that he's the only one watching us*, she thought to herself. She had told Blake and Ashley that Blair was concerned about the FBI watching both her apartment and Hunter's dad's place. Blair was trying to find out what was going on. Both of them said that they wanted to help. "Blair knows that you want to do something to help. She might call one of us later tonight."

"Do you have any idea what is going on?" Blake asked.

"I'm not really sure, but she had to go to Bridgewater to check on Hunter's dad."

"Is he okay?"

"Yes, but the FBI is also involved in searching his place and Blair wants to get to the bottom of this."

"We don't blame her," Ashley answered.

Blake said, "When I came out of my apartment I noticed a man sitting on a park bench and figured he was watching the place. You could tell he wasn't a tourist by the way he was dressed."

Olly said, "I do know that the FBI has been watching her place and The Pub looking for her."

"If we could pretend that she's around that might help,"

186

Ashley said. "I still have her apartment key. Why don't I go there? They might think I'm Blair."

"That might work Ashley, but your hair color would give you away."

"I'll wear one of those crazy hats that Blair loves. It can't hurt."

Olly thought for a minute. "Okay but wait until near midnight. If you go in the apartment, stay there for about an hour. It might cause them to be thrown off the trail here at The Pub."

"What if I spend the night in her apartment?"

"I don't think you will want to do that, Ashley."

"Why?"

"I don't think anyone has cleaned up after the shoot-out yet."

"I forgot about that."

Olly said, "The main thing is we want to throw them off the trail. Ashley, why don't you go to the apartment about midnight, then Blake, you go and pick her up around one a.m. like you're going out somewhere together. Head off toward Venice, you know, around The Whaler on the corner of Washington down by the beach."

"How about the Halo Bar upstairs?"

"Yes, it's always jumping about that time. I know Blair would go there after we closed sometimes."

"You think they're watching us too?"

"No, I think they're watching the places she would normally go, like work and home."

"At least we'll feel like we're helping her." The plan was set. Blake and Ashley would try to throw off the FBI by pretending that Ashley was Blair. That might help her get to The Pub and get the package. Olly didn't tell them that Blair was coming back from Philly that night. She just hoped that their two friends could help buy her some extra time. They would understand. She was not sure what was happening, but she was sure that Blair was in too deep and not experienced enough for this type of espionage.

****

187

Blair got out of her seat and went into the bathroom at the rear of the plane. It was about ten-fifteen p.m. Pacific Time. She would be in Los Angeles in less than an hour. She wanted to make sure that her disguise was okay and didn't bring her too much attention. She had her hair pushed up under the hat she found in Hunter's room and the boots added a flair that was almost stylish. She came out of the bathroom and looked down the aisle to peek at the soldier four rows ahead of her. He seemed to be sleeping. Should she take a chance on walking past him? She wanted to get a look at him in case they ran into each other. She walked down the aisle looking forward only to peek at the soldier as she made her way up the aisle. She noticed that he was sleeping but there were some papers on his lap. She continued past the row he was in and stopped about ten rows past him. She looked back and saw that very few people were awake. Those who were seemed to be reading or looking out the windows hoping to catch a glimpse of the Grand Canyon or the lights of a big city they were flying over.

Blair saw that the soldier hadn't moved. She headed back toward her seat and slowed as she passed him. The papers were in a folder on his lap but she stopped dead in her tracks when she saw a picture of her and Hunter on top of the folder. She wanted to grab it off his lap. Why did he have a picture of them? Who was this soldier? She continued to walk down the aisle toward her seat in Row 32. She stood in the aisle for a few minutes and almost jumped when one of the attendants asked if she needed anything.

"No, thank you, just a little stiff from sitting so long."

"One of the girls said you asked about Captain Montgomery."

"Oh I was just curious."

"I'm Tammie. I talked to him when he came aboard. He said that he had been flying from Iraq to London and then to Philly before boarding our flight."

"Without stopping?"

"That's what he said."

"I wonder why he would do that."

"I asked him and he said that he was going to the Los Angeles area to see a friend. Must be a chick; why else would you

188

go to LA when you're from Georgia?"

"I was just interested because I have friends in the military."

"Oh, can I get you anything?"

"No, I'm fine, just looking forward to getting home." Blair sat down in her seat. She wanted to find out what the soldier had to do with all of this. She couldn't think. How much more could she take? But now her main objective was to get the package.

The plane was about to make its final approach into the Los Angeles area. She had one small carryon and it was in the luggage bin above her seat. It was a duffle bag that she found in Hunter's room. She wanted to bring a few things to change into as a cover. She stood up and grabbed the bag. She pulled a makeup bag out and put the carryon under her seat. She needed to make sure she looked different from the photo that Captain Montgomery had on his lap.

"Do you think I could use the bathroom before we land?" She asked the flight attendant.

"Sure," she said, "we're probably about thirty minutes out."

Blair opened the bathroom door. The term bathroom on a plane was almost an oxymoron. It was more like a closet than a bathroom. She opened her makeup bag and got out her hair brush and some mousse. *Maybe if I get all this hair under the hat and put a little make-up on I'll look different from that picture.* She tucked all her hair under the hat and looked in the mirror. She thought about the picture that the Captain had. It was from a trip that she and Hunter had taken. They had just finished changing after skydiving and the pilot had snapped their picture. The skydiving trip was a real rush.

She finished with the makeup and looked in the mirror once again. No one knew where she was except for Olly. She didn't tell Allisa that she would be flying somewhere just that she had to go out for a while. Hunter's dad would not tell anyone and she just had to know more about Captain Montgomery. She was going to follow him when they landed. Blair was determined to find out what he was doing and why. The pilot's voice came back across the loudspeaker. "We would like everyone to please place your

189

seats in the upright position and return your tray tables to the back of the seat in front of you. We should be on the ground in a few minutes." *So much for thirty minutes*, she thought. *I couldn't have been in here that long.* Blair opened the door only to jump back. Captain Montgomery was standing in front of the bathroom door.

"I'm sorry miss. I didn't mean to startle you," he said.

"That's okay." Blair bent her head down and turned away from the soldier. She headed back to her seat and made sure that she was watching for him to come out of the bathroom. Did she seem too obvious when she walked away? Did it appear that she was hiding something? *Holy cow, that was close.* Captain Montgomery came out of the bathroom and walked back to his seat. Blair noticed that he just looked straight ahead and she felt relieved. The plane glided to the right and made a large sudden turn. The movement seemed to be a harsh maneuver. The pilot came back on the intercom and asked everyone to please continue to stay seated and keep their safety belts on. Passengers had worried looks on their faces. Was something wrong? The pilot came back on the intercom.

"Folks, we were waved off our approach and I'm sorry that I had to make such a sudden turn. Please be assured that everything is fine. It appears another flight had been on the same approach and we were too close to their airspace."

All the passengers seemed relieved. There was a little laughter and conversation after the announcement. Blair also felt relieved. She never thought about crashing but when something like this happens, it's her first thought. She leaned out of the aisle to check on the soldier. He was talking to the couple who were sitting across the aisle from him. They seemed to be having a conversation and he was demonstrating something with his hands. The pilot came back on and said, "We have been cleared to land on the western runway. I'm sure we are the only plane on this approach."

Everyone laughed.

He added, "At least I think we are."

That made everyone on the plane laugh even more. It was a good idea to make a joke of it and it did relieve the tension. The landing was smooth and everyone applauded as they glided to a stop. The pilot came on and thanked everyone.

"Guess this wasn't too bad, especially since it's my first flight."

The laughter was contagious. Blair chuckled as she stood up to get her bag from under her seat.

The attendant said, "The pilot, Dan, is a twenty-year veteran and he always makes jokes; it helps to keep people calm."

"I'm sure he has seen many strange things and laughter always makes people feel less stressed."

"Tammie said that you're with the FBI."

"Yes, but I didn't want everyone to know."

"I understand. I bet that's real interesting."

"Not really, I spend most of my time on background research. Not all that interesting."

"Are you on an assignment?"

"No, just headed home." Blair had almost forgotten that she had to show her FBI identification to board the plane. *Guess they don't get too many FBI people on their flights,* she thought. She tried to keep watch on Captain Montgomery as she waited to get off the plane. He turned toward the rear of the plane and she looked down. She was in the last row and although the plane was just a little over half full it still took about ten minutes for all the passengers to collect their bags. She walked about ten feet behind the soldier as they all made their way to the baggage area. She didn't have any luggage just the carryon but she was determined to follow him.

She dialed her cell phone. "Hi Olly, I just landed and will catch the limo to the Holiday Inn as planned."

Olly told her about the plan she worked out with Blake and Ashley.

"Sounds good, anything to throw someone off the trail will help."

"Blair, they have a man watching The Pub and we are sure one is watching your apartment. Officer Tuttle came by earlier and asked about you."

"What did you say?"

"I told him that you needed some time and that you maybe

had taken a ride up to Santa Barbara."

"I really could use a trip like that."

"I'm sure once this is over you could use a long trip alone."

Olly told her, "I'm using Sonia's car in case they're watching me." The Suburban would still be parked in her spot behind The Pub.

Blair didn't tell her about the soldier. She just wanted to follow him and see if she could get any information that would help her. "I'll call when I'm close to the Holiday Inn."

"Sure, just be careful."

They approached the luggage area and the soldier seemed to be looking for someone. Blair watched from a distance and saw him approach a tall man in a suit. *Wonder who that is,* she thought. She took her phone out and pretended to be dialing and pointed it toward the two men. She took three pictures and put the phone away.

She headed out of the terminal toward the limo pickup area. The limo ride was always the quickest way back to Santa Monica. She would often tell her friends, "Don't pick me up; I'll just take the limo." LAX was always a nightmare to get into and out of especially with the tightened security. The limo headed toward the pickup area and she saw that there was only one other person waiting there. When the limo stopped Blair turned back to make sure no one was watching her. She put her bag on her lap as she slid into the back seat.

"Where's everyone going to?" the driver asked. He was making his drop-off plan. Many of the passengers were regulars and knew the route.

"Going to the Shutters on Pacific," was the first passenger's response.

"The Holiday Inn on Second," Blair said.

The limo driver made a right and turned down Lincoln toward Santa Monica. The ride through Marina del Rey and Venice was always nice. He turned on Ocean Park in Venice and then turned right on Neilson. That would lead into Ocean Avenue and the first drop off at Shutters. It was an exclusive hotel on the beach side of Ocean Avenue where many Hollywood types would stay. The first passenger thanked the driver and got his bags out of the trunk. The driver got back in and said, "You're next, honey."

She said, "Thanks." The limo pulled off of Ocean onto Colorado and stopped in front of the Holiday Inn. She got out and grabbed her bag. She tipped him five dollars and headed into the hotel.

Blair walked into the lobby and pulled out her cell phone. "I'm here."

"I'll be there in ten minutes to get you. Remember I'm driving Sonia's car."

Twenty-Five

Captain Douglas was excited. The call had just come into the station and he was rounding up his men to head back out to the field along Apple Lane. He headed to his squad car and thought about calling the FBI but figured that it was late and he would wait to see what his men had found for sure. He had gotten the call about twelve-thirty a.m. and would usually be at home, but with all that had happened he decided to stay in the office later that night. He was monitoring the car that had been covering the Adams' house and had talked to Jerry McCarthy after Jerry had the altercation with Jon David at the all-night diner and coffee shop. Douglas turned onto Apple Lane and slowed down when he saw the two squad cars parked along the north side of the street. He grabbed his flashlight and headed toward the wooded area.

"Captain, hope it wasn't too late to call but I knew that you would want to be here."

"You're right. We needed a break of some sort in this case."

The Bridgewater officer and the state police were pleased that they were the ones to find the body. As they headed off into the woods two more squad cars pulled up. This was the first break in the disappearance of the second fugitive from the Adams' shooting. The team of police officers had combed through the wooded area for over a day and a half with no results. The heavy rains had flooded the woods and made it almost impossible to search too close to the abandoned car. After the rains had stopped, the spring winds and a good sunny day helped dry the ground around the abandoned car so they could resume the search for the missing fugitive. The officers led everyone to a spot about thirty feet from the abandoned car to a ravine. You could see a partially exposed body laying in it. The legs had been seen under some tree limbs that covered the rest of the body.

"Let's get down there and see what we have."

"We didn't know if we should disturb it before you got here, Sir."

"You did the right thing."

It was a drop of about four feet to the body and it looked like a large tree limb was on top of the chest area. The two officers who found the body moved down into the ravine to remove the tree limb and see if they could pull the body up. Captain Douglas told them to take care in case something fell out of the clothing. It might give them a clue as to who this was. While they were bringing the body up, Jon David called out to the captain. Captain Douglas was startled to hear him.

"We're over here, Jon."

"I was on my scanner and heard your call. I figured that you probably already called my boss but I thought I should be here too."

"I didn't know for sure what we found so I haven't called him yet."

"Guess that makes sense. Do you want me to call him for you?"

"Let's get the body up here first and make sure it is who we think it is. It might not even be related to our case." The local police had a good feeling about Jon, maybe because he was once a local cop in Philly and he understood them. He didn't seem to talk down to them like the other FBI personnel.

The body was laying flat on the edge of the ravine and the captain and Jon bent over to check out the face. They realized that this was their man. He matched the description Andy reported of a man being dragged through the woods. He could not have been dead very long.

"Jon, you go through his pockets and I'll call your boss."

"Thanks Bob. That will sit well with Dino."

When the phone rang, Dino jumped. Who would call at this hour? He had just gotten back in the Suburban after looking around the abandoned truck at the Crosswicks' rest stop. He didn't recognize the number on the phone's screen.

"Mr. Tuchy, this is Captain Douglas."

"Oh yes, Captain, what can I do for you?"

"Hope it isn't too late to call but we believe we've found the body of one of the missing fugitives."

"That's great news. I appreciate your calling me."

"Your man, David, is here with us and he's going through the personal effects of the man as we speak."

Dino wasn't surprised that Jon was on the scene. He knew that Jon was good with local authorities and that was one of the reasons that he left him in Bridgewater. "Can I talk to him?"

"Sure, but after I give him the phone I want to take the body to the local hospital for examination."

"That's probably a good idea. I can get our crime lab people over there to help with the identification if you want."

Bob Douglas knew that the FBI would want to be in charge but Dino asking him if it was okay made him feel better. He also knew that it was his men and the state police who had made the find and was proud of his people. He would tell them that when they all got together to cover the details of this on-going case. Bob handed the phone to Jon. "Mr. Tuchy wants to talk to you."

"Good job, Jon. Glad you were on the spot with those local guys to make sure everything went okay."

"They found the body, Sir, and were good enough to call me so that we would be involved." Jon wanted the local authorities to know that he appreciated what they did and hoped to be able to have them keep him in the loop. He was a good politician.

"Don't let them screw this up, Jon. We're just leaving Crosswicks and should be in Bridgewater in about thirty minutes."

"Boss, this is the guy. He was down in a small ravine and covered with branches. Looks like his partner tried to hide him."

"Okay, I'll call the crime lab people and get a CSI team out to the field. Get it all staked out; I want you to stay with the body the whole time."

"No problem, Sir, but now no one here is covering the Adams' house."

"Allisa is in there so I'm not too concerned. She's a good agent and will watch out for any funny stuff. Maybe you could ask the captain to keep sending a car past the house."

"I'm sure that's not going to be a problem."

Dino turned to Steve and said that they needed to get back to Bridgewater.

"What's going on?"

"They found one of the fugitives' bodies in the woods. Either you or Frank must have shot him like you thought."

"Maybe we will have that break you're looking for, Boss."

Dino wanted out of Bridgewater and onto the bigger action in New York. His early career was solid with a few high spots. The last big case he was involved in was when Allisa worked with him and they made the major bust of a group selling documents to the Russians. That was a few years ago and he needed one more big case to get to the next step on the ladder. A possible terrorist cell in New York and something to do with Yankee Stadium would be the ticket. Dino was in his mid-forties and time was running out. This could be the break he was waiting for.

Steve was happy that they may have gotten one of the fugitives. He was still hurting over the loss of his partner, Frank, but maybe now they'll get some answers. He headed back to the interstate and was glad that there was no traffic this time of night. The traffic would be heavy later on during morning rush hour. Many commuters used I-95 to get into Philadelphia for work each day. Southern Jersey was a bedroom community for those that worked in the Philadelphia area.

Jon appreciated that Captain Douglas was willing to have him ride along with the body. He made sure that he gathered any loose items found at the scene in case they belonged to either fugitive. He looked at his watch and figured that Dino and Steve would be in Bridgewater in about a half hour. He was hoping that he could get some key information to help the case along.

****

Yawer was getting close to New Brunswick and the intersection of Highway 130 and Highway One. He was planning on staying on Highway One the next ten miles until he could get on Interstate 278. That would lead him to the crossing at the

Narrows. He would call El Jaafi from Staten Island. Yawer looked down and saw that the truck still had over a quarter tank of gas and he hadn't seen any sign of the police.

****

Everything was quiet in the safe house. It was tucked into a residential neighborhood that had a mixed population of mostly Hispanics and Arabs. El Jaafi and Abdullah knew that they were only hoping to be there for a few days. The group that was there had their mission and was not part of their plan. They knew that things had gone wrong in Bridgewater. Yawer would make his way back to them and they needed to make their next move. El Jaafi wanted to head to California. He felt that Blair Adams was the next step in their search.

The group in the Bronx kept constant lookout because they were always suspicious of everyone. They had noticed that police cars had traveled along the street a little more than normal that night. They never stopped or seemed to be going slow like they were searching for something, but seeing police cars made everyone nervous.

Yawer had just made his way to Perth Amboy and crossed into Staten Island on 440. He wanted to avoid I-95 and hoped to find a spot to ditch his latest ride. He continued on Highway 440 and looked for an exit that appeared residential. He got off at Arden Avenue and pulled onto a quiet street. He dialed his contacts. "I am close and will be there in about an hour."

"We must make our next move. I will start our plans to travel to Los Angeles." Yawer wanted to tell El Jaafi about the papers that he left in the truck but wasn't certain which ones he had left. Maybe once he was in the safe house he could look through the documents that he had and then he would know what he left behind.

"I must get a new ride," he said to Jaafi.

"You could ditch that one and take the subway here."

"That's a good idea. I have been afraid that the truck would lead someone to the safe house."

"Get into an area that the subway runs to and leave the

198

truck."

"I'll call when I'm closer."

"You need to follow the subway to Yankee Stadium. We can come get you if you need."

Yawer felt that was a good plan. Jaafi was rested and he was exhausted. Jaafi helped him keep focused. He got back on Highway 440 and headed up the interstate and the crossing at the Narrows. The ride had been without incident since he headed off into the woods. He knew that he must have covered his tracks pretty good at the barn where he found the truck and some fresh clothes. He continued along Highway 278 after crossing at the Verrazano Narrows Bridge. Yawer was in Brooklyn and had to get off the highway to look for a subway entrance. This was a highly residential neighborhood that ran along Prospect Park and the Zoo.

He parked the truck along Coney Island Avenue and started to walk toward the subway entrance. He would travel by subway through Manhattan to the Bronx. The idea that El Jaafi had was a good one. He made sure that he cleaned the interior of the truck so that no fingerprints remained behind. He left the keys in the ignition and hoped that some kids would take the truck and when they were caught it would throw the authorities off his track. He had his documents in a saddlebag and tossed it over his shoulder like a backpack. It was about three in the morning and not many people were around. The subway line was about a half a mile away and he could see the entrance ahead. He checked to see that he had change to go through the turnstile. He walked down the steps and entered the tunnel to head toward the Manhattan line. Yawer was very tired. It had been a long time since he had any rest.

****

Jon arrived at the Bridgewater hospital and walked with the two ambulance attendants to the morgue. They entered an elevator and went down two flights to the basement. It was a dark and dreary hall that led to a large room with sinks around the perimeter. Jon felt creepy as he watched them move the body from the gurney to a steel table in the center of the room. It was cold in the room and they left him alone once they had completed their job. Jon looked around and noticed the instruments that were on a roll-around steel table near a large sink. He figured that these were the tools that would be used to carve the body of the fugitive open. He hoped that Dino and Steve would arrive soon. Being in the morgue alone was not something he relished. While on the Philadelphia police force, he had been involved in a double homicide investigation. It appeared that a man had shot his wife and then killed himself. The wife had been shot numerous times and they had to get the bullets for evidence. Jon was assigned the task of overseeing the autopsy and making sure he gathered any evidence from the body. He never forgot the sight of the medical examiner sawing the breast bone of the woman open and removing vital organs. There were three bullets lodged in her body. One in the skull and the other two in her torso. The bullets matched the gun found near the husband's body. They also matched the bullet found in the husband's skull. Jon hoped that he would never have to view something like that again.

****

Steve crossed the Delaware River at West Bristol and headed toward Bridgewater. He and Dino had been talking about the possibility of both of them heading to New York to continue the investigation. They felt that there was a definite connection with the fugitives and the map that had the area of Yankee Stadium circled. What did this have to do with the Adams' investigation? Why did the fugitive who got away have a map to the New York area? Steve and Dino had discussed many possible connections but neither of them came up with an idea that made any sense. The ride to Bridgewater was short from West Bristol and Dino dialed Jon. "Where are you now?"

"I'm in the morgue with the body of the fugitive."

"Are the local guys there?"

"No, I came in the ambulance with the body and have been here alone."

"We'll be there in a few minutes. I called the crime lab people and they have dispatched a team back to Bridgewater to meet you at the hospital."

"See you soon, Boss." Jon knew that Dino was happy that he was with the body. Dino never trusted the local police. He would often say that they could not find their dick with both hands in the dark. Jon wanted to make sure that he covered his ass with Dino but also wanted to keep open the lines of communication with Captain Douglas and the state police. They might have some useful information and they would be more willing to pass it along if he showed respect to their investigation.

The captain came into the room with another man.

"Jon, this is Sandy Banks. He is the Bridgewater medical examiner. It will be his responsibility to do the autopsy on our fugitive."

"That's great captain. I just heard from Mr. Tuchy and he'll be here in about five minutes. I hope it will be okay if we wait for him to be present."

"Shouldn't be a problem, it's not like our guy is going anywhere."

"You've got that one right."

Captain Douglas had done some research on the FBI guys that were on this case. He found out that Jon had been a local cop in Philadelphia and was highly regarded by his peers. He liked Jon and was willing to make sure that he looked good to his boss, even though he didn't like Dino.

It was close to three in the morning and everyone was tired. Finding the body gave them all an adrenalin rush but that was now starting to wear off. Douglas had sent his men home. He knew that tomorrow would be another day of searching for more clues.

Jon sat on a small round metal chair that spun around. It was on wheels and he was moving around the room nervously as he waited for Dino and Steve to arrive. He was concerned that Dino would raise holy hell when he saw the local medical examiner there. He had already put in a request for the FBI crime lab team and they would be there soon.

Dino and Steve parked in front of the Bridgewater Hospital and walked inside. They stopped at the front desk and asked for directions to the morgue. The attendee said that he would take them there. They got in the elevator and Dino looked at Steve. "Guess there is more than one floor to this place."

The attendant looked back and said, "We have four floors plus two lower levels." He knew that Dino was being a smart ass and didn't mind answering him back. He walked them down the hall and they entered the morgue.

"What's going on here?"

Before Jon could answer, Captain Douglas spoke up.

"I asked our medical examiner to be here to perform the autopsy on our man. Your guy insisted that we wait until you arrived."

"I know that this is important Captain, but I would like our CSI team involved too. The director feels that this is a multiple-state investigation and that the FBI should take the lead."

"When do you think your team will arrive?"

"I talked to them a few minutes ago and they are only ten minutes away."

"Mr. Tuchy, we need to come to an understanding. I am responsible for anything that happens in Bridgewater. You and your people are my guests. We will be every bit a part of this investigation."

Dino didn't like his statement. He wanted to push the FBI issue down their throats but knew that the director John Martin was interested in results and that arguing would only slow those down. He also had his sights on getting out of Bridgewater. "Of course your team will be an integral part of this investigation. I just want to make sure all the resources of the FBI and our forensic team is available to help solve this case."

Everyone was surprised to hear what Dino said. It was not like him to be so cordial.

The captain leaned back and smiled. "Okay, we'll wait for the FBI team to arrive. I'm glad that you see that we would be more successful together than each of us handling this case separately."

"Sure," Dino answered. He turned to Jon and said, "Why don't you come with me so you can fill me in on what you found in the woods."

Jon didn't like that idea. He was sure that Dino would eat

his ass out for something.

"Sure, Boss." They walked into the hall leading to the morgue.

"Jon, I'm glad that you were here to hold those assholes off. I wish I could shoot the son of a bitch instead of having him think it's his case." Jon knew that Dino was mad, but at least he wasn't mad at him. "I'm going to have Steve head upstairs to wait for our guys. You stay with the body and don't let them touch anything until I get back."

"Yes, Sir."

"Send Steve out here."

Jon walked back into the morgue and told Steve that Dino needed him in the hall. He waited for Steve to leave and then thanked Captain Douglas for working with him.

"Kid, I've seen these FBI types before. You seem like a nice guy; no sense both of us going down in flames."

Jon smiled at him. "Thanks."

Twenty-Six

The traffic along Fourth was very congested as Olly pulled out of her spot to head for the Holiday Inn. This was the first time she had driven Sonia's car. Her plan was to drive toward Arizona then down Ocean. She kept an eye on the rearview mirror to make sure she wasn't being followed. It was a warm night and there were a lot of people still walking on the Promenade. The Santa Monica Pier was crowded with people coming from the amusement rides and carnival attractions, as she made the left turn off Ocean onto Colorado Boulevard. She pulled up in front of the Holiday Inn and Blair came out to meet her. "I'm so glad to see you," she said.

Blair jumped in and Olly looked at her.

"What's with the boots and hat?"

"I wanted to get out of the house and to the airport without being seen. When I was on the plane a strange thing happened."

"How many more strange things can happen to you?"

"There was a soldier on the plane who was just returning from Iraq. The strange part is when they announced where he was from, it was the same group that Hunter was in."

"You're kidding. Did he know Hunter?"

"I didn't want to take a chance on talking to him but when I walked by his seat he was holding a picture of Hunter and me on his lap."

"What?"

"Olly, I almost froze. I looked down and could not believe that he had our picture. I kept away from him on the flight but followed him to the baggage area."

"Why would you do that?"

"I just had to know what he was doing and why he had our picture. I got a good picture of him with my camera phone. Maybe

Allisa will know who the man was that he met at the airport."

They continued along Colorado to Fourth Street. Olly pulled into a parking garage and found a spot on the first level.

"Okay, what's the plan," she said.

"I left a package at The Pub on the day I was supposed to meet with the FBI Agent, Allisa Jones. I had just picked it up at the post office before I got there and I remember leaving it behind the bar. I think that package is what everyone is after."

"I remember, Ashley left me a note that she put in my office. What's in the package?"

"I never opened it. It was from Hunter's address in Iraq and I couldn't bring myself to open it up. I need to get that package and see what's in it."

"I could have opened it for you. It would have saved you this trip."

"I have to open it myself."

Olly understood. Everything that had happened could be related to the package and Blair needed to see its contents.

****

The CSI team from Philadelphia arrived at the Bridgewater Hospital. Steve met them and escorted them to the morgue on the lower level. He explained the situation and that the local medical examiner was also waiting to perform an autopsy. They were accustomed to friction between local authorities and the FBI. It seemed that anytime there was the possibility of a case being solved, everyone wanted to take credit. Sandy Banks was the local M. E. and had never worked on an autopsy with these types of implications. He actually was relieved that the FBI was sending an experienced team to help with the process. Sandy would often be called in on an accident or a questionable death but never in his ten years in Bridgewater for a murder. Bridgewater was a normal small town. It had its share of problems but all of them were minor compared to those that the FBI handled.

Steve walked into the morgue and Jon was sitting on the steel roll-around chair. Steve looked at him the way he would look at a child. "What is it with the damn chair?"

"I don't know. Just a place to sit I guess."

Steve smiled. "If it's just a place to sit why are you wheeling around the room?"

"Just nervous I guess."

Captain Douglas had left the morgue and Dino was still outside. The two agents knew that Dino would want them to be present during the autopsy. Jon introduced himself to the CSI team leader. The medical examiner and the FBI team seemed to be just fine together and were in the process of getting ready to start their investigation. Both Jon and Steve moved to the back of the room. This was a task that neither of the agents was anxious to see.

Dino looked at his watch and figured that they should have some results in the next couple of hours. He wanted to go to the scene in the woods where the body was found. It was a little past three a.m. and he was dead tired. He remembered that he told Allisa that he would be at the Adams' house around noon. That was before this development and he would call her in a little while to change that plan.

****

Yawer had transferred from the Manhattan subway line to the one that would take him to the Bronx. He would get off at the Yankee Stadium stop and walk the last three blocks to the safe house. He looked at his watch and figured that he would call El Jaafi when he got off the subway. There were always people riding the train regardless of the time of day. He sat in the corner of the car and closed his eyes. It had been a long night. Yawer had not been to sleep for close to forty-eight hours. He still had to go through his backpack to see what documents he may have left in the truck at Crosswicks. He needed to let El Jaafi know in case it would compromise the safe house location. He fell asleep in the corner of the subway car as it rocked on its way to his final destination.

****

Olly and Blair had set their plan. The Pub would be very

busy. It was always busy on karaoke nights. Big John, the bouncer, usually had his hands full with someone drinking too much and thinking they were Elvis. Tommy would be behind the bar and not many people would be paying attention to Manuel, the cook. The fun always started slow but as the patrons had a few more drinks it seemed that you could not get them off the small stage in the front corner. Olly called back to The Pub to tell Manuel that there was a package in her office with Blair's name on it. "Just bring it out the back door and put it in the dumpster." He was confused but would follow her request. She figured if she had him do this it would look normal because every night he would take items out to the dumpster from The Pub. She also didn't want to get anyone else involved because they would ask a lot of questions. Manuel was a good employee. He had been at The Pub for over three years and was a hard worker. His English wasn't very good but he managed to get by.

He went into the office and found the small package that had a lot of foreign stamps and Blair's name across the front. It was wrapped in plain brown paper with string around it. He took the package from the office and put it on top of some trash that he had collected from behind the bar. He walked to the back door and headed for the dumpster. The dumpster was a large metal trash bin that the city of Santa Monica had stationed behind restaurants along the Promenade. It was about six feet long and four feet tall. It would be easy for them to retrieve the package.

Blair had checked with the United gate agent before she left the airport to review the schedule for return flights to Philadelphia. There were two direct flights. One scheduled at six twenty-four a.m. and the second one at eight-fifteen. The goal was to get on the earlier flight. With the time change and help from a western tail wind, she would be in Philadelphia before two in the afternoon. She would have to call Allisa and see if she could buy her some extra time.

****

Captain Montgomery had settled in his hotel room. He had been flying for over thirty-six hours from Baghdad to London then

Philadelphia and finally to Los Angeles. Dean Curry, the Los Angeles FBI bureau chief, had taken him to his hotel. He was going to catch some sleep before Dean picked him up in the morning. He had studied the documents that were sent to him and he planned on using them to help find Blair Adams and to use his relationship with Hunter to get information about the missing documents. Captain Montgomery had been an undercover FBI agent for many years. He had been recruited while at West Point. As a young military officer he was highly regarded by his commanding officers. The opportunity to join the FBI was a tough decision to make. He loved the military but thought that he could serve two masters and help protect his country. Being from rural Georgia, he had a deep love for his country. He felt that young southern men had a deeper feeling of patriotism than people from other parts of the country. Montgomery was a conservative and religious individual. He also was a fierce fighter. He would find Ms. Adams and use the pretense that Hunter asked him to visit his wife if anything happened to him. He would get the information and those documents if she had them. Dean Curry had informed him that Mrs. Adams had not been seen for close to thirty-six hours. They heard that she had gone to Santa Barbara but one of his men spotted her coming out of her apartment a few hours ago with her friend Blake. They went down to Venice Beach and a bar called The Whaler. His men were watching the place to see where she went next.

****

Dino took the elevator back down to the morgue. The CSI team would be involved in the autopsy. He'd get Steve to go with him to the woods where the body of the second fugitive was found. Maybe they would find a clue that would move this case along. Dino wanted results and to be able to get to New York. He knew the FBI chief in New York pretty well. They had been together in Washington early in their careers. Dino knew that he would be able to work with Don on this case. Don was in a secure position. He had been promoted to the New York post after 9/11 and had been instrumental in helping gather critical information in the aftermath of the Twin Towers being hit by the two airplanes. Don was respected by the other agents and John Martin trusted his judgment.

Dino told Jon to stay with the CSI team and to call him with any updates. He hoped that the CSI team would come up with an identification of the body. He knew that the two men found in Mrs. Adams' apartment that Agent Baxter had shot had been identified as Iraqi nationals. One of them had been identified as Ahmad Aswar, who had close ties to Saddam. Ahmad had been held at Abu Ghraib prison by the U.S. Army but released just a few weeks earlier. The other body was that of El Hassen also an Iraqi national. The identification of the two men in the Santa Monica shoot-out had caused a red alert by the Homeland Security Department. Dean Curry and his agents had been on twenty-four-hour duty making sure these were the only two men involved in the incident at Blair Adams' apartment.

There was still no motive but the desire to find the missing documents grew with the identification of these men. Could there be a link with the body found in Bridgewater? Dino had to know and wanted that information as soon as possible. The CSI team had a direct link to both Washington files and those of Interpol.

The trip out to the scene in the wooded area off of Apple Lane was short. It was still very dark but Dino and Steve had brought extra equipment. Captain Douglas had one of his men stationed at the scene. Dino called out to him as they approached. Steve showed him his badge.

"Captain Douglas said you would be coming. I'll help in any way necessary if you want."

"No thanks. We can handle this," Dino answered.

"I understand but I will have to stay until my captain tells me differently."

Dino just gave a look of distain and walked by as Steve followed. Based on the information from Jon, they walked past the car that had been found the night before the ravine was about thirty feet beyond the car. It was still muddy around the area but you could see where the body had been hidden. It was about four feet down to the place and the tree limbs still lay on the ground.

"I'm glad that Jon was here," Dino said. "The bag of items

209

he retrieved may help us in this investigation. It might be better to send the CSI team out here in daylight to see what they can come up with."

"That's a good idea, Boss."

Both men searched around for a few minutes but found nothing new. The mud had caked over their shoes and Dino struggled to pound it off. They walked past the police officer to their Suburban. Neither man said anything as they got into their vehicle. "Dumb shits, only thing they found was mud."

Dino wished that they had found something that would move the investigation along. He was tired and Steve knew that they should rest because it would be a few hours before the CSI team had anything.

"Boss, we should go back to the hospital and wait for results. I could use a nap." Steve thought if he suggested it then Dino could blame him for the needed rest.

"That's a good idea. I'll give the team the location of the wooded area so they can head here to continue the search at daylight."

Meanwhile the team at the morgue was busy at work. They had fingerprints faxed to the FBI central bureau in Virginia and to Interpol in London. Photos were taken and sent along with the fingerprints. The medical examiner from the hospital had waited until the FBI team had the information they needed. Sandy Banks was pleased to be involved with such a high profile case. The team also was going through the items that Jon had retrieved from the scene. There was a gun that had been tucked in the back of the fugitive's belt along with a few items from his pockets. Dino went in and talked to the team leader. He gave them a map with the location of the wooded area off of Apple Lane. They would go over to the scene that had been roped off by the Bridgewater police. He told them to call him as soon as any update came in. He covered the plan with Jon who was still sitting on the metal chair. He was in a corner of the room nearest the entrance. Everyone was tired but there was still work to be done. Dino said that he and Steve were going to catch some rest and that they would relieve Jon in a few hours.

Jon said, "Thanks, I'm fine."

Steve found a spot in the hospital waiting area where they could catch a nap. It was empty and they both needed some rest. Once they had some positive information they could plan the next step.

****

The alley was dark and a few drunks came swaggering down the lane as Olly walked by.

"Hey baby, wanna dance?" The two men laughed and she just smiled and quickly passed on by. It was still busy on the street ahead. She ducked in behind The Pub and looked in the dumpster. There it was, the package Blair had left a few days ago. It had a lot of foreign stamps across the top of it and had Blair's name in the center. It was about ten inches long and maybe weighed three pounds. What was in it she thought? She could hear the music from The Pub. Karaoke had been starting up when she left and it was really cooking now.

Santa Monica was full of Hollywood hopefuls and many of them found their way to The Pub on karaoke nights. Never know when that big break would come. She retrieved the package and headed back down the alleyway to the parking garage. Soon they would have the answer to the package contents.

She held the answers that Blair, and obviously many others had been looking for. What could it be that Hunter sent her that would have caused such a high level search from the FBI? The parking garage was almost empty at this time of night. Many of the tourists would have headed back to their hotel rooms and those still on the Promenade would be locals who could walk home or take public transportation. The Pub was the busiest place because of karaoke. It had been very popular and getting in was always tough. When she entered the parking structure on Fourth Street, she got into the car and handed Blair the package. Holding it on her lap, Blair just studied the outside. The package was fairly heavy for just papers. It was not Hunter's writing. He always made a little heart over the letter I in her name. The address in the right hand corner was that of the APO Battalion location that Hunter was in. She looked back over at Olly.

"I'm not sure what's in here, but it's not from Hunter."
Olly looked surprised. "How do you know?"

"He always had this funny way of writing my name and this isn't his handwriting. I'm not sure who sent this but it wasn't him." Blair turned the package over and studied the bottom. It had been taped up with the two-inch type of package tape that you could buy at any FedEx store. She turned it back over and again looked at the front of the package. It was unquestionably from Iraq. The foreign postage in the right-hand corner was very prominent.

"You're killing me," Olly said. You have to open it so we can see what the fuss is about."

"I know, but I'm afraid to."

"Do you want me to open it for you?"

"No, I have to do it."

Olly opened her purse and took out a small pocket knife. "Here you can use this to open the package. In case it has something important, you don't want to damage the front. The FBI will want it as proof that Hunter didn't send it to you."

"That's a good idea." Blair took the pocket knife and slit open the side of the package so she could remove the contents without damaging the outside. There was a cardboard carton inside the brown wrapping. She removed the carton and put the outside wrapping on the dash of the car. Olly watched with great anticipation. She wanted to help Blair or at least hurry her up. The carton was folded at the top and easy to open. Blair pulled open the flaps and removed two rubber banded packs of letters. They were all in envelopes and the one on the top was addressed to Hunter from her. She looked over at Olly and said, "These are letters that I sent to Hunter. This doesn't make any sense."

There was a note on top of them. She held the note and studied it.

"Come on," Olly said.

Blair's eyes filled with tears as she slowly read the note aloud.

Blair,

I know that you must still be hurting with the loss of Hunter. Although I had just met you for the first time at his funeral, I could see how much you loved each other. I found these letters in his foot locker and felt you should have them. I hope that when I get back to the States we can get together. I would like to share some stories of Hunter with you. He was a great friend when we were growing up and a brave soldier.

Your friend,
Brian

"Olly, these are just my letters to Hunter. His friend Brian sent them to me. There isn't anything in here but my letters. I don't understand."

"Who is Brian?"

"Remember I told you about Hunter's friend, Brian, who was with him on the rooftop. He accompanied Hunter's body home from Iraq. They went to high school together. I introduced you to him at the funeral."

"That was such a difficult time, Blair, I just don't remember."

As she looked at the front of each letter she noticed the dates were almost in order. She wasn't sure if Hunter or Brian had done that. They were in two bundles banded together. Blair was looking at the front of each envelope in the first bundle and Olly watched her. Neither of them spoke. Her friend could see tears in Blair's eyes as she fingered the envelopes. Love letters that she had sent to her now- dead husband. The words that she shared with Hunter were now in her hands. Olly too had tears in her eyes and didn't know what to say. Blair reached for the second bundle when a small brown manila packet fell on the floor. She leaned over to pick it up. It was sticky on the front and appeared to have stuck to the bottom of the top packet of letters. There was nothing on the outside of the packet.

213

"What is that?" Olly asked as Blair held it in her hands.

"I'm not sure, it was stuck to the last letter."

The packet was about five by nine. It had a sticky substance on the front but no address or other writing that identified its contents. Blair held the packet and looked over at Olly. "This isn't something that I sent to Hunter."

"Open it up."

Blair held the packet and studied it again. She flipped it over and saw that it was closed with two metal tabs. She pulled them up and opened the packet. There were papers folded in the packet and she slid them out. The top paper was written in a foreign language. She looked over at Olly and had a puzzled look on her face.

"I'm not sure what this is; it's in a foreign language."

"Let me see it."

Blair handed the contents to Olly and she looked at the top piece of paper.

"This is Arabic, Blair."

"How do you know?"

"Remember Mr. Thomas who comes in every Friday morning for breakfast? His brother lives in Saudi Arabia and often sends him letters. Mr. Thomas was showing me some pictures from his brother in a letter sent to him and the writing was the same as this."

They started to look through the rest of the contents of the packet. Blair took out a folded brown piece of paper that looked like a map. There was a small metal key taped to the corner. All the documents appeared to be in Arabic.

"Olly, this is probably what the FBI is looking for! Why would Brian send it to me?" Neither woman had any answers and continued to look through the documents in the packet. Blair put all of them back into the manila envelope and looked over at Olly.

"I need to get back and see if I can find the answer to what these mean and why I have them."

"Blair, we know that there are people killing each other to get this information. It will be dangerous. Maybe you should just call the FBI and let them handle it from here."

"I can't because I still don't know why I have them. Did

Hunter want me to get these or did Brian do this? I have to get more answers before I give this to the FBI."

"Yeah, I guess you're right. You have to be careful."

"Olly, please get me back to the airport."

Olly started the car and headed back out of the parking garage. She turned right on Fourth Street and left on Colorado to Lincoln Avenue. She would take Lincoln all the way to LAX. Neither of them spoke for quite a while. Blair put all the letters and the manila packet back into the larger package that they came in.

"I will call you once I get back to Philly. The plane ride will give me some time to think of how to handle this information. I think I can trust Allisa but I will have to see what has happened in Bridgewater before I tell anyone about what I found."

"How are you going to get back to Bridgewater?"

"Thomas' brother, Bill, will pick me up and get me back. Allisa is covering for me. If I can make the six twenty-four flight I will get back close to noon Eastern Time."

"Blair, you still have a few hours before that flight leaves. Let's stop at the little diner that you like on Lincoln and Rose and get something to eat."

"I'm too worked up to eat."

Olly insisted, "You have to eat. There's a lot going on and you have to keep up your strength."

"Okay, but I can't miss that flight."

They stopped at the diner and got something to eat. Olly was trying to keep Blair on an even keel. This was a good idea because she could help Blair put her plan into a clear thought process. She knew that Blair was in an emotional turmoil and that she needed some time to think. Olly suggested that before she got the FBI involved in the packet she should find out what the material was about.

"I don't know anyone who reads Arabic."

"Maybe Hunter's dad will know someone who does."

"That's a good idea. I'll see once I get back."

After they finished, Olly and Blair headed to the car. "Breakfast was a good idea; I guess I was a little hungry after all. I needed some direction and time to think. Thanks."

"Blair, with all the mental and physical stress you're going through, you need to stay healthy. I can still get you to the airport in about ten minutes." The two friends sat quietly as Olly drove to LAX. Blair held what she thought might be the reasons for all the break-ins and FBI intrusion into her life. She wasn't sure exactly what she had but knew she shouldn't have them. Olly pulled up to the front of LAX and Blair leaned over and hugged her.

"Call me when you get back."

"You know that I will."

"I'm worried about you. You're taking too much on and this is very dangerous."

"We've been broken into; men have had a shoot-out in my apartment and Thomas has had a shoot-out in his yard. How much more danger could there be?"

"Just be careful, girlfriend."

Blair got out of the car and headed toward the terminal. Maybe she would get some answers with this new information.

Twenty-Seven

The subway car rocked back and forth as Yawer leaned in the corner sleeping. It had been close to two days since he had any sleep and being on the run for the past twenty-four hours had taken its toll. The next stop was at 135th Street. Three young men entered the subway car and looked at each other as they watched the man sleeping in the corner. Two of them wore local gang colors. The third seemed to be an underling of some sort because the other two were telling him what to do.

It was not unusual to see someone sleeping on the subway but this passenger had a large backpack that had slid to the floor. One of the men moved across from Yawer and another sat on the seat next to him. The third man, the underling, stood as the car rocked on its trip through Manhattan toward the Bronx. The next stop was at 145th Street. As the subway slowed to its stop, the man standing reached down and picked the backpack up off the floor. They kept an eye on the man sleeping in the corner, he didn't move. The doors of the subway opened and the three men ran out of the car and headed up the stairs to the street level.

Yawer moved as he heard the noise of the doors closing and looked to his side for the backpack. It was gone! He jumped up and looked around hoping that the bag had just fallen under his seat. There was no sign of the backpack. Where was he? What was the next stop? It was the exit for Yankee Stadium. He ran back and forth in the subway car but there was no sign of the backpack. He remembered that the safe house was a few blocks east of Yankee Stadium. He would have to get off at the next stop, but where was his backpack and who took it?

The three young men ran down 145th Street toward Lenox. They looked back and saw that no one was following them. They stopped on the corner of 145th and Lenox. The man holding the backpack opened it and looked through its contents. The first thing he found was a silver pistol. None of them recognized what type of gun it was. The rest of the contents were papers in a foreign language. There was a map and the name of someone in Bridgewater. They studied the papers and none of them could make out what they were but they thought that it might be Arabic. The neighborhood was very ethnic and many Arabs had moved into the area. They pushed the papers back into the backpack and tossed it into a trash can on the corner. The men took off toward St. Nicholas Avenue. They were hoping that they could sell the gun. This one looked expensive.

****

Jon found Steve and Dino sleeping in the waiting room off the lobby in the hospital. He tapped Dino on the shoulder. "Sir, they have an identification of the body."

Dino moved slightly but Jon realized that he would have to physically wake him up, so he put his hand back on his shoulder and pushed. "Sir, I hate to wake you so soon but they have identification."

Dino was startled and jumped to a standing position. "I was just about to get up. What did you say about identification?"

"They have the identification on the body, Sir. Interpol was able to trace the fingerprints that the crime scene people sent them."

"Holy shit!"

"He is an Afghan rebel with a long association to the Taliban. His name is Omar Kabole. His father is Mohammed Kabole, the former Taliban deputy interior minister."

"What the hell! Now we got a Taliban rebel involved? The men in Santa Monica were Iraqis. The shit will hit the fan in Washington with this information."

Dino yelled at Steve. "Steve, get up. We've got to go to the office. The director is going to go nuts when he has the news of this I.D. He'll want to mobilize as many men as possible."

Steve looked dazed. He got up and almost stumbled over his own feet. "I'm with you, Sir." Steve had no idea what had

218

happened but he knew Dino was headed out to the Suburban and he was going to follow him.

"Jon, stay here and keep the situation together. I'll call Allisa in a little and let her know what's going on."

Jon stood in the lobby and watched as they jumped into the Suburban and drove off. What was he supposed to do? What situation? The one last fugitive had gotten away and the identification made this chapter of the case closed. He headed back toward the morgue to see if there was any follow up to the information he gave to Dino.

****

Blair entered the LAX terminal and headed for the United desk. She was able to get on the early United flight to Philadelphia. "Not many people on this flight," the attendant said. She used her FBI identification again when she was at the desk and was getting used to showing it. The desk clerk, a young man, smiled at her and tried to strike up a conversation. Blair was tired but now had a purpose and didn't feel like talking. She thanked the man and took her boarding pass. She started walking down toward her gate when she was startled by someone calling out her name.

"Ms. Adams."

Panic struck her. Who was this and why did he call her by name? The voice was not familiar and she was afraid to turn around. She knew that the FBI had men looking for her; did they have someone at the airport? Should she run? The voice sounded closer and she had no choice but to stop and turn. Blair turned and was relieved to see that it was Allisa's friend, Steven, whom they had talked to when they left LAX a day ago. She was sure that he would question why she was flying again from Los Angeles to Philadelphia just two days since her last trip on the same route.

"Oh hi," she said.

"I'm so surprised to see you again so soon. Is Allisa with you?"

Blair was glad that the subject of Allisa seemed to be what Steven wanted to talk about. She remembered that Allisa told

Steven that she would look him up when she was back in Los Angeles.

"No, she stayed on the East Coast. I had to come back and get some documents that were necessary for her case. They were too important to put them in the mail."

"Please tell her that I am looking forward to seeing her again."

"No problem, Steven. I'm hoping to get a seat in the back of my flight to Philly. Need to catch a few ZZ's."

"I can help you. What flight are you on?"

"I'm on the six twenty-four flight to Philly."

"Would you like me to get you a first class seat?"

"I don't want to be a problem. A seat in the last row would be just fine." Blair didn't want everyone on the plane walking by her. Never know who you might see. Having run into Steven was proof that you might meet someone that you just don't want to see, or want them to see you. The memory of the soldier on her flight out to LA was still in her mind. She had to find out who he was and who it was at the airport that met him.

"I'll walk with you to the gate."

"That's very nice of you."

Blair thought people would think they were a couple going on a trip and pay less attention to them. She didn't know if the Los Angles FBI had put out an APB on her whereabouts. They walked to United's Gate 26 and Steven went up to the desk and started to punch in some information. He came back with a new boarding pass and handed it to Blair.

"Please don't forget to tell Allisa I said to call me."

"I won't, thanks so much for your help." Blair could tell that Steven was pleased that he had helped her. She also knew that he could be used for this sort of assistance and figured that is why Allisa kept him on a string. She settled in a chair that was empty near the next flight gate. Steven asked if he could do anything else for her. "I just wish I could get on the plane first so that I could settle in before all the other passengers."

"I'll come back in about forty-five minutes before they start boarding and get you on the plane."

Blair said, "Thanks," and gave him a peck on the cheek.

Steven smiled and strolled away. She had close to an hour before her flight was scheduled to depart. She looked at her watch and saw that it was five twenty-five a.m. She got her cell phone out and dialed Allisa's number. It was three hours later in Bridgewater and she was sure that she would be awake.

"Blair, I'm glad that you called. A lot has happened here. Did you find what you were looking for?"

"Yes, and you will be happy with my results."

"What is it?"

"I don't want to say over the phone but I'm on my way back. It might be a little later than noon."

"You're going to be okay because they found the body of the missing fugitive in the woods and have discovered his identity. He is a son of a high ranking Taliban minister. Dino and Steve had to head to Philly and are probably going to New York soon. It looks like the investigation here in Bridgewater is close to being over."

"You're going to want to stick around to see what I found, Allisa. You and I can break this thing wide open. I also have a picture on my cell phone and I will need your help to identify the individual who was on my flight out to LA. He might have been from Hunter's battalion in Iraq."

Allisa was silent for a moment. She wanted to be involved if the case was headed to New York but she knew that she would have to be in the background because she was still supposed to be in Santa Monica. If Blair had information to solve the mystery she could be in the lead role. "Blair, I have to at least get an idea of what you found."

"What if I told you that I found a map and a key?"

"Oh shit, that's got to be what everyone has been looking for. Where did you find it?"

"I will give you all the details when I get there. You have to promise not to tell anyone until we're together and I know what these documents are about. One problem is they are all in Arabic."

"That's not a problem; I have a friend in the bureau that can help us."

"Wait until I get there and we can handle this together."

221

"That's a deal, Blair. Do you need us to come and get you?"

"No, I have that arranged."

"Where are you now?"

"I'll tell you all that in a few hours. Give me until around two o'clock." Blair hung up and dialed Bill. She had told him when he dropped her off at the airport in Philadelphia that she would let him know about picking her up. She gave him her flight information and he said he would be there to meet her in Philadelphia. Everything was set for her return. She was sure now that she could trust Allisa and knew that she had what was possibly the key piece to the puzzle. Blair figured that if she had what the FBI and everyone else was searching for it would be important enough for Allisa to keep it quiet and to want to be the one to reveal the finding.

Allisa was excited about the information that Blair had told her. This could be the break she needed. She would tell Dino when he called that it would be best if she stayed out of the picture and kept an eye on Blair in Bridgewater. She knew that he would want to grab some glory and if he didn't have to worry about her being along it would be easier. She was in the kitchen drinking coffee. Thomas was outside getting the newspaper. He always took a stroll around the yard in the mornings. It was so nice to hear the birds singing and he stopped to watch the small field animals that were making their summer nests and homes. The wooded area behind his house was teaming with squirrels, raccoons and rabbits. Thomas had been so sad the past few weeks that he had not paid much attention to this rite of spring. He had some excitement now with Blair bringing him into a bit of espionage that he forgot about his sorrow and was nervous about her findings. Thomas came into the kitchen and saw Allisa at the table.

"I'm surprised that we haven't heard from Blair yet."

"She just called to let us know that she was on her way back and would tell us what she found."

"I hope that she's being careful," Thomas said.

"She's a bright girl and very smart. I'm sure she'll be fine."

Just then the phone rang. Thomas answered; it was Dino calling to talk to Allisa.

"The director has given me the assignment to head to New York and to work with them on the suspected terrorist cell. Because we have the background on the escaped fugitive we will be in a lead position."

"That's great, Dino. I don't want to mess you up by being involved. How about if I stay here and keep an eye on Blair and Mr. Adams for you?"

"Are you sure that will be okay with you?"

"Too much could go wrong if I'm discovered with you in New York. Too many people know me there."

"I promise, if we solve this Allisa, I'll give you some of the credit."

"Thanks, Dino. You've been very special and I want to wish you good luck in New York. If you get a chance to call me with an update, I'd appreciate that."

Dino was relieved that Allisa had let him off the hook about going to New York. He wanted to be able to handle the assignment without the fear of people finding out that he had her involved. "You know that I will keep you in the loop if we have something."

Allisa didn't feel guilty about not telling Dino about the documents Blair found. She wasn't sure what they had but it could be as big as Dino's search for the terrorist cell. She knew that they could all have success if things worked out right. She would start watching the time with excitement waiting for Blair's return.

The flight was about half full and Blair had a seat in the back of the plane. She had taken a bottle of water from one of the attendants when they first came down the aisle and settled in to catch a nap. She clutched the bag she was holding. It was lodged against her left side toward the window where no one could even see that she had anything. The row ahead of her was empty and no one was across from her. She needed the nap just like she needed the breakfast that Olly had forced her into having. The flight was a direct one and she should land in Philly around one-fifteen p.m. Allisa said that the coast was clear and Dino would be headed to New York. Blair slept the best rest she had in a long time. There were still questions to be answered but she felt that she had some

223

of the answers with her.

****

Yawer walked up and down 155th Street hoping to find evidence of his missing backpack. He would have to call El Jaafi and tell him what had happened but did not want to make that call until he had time to search for the backpack. He only knew that when the subway door closed, he saw some young men running up the stairway. He could get back on the subway and head back in the opposite direction. It was just one stop back where they got off the train. Did they take his backpack? He thought that they had to be involved. He needed to get the documents that were in the backpack back as soon as possible. It was about five in the morning and not too many people were on the street. He headed back to the subway station and entered on the other side of the street to head back into Manhattan.

Along the same area, Pat, who was usually up early but never ventured out at this time, strolled the neighborhood with a dog in tow. She was watching her sister's dog and he was crying to go outside. It was not exactly what she had planned this time of the morning but here she was, out of her brownstone and down the street with the puppy leading the way. She turned off of 7th Avenue toward Columbia University. It would be a good spot for the puppy to run around. She crossed the corner on Lenox and saw what looked like a backpack in a trash can. The puppy stopped to perform his morning duty while Pat retrieved the backpack. The bag looked fairly new and was full of maps, books and papers. Maybe a student from Columbia had been robbed and needed it back. She opened the backpack; there were a number of documents, all in Arabic, and maps. She figured that it was important to someone and would drop it off at the local police station on the way to the campus. The puppy was done so Pat put the droppings in the plastic bag she carried and left it in the trash can where she found the backpack. She continued on her walk with the backpack over her shoulder.

Yawer got back off of the subway at 145th Street and started walking toward the west. He came to Lenox and turned south. If only he knew that at the exact same time, Pat was walking on St. Nicholas headed in the same direction. The Columbia campus would be quiet at this time and there was a police station on the corner of St. Nicholas and 135th Street. Pat saw two officers standing on the steps of the police station.

"Good morning officers. I found this backpack on the corner of Lenox just off of 7th in a trash can. Looks like it might belong to a student."

"Thanks Ms. We will get it to the lost and found. It might have some identification inside."

"I thought so too, so I looked but it is all in Arabic." Pat was happy that she may have done her good deed for the day. She continued her walk toward the Columbia campus on Cathedral and St. Nicholas. She passed a man who looked suspicious headed in the opposite direction. He had farmhand clothes on and looked out of place. He was looking around like he had lost something. Pat continued on her way, puppy in tow.

The officer at the Columbia University Campus Police Station took the backpack into the station house. He gave it to the desk clerk and said a lady found it on the street. It probably belongs to a student. "I looked through it to see if I could find any identification. There isn't any." The clerk opened the package and saw that all the documents were in Arabic except for a local map. He put it on the floor and called upstairs to one of the detectives. He was Arabic and might be able to help. He was told that Wahid would be in around ten a.m. The backpack was left on the floor of the station house with a note to be delivered to Detective Wahid upstairs.

Twenty-Eight

The flight from LAX to Philadelphia seemed shorter than expected. Maybe it seemed that way because she had slept most of the time. Blair held her package tightly as they were making the approach into the Philadelphia area. They should be on the ground in about thirty minutes. Blair was looking forward to getting back to Bridgewater and finding out what the documents she found held. She had told Bill that she would meet him in front of the United terminal. She would call his cell number when the plane landed. It was about forty-five minutes to Bridgewater and she was rested and excited.

Allisa looked at her watch and figured that Blair's plane should be landing soon. She called to her friend, Baltazar, who she went to NYU with. He had moved to Philadelphia and majored in Middle Eastern studies. The FBI had used him many times as an interpreter and she knew that she could trust him. He said that he would be glad to help with some documents and for her to call later when she had them. They would meet wherever necessary. She had been pacing and Thomas said she was making him nervous.

"I can't help it. Blair is due back any minute and I hope she has found something that can help solve this."

"So do I," he said.

Blair found her way out of the Philly Airport and called Bill to tell him that she would meet him in front of the United Airlines terminal. She hurried through the airport and out to the pickup area. She stood on the corner and watched for Bill's car. He pulled up and Blair jumped in.

"I'm so glad to see you," he said. "I can't believe that you were able to make it out there and back so quickly."

"I was lucky that the flight schedules worked in my favor. I

226

can't tell you how much I appreciate your doing this for me. I need to get back to Thomas' house as soon as possible."

"I talked to him this morning and he said that the other FBI people were leaving Bridgewater. I hope it's good news."

"I think they've headed to New York because of developments in this case."

"Do you want me to drop you off on Blue Bird or in front of the house?"

"Just to be safe, drop me off on Blue Bird Street. I can walk through the woods to the back of the house. No sense taking any chances now. Plus I don't want to get you involved."

"I'll do anything for you and Thomas, Blair."

Blair leaned over and gave Bill a hug. They rode along without saying much the rest of the way. Traffic was a lot heavier than on the ride the night before but they were making good time. Blair never wore a watch and she asked Bill what time was it. He looked down and said it was one fifty-five p.m. They were just about fifteen minutes from Bridgewater and Blair felt the excitement of her findings tingle through her. Finally, she would have some answers to the mystery. Bill slowed down as he drove along Blue Bird behind Thomas' house. Blair leaned over and kissed him again on the cheek. "Thanks so much for everything. You've been such a great help and we'll call you later. Thomas will fill you in on my mission."

Bill didn't ask much about the reason for the trip but he knew that it must have been crucial. Blair got out of the car and headed through the woods behind Thomas' house. She went in the back door behind the garage and into the kitchen.

"I'm back!"

Allisa came running into the kitchen and Thomas was not too far behind her. They all hugged. She told Blair that Dino and Steve were probably on their way to New York and that no one was looking for her here. Allisa said, "I got nervous when Dino called and told me the L.A. office had spotted you coming out of your apartment last night. I was afraid that they would stop you from carrying out your plan."

"That was a setup my friend Olly had planned to throw

227

them off the track. They saw my friend Ashley who pretended to be me. She and my other friend Blake helped with the diversion."

"That was a great idea."

"They said that the bureau guys had been looking for me and that the local FBI had men watching The Pub and my apartment. My friend figured that if she could throw them off the trail it would be safer for my arrival in Santa Monica."

"I'm so glad that you're back safe," Thomas said.

"We have to sit down and I can go over what I found."

Thomas turned and headed into the living room. They followed him. He sat in his rocker and Allisa and Blair sat on the couch. Allisa moved to the edge of the couch and Thomas slid his chair closer as Blair opened her bag and brought out the package with the two bundles of letters inside.

"The package was addressed to me from Hunter's unit in Iraq but it was not his handwriting. It was addressed to Mrs. Blair Adams and the return address did not have a name, just the unit number on it. The only thing inside were these two bundles of letters, letters that I sent to Hunter. He must have kept all of them. I didn't open any of them but when I got to the end of the first bundle, I found this manila envelope stuck to the bottom of it." Blair held the manila packet up for both of them to see. I opened it and this is what I found."

Both Allisa and Thomas were now standing over Blair as she emptied the contents on the coffee table. No one was talking as Blair removed some papers and then a map. The writing was all foreign and there was a small key taped to the lower right corner of the page with the map on it. Blair continued to tell them about the contents. "I looked at everything inside. It seems that someone had hidden this packet between my letters so that it would not be found. Allisa, you said that Hunter was sent on a mission the day after he led a search of one of Saddam's castles. I think he wanted to make sure this was in a safe place so he stuck it in between my letters until he had time to get it to the proper people."

"That makes sense, Blair. The information we have is that he always followed through himself on every mission. He was supposed to go Riyadh, Saudi Arabia, for a debriefing the next day. Instead they asked him to go on another mission because one of the men in his group had been injured in a mine explosion."

Thomas picked up the map and studied it. "I'm not too familiar with the writing but I can tell you that there are two spots marked on this map that designate something hidden or buried."

Both women looked at Thomas.

"How do you know that?" Allisa asked.

"When we were in Greece, our command was always doing search-and-rescue missions. Every once in a while we would find a map with some designation like this. It usually was a symbol for items that either had been buried or hidden during raids on villages. The locals would bury valuables so that invading armies wouldn't steal them."

"Blair, I have a friend that I went to NYU with; his name is Baltazar and he does a lot of interpreting for the FBI. He is willing to come and look at these for us."

"How do we know that he can be trusted?"

"I know him very well and he will look at everything here and give us the answers to what's inside these documents. We can decide what to do once we know what they say."

"That makes a lot of sense. Give him a call." Thomas agreed.

While she called Baltazar, Thomas and Blair continued to study the documents.

"He said he will be here in a few hours. He'll call when he's on his way so I can give him directions to the house." All three of them sat around the coffee table looking at documents and thinking about what they held.

"Allisa, I also took this picture in the LAX airport. Do you have any idea who these men are?"

She took the cell phone from her and studied the picture.

"The man on the right is Dean Curry, the FBI bureau chief in Los Angeles. I don't know who the soldier is. Dean's the one who they told me to turn over all my information on you to him. I told you that they were taking me off the case and he was going to handle it from where I left off. He isn't a nice guy. I'm not sure why he's meeting Curry at the airport."

"The soldier's name is Captain Montgomery. He was on

my plane to LA. He had flown in from Baghdad."

They were baffled why Dean was meeting Captain Montgomery at the airport. "Blair, Dean is usually up to something and you may have just ruined his plans." Allisa smiled at that thought.

****

Dino told Steve that when they got to New York they were supposed to meet Don Goth at the FBI headquarters in Manhattan. "We can coordinate our search with his team and the team from the Bronx." New York had one of the largest groups of FBI personnel in the country. With its heavy population, and after 9/11, the Office of Homeland Security made sure that the ports of entry on the East Coast and the City of New York would be as secure as possible. The possibility of a terrorist cell operating in New York City had many of the agents mobilized and the city teaming with Code Red security measures.

****

The desk officer in the Columbia University station had the backpack that Pat had turned in taken to the office and put on the desk of Detective Wahid. He would be in soon and could look through the documents so that they got to the right person. The shift of detectives arrived a few minutes before ten a.m. and Wahid was informed that a package was on his desk. "Why did they bring it to me?"

He was told the material inside was in Arabic and that he might be able to help figure out who it might belong to. When he went upstairs he saw the backpack. He walked past his desk and got a cup of coffee and a donut and saw some of the other detectives that were on his shift laughing.

They were ribbing him as he came over. "What's in the backpack on your desk, Wahid? Forget your homework?" They all laughed.

"Funny guys, you should all be on television." He tossed the backpack on the floor and went through his reports from the break-in that he had been working. *Bunch of comedians*, he thought.

****

In another area of Manhattan, Dino and Steve had arrived and parked in front of the FBI center. Dino put his FBI card on the dash and they locked the doors. "Just let me do the talking," he said. "Don is a great guy and we can be a big part of this thing." It was close to noon and Don had just gotten off the phone with the director about sending men from the original investigation site to help with the search for the possible terrorist cell. Dino had the copy of the documents that Jon had found at the Crosswicks' rest area. He hoped that Don would not be offended that the director had sent him in to help with the investigation. Don came out of his office when he was told about the guest who just arrived. "Welcome to New York. I just got off the phone with John Martin and he said that you would be here to help with the situation. I understand that you have some key information that should help us in the search for possible terrorists operating in our area."

Dino was happy that Don was greeting them himself and he thanked him. He showed him the map that he had. They camped over the map with two other agents. "You can see the area around Yankee Stadium is circled in red and there are arrows leading to the streets to the east of the stadium."

"We have added about thirty agents to help with the search area and I have sent an APB to every police station in the five boroughs to be on the alert for anything suspicious. The director has also issued a Code Red for the metro area."

****

Back at the Columbia University police station, Detective Wahid was sitting at his desk when his captain called all his men in for a briefing. "Folks, we have been put on a Code Red Alert for possible terrorist activity. Anyone who has anything suspicious, report it to me immediately. It appears that a cell may be operating

231

in the area and we need to be on the lookout for anything that may help solve this case."

Wahid went back to his desk and reached for the backpack that was on the floor. "I might as well get this out of the way," he told his partner. He opened it and pulled some of the papers out. "Christ, there's a map with all kinds of red circles and writing, all in Arabic." He immediately realized that he might have critical documents that the captain had just told everyone to be on the lookout for. The map detailed the location of a two-story house about three blocks east of Yankee Stadium. The writing also detailed a search in Pennsylvania that the owner of the backpack was involved in. The names that were highlighted were that of Blair and Thomas Adams. Wahid immediately took the backpack into the captain's office. "Captain, I was delivered this backpack from the desk downstairs and I think you will want to see what's inside." He took out the map and translated the material for the captain.

The captain was excited. "This may give us critical information on this search." He contacted the New York FBI headquarters in Manhattan and faxed them a copy of the map. The captain put Wahid on the phone so he could interpret the other material.

Don waved Dino and Steve into his office and told them about the map that was being faxed over from the Columbia Police station. They were excited that some possible leads were already coming forth. He told them, "I've been told the information contains maps and details that may be the key to our terrorist cell." When he said that the detective also found information about Blair and Thomas Adams, they knew that this was the real deal. It was all coming together Dino thought. The papers must have belonged to the escaped terrorist from the break-in at Thomas Adams' place. This was the only conclusion that they could come up with. The men stood at the fax machine and studied each document that came across. Dino was pleased and he and Don would consult the director before they made their next move.

Just a few miles away, Yawer walked all through the neighborhood without any luck. He had to finally call to El Jaafi to let them know that he was close but had lost the backpack with all

232

the documents inside. El Jaafi said he would inform the men in the safe house but first Yawer should get to the house so they could plan their trip to Los Angeles. He knew that his friend was upset and felt that he had failed in his mission. "Our mission is not complete. We will head out as soon as you arrive. I want to head to California to continue the search."

****

Baltazar made it to Bridgewater about three thirty. He called Allisa when he got off the freeway to get directions to the Adams' home. He was in his mid-thirties and had been called by the FBI office in Philadelphia many times for assistance in interpreting documents that they had found. Baltazar was a first generation United States citizen. His parents had traveled to the U.S. from Lebanon during the war with Syria. He studied Middle Eastern History at NYU and he had been asked during his senior year to help the local New York police with a case that required an Arabic interpreter. Baltazar was proud of his involvement and the help that he had been to local authorities. He got to the Adams' home and was introduced to both Thomas and Blair. Allisa explained that she was working on a case and they were part of that case. She also told him that the importance of the documents was not known to anyone and that she was to inform the director of the FBI herself. The information would be top secret. He was stunned to see the documents that they showed him. He took a deep breath and started to explain what they held. "The map must have been drawn by a close member of the inner circle in Iraq," he said. "It may have been done by Saddam himself. It has two specific areas that seem to show the location of a cache of great wealth, probably gold, and the other of massive weapons stored outside of Baghdad."

Blair and Allisa were looking over his right shoulder as he explained the map's details. Thomas sat across from him with a grim look on his face. The letters that accompanied the map had a detailed legend of the map with locations spelled out. "From the dates on the side, I would say this map looks like it had been

233

drawn out about three months before Saddam's fall from power. He must have felt that there could be an invasion and he wanted to move stockpiles of weapons and gold to a safe hiding place."

Blair was close to speechless and Allisa was alive with excitement. "This is the key to why those men were searching your apartment and Thomas' house. They must have known that Hunter found these documents and thought since nothing happened for weeks after his death that he never turned them in to his commanders. They probably felt he was planning on keeping the treasure for himself." Both Blair and Thomas knew that could not be true.

"He would never do that," Blair said.

"That's for sure," added Thomas.

"I agree," said Allisa. "If he had planned on sending these items to you he would have attached a note with an explanation. He must have just hid them like you said between your letters for safekeeping."

"What do we do now?"

"Blair, we have very important documents that can help the FBI with their mission and obviously help the war effort. I think I should call the director and give him some idea as to what we have found. We could deliver them to him personally."

"Allisa, I want to think about this for a little first. It is important that Hunter gets credit for this information and not thought to be a traitor."

"Blair, I agree with you. With this information and especially the fact that Hunter did not send it to you but it was in the middle of letters that someone forwarded to you, no one could think he was a traitor. Hunter will be a hero and you and I will be off the hook. We may have found the answer to the mystery."

Blair thought for a few minutes and asked Thomas for his opinion.

"I agree with Allisa. You and she need to take these to the number one person in charge. Don't let someone else take credit for it. You will make sure Hunter gets credit for finding them and it would make me feel a lot better."

It was settled. Allisa said she would contact the director and would just tell him that she had found some very important information to solve the case. "He doesn't know that we are together here but the fact that we have critical information will be the key to the meeting. "We'll go to Washington together. You can give him the documents and we will explain everything. We're going to have to let him think that we are coming to Washington from California. Everyone still thinks that we're there."

****

Dino knew they had important details as he looked at the material that was faxed. There was definitely a location highlighted. It might be the possible safe house in the Bronx. Don was putting together his team that would head off to the Bronx and they were getting the military that was stationed in the Port of New York put on alert to their plan. Don contacted NYPD headquarters to advise them that the FBI would be carrying out a special high-level mission. He asked the police chief, Charles Allen, for support. "Your men could set up a perimeter around the suspected safe house." Charles said the NYPD was on board.

Don had Dino contact the Commander of the National Guard so that they could supply the necessary manpower needed for this mission. They took the map and other documents that were faxed to them and made copies so that they could be distributed to the other agencies involved. They would take Madison Avenue across to the bridge on Third Street in the Bronx. The local police station was on 149th Street and they would set up command there. It was just two blocks from Yankee Stadium and gave them easy access to the neighborhood east of the stadium.

****

Yawer arrived at the safe house and he and El Jaafi were in deep conversation. The leader of the other group wanted to know what had happened. His men had noticed a heavier concentration of police in the area. At first they associated it with the upcoming night game between the Yankees and Red Sox, but it seemed too early for this much police action. Yawer told him that they just needed to plan their exit and get to California.

This was an important day for the group's plan of action. They had all of their operatives in place and planned to plant explosives in trash cans around the stadium. The timing of the explosion would be about twenty minutes before the ballgame and many people would be trampled to death both outside and inside the stadium. They would create not only a monstrous moment for their cause but it would disrupt most sporting events around the country for a long time. They knew that the American people loved their sports but the constant fear that a bomb might be planted at any stadium would be in the back of most people's minds. Every sporting event had increased security and people were always checked before entering stadiums. The group understood this that is why they decided to plant their explosives around the outside of the stadium. If their plans worked out, the people inside would hear the explosions and start to rush out and trample those trying to enter. There would be thousands of people crushed. They also hoped that their next step would be to duplicate the bombing that took place in London at subway stations in the New York area.

The two men were happy that the local group was going to destroy American infidels. "We will leave so you can carry out your plans." Jaafi turned to his friend. "We should get Abdulla and leave for California. They began to pack and make reservations for the next flight to LAX. They would be using the new set of identification that they had forged. They were sure that they could still succeed.

****

It was now close to five and Dino checked in with the director. "Sir, we are closing in on the terrorist group in New York City. It appears that they have a safe house just east of Yankee Stadium and Don and I have mobilized both the National Guard and the NYPD. We're going to get them, Sir." The director was pleased with the progress.

Just after he hung up with Dino, his secretary said, "You have a call from Agent Jones, Sir." He wondered why she was calling him. Dean Curry advised that she was officially off the case.

"Sir, I know that my bureau chief advised me that they will handle the case from here, but I had a follow-up with Ms. Adams to tell her I would no longer be the one contacting her. While we were together she remembered about a package that her husband had sent, and that she had left at her work. I have the package and want to bring it to Washington. I know you'll want to see the contents yourself."

John Martin was puzzled but knew her previous successes and asked, "Why don't you just deliver the package to Dean?"

"Sir, Ms. Adams and I want to bring it directly to you."

"We have a major issue going down in New York. Does your information reflect anything there?"

"No, but it's critical to our Iraqi involvement."

With that, he agreed and said he would contact Dean back in Los Angeles that she was back on the case."

"Thank you, Sir. We'll catch a flight and call when we arrive."

The director contacted Dean in Los Angeles to inform him that Allisa was back on the case and it might not be necessary for Dean to get Captain Montgomery involved and blow his cover as an FBI agent. Dean Curry was mad that he was again being put on the back burner and that Allisa had found favor with the director. John Martin did not give Dean any other details and said that he would send out a memo to all the FBI offices once he had studied the material that had just been made available to him.

Dean had to contact Captain Montgomery and inform him that they were being put on hold until there was further direction from Washington. John Martin wanted to let the president know that his team was close to solving the case and that he had further information regarding possible activity in New York as well as Iraq. He would contact the director of Homeland Security. Martin wanted to make sure that it was his team that got credit for solving this crisis.

Twenty-Nine

El Jaafi had carried his bag out to the car when he noticed a police car at each end of the street. He walked down the street toward the corner to see what other activity was taking place. He saw that there was a military Jeep parked on the next corner and that it appeared that the lights were turned on in Yankee Stadium. It seemed too early for the lights to be on. He walked down Second Street closer to the stadium and could see that vendors had set up carts on the streets that led to the stadium entrance. There were a lot of people on the street around the stadium. It was at least two hours before the big game but he knew that the group at the safe house had said that close to sixty thousand people would be in attendance at the game. He didn't understand Americans. Even when he was in New York before 9/11 he found Americans to be superficial and preoccupied with sports and sex. He walked back toward the safe house and passed three NYPD officers who were walking toward the stadium. Although he was concerned, he connected the activity to the big game. He went into the safe house and told his two men that they should get going.

The terrorist group in the Bronx was lead by Fahim Wazir. His team was meeting in the large front room on the lower level making their final plans for that evening. His men all had their backpacks loaded with detonation devices. They would set the times to go off in a sequence so that as people ran away from one explosion they would run directly into another. The dirty bombs had nails, metal and fragments that would cause great damage and loss of life. This was the same type of bombs that were used in the Madrid and London bombings. The plan was to get all the bombs deposited around the stadium about an hour and a half before the game. Fahim informed them that they should start leaving in groups of two with their backpacks in ten minutes. He issued both

Yankee and Red Sox caps to all of them. The cover had to be convincing. They had to look like fans on their way to the big game. Once they had planted their bombs, another group would place more bombs at subway stations around the stadium. They were set to go off about an hour after the stadium bombs struck. The goal was planned to create havoc and disrupt all future sporting events in America.

El Jaafi wanted to bid them good luck in their attack on the Americans. He was thinking back to the group he participated in before the 9/11 events unfolded. His group had similar goals that were centered around the financial district in New York. Yawer and Abdulla went outside the safe house to wait for him. Yawer looked down the street toward the stadium and could see a large group of men standing on the corner. Abdulla pointed to a dark, high-cube van on the street a few houses from where the men had gathered. The van had what appeared to be a radar dish on the roof. Yawer moved away from the car parked out in front and toward the men on the street corner. He had a Yankee baseball cap on and was following another group of fans who had found parking spots along the street. One of them turned and asked him if he knew if Giambi was back in the lineup. He figured that he could walk along with them and appear to be part of their group. "I haven't seen the paper today but, I hope he's playing today," he answered. He knew they were Yankee fans and thought that was the best answer.

They continued their conversation and he walked alongside of them listening. He had to get a closer look at the men on the corner. When he got closer to them he saw that part of the group of men had weapons that weren't related to the game. Yawer told the two men he was walking with that he had to meet a friend. They waved as they continued toward the stadium. The men on the corner watched the group of guys who just separated. Yawer moved back down the street toward the safe house. He then walked up to the porch of a house that was about four houses from the corner. He sat down on the stoop like he was waiting for someone. He took his cell phone out and started to call back to El Jaafi.

Back at the safe house, Abdulla had gone back in when

Yawer headed to the corner. He wanted to alert Jaafi that more action was happening at the corner and it seemed unusual and that Yawer was heading down the street to check it out.

****

Dino and Steve were manning the surveillance truck parked down the street from the house in question. The FBI had been using audio-transmission surveillance of the neighborhoods around Yankee Stadium. They had picked up the conversation from the house via radar and knew the exact location and had an idea what their plans were. They had to move in and move in quickly before any of the men escaped with the bombs they planned to plant. Orders were given by Don who had been on the corner of the block with the NYPD police chief. They mobilized all the men available from both the NYPD and state unit. They had close to a hundred men stationed on the street behind the safe house and they were now moving into position to surround it. The goal was to arrest the men that were plotting this evil deed and not have any civilians injured. Orders were given to block the street and detain everyone who was walking down the street.

The group of men who were watching fans walk down the street was now getting their orders. They called back that a small group of about three men just separated and two had just turned the corner and headed toward the stadium. One of them stopped and appeared to be waiting for someone. They were given orders to detain the man who was still on the street and find the other men who had turned the corner. They should all be searched as a precaution. The National Guard had set up a perimeter around the stadium and was on the lookout for anything or anyone suspicious.

Don gave the order to move in and not let anyone out of the house. They had made sure that all the people on both sides were taken out of their houses and put in a safe area. El Jaafi and Abdulla exited the safe house when a loud speaker announced that they should put their hands up and lay face down on the porch. Abdulla jumped over the small wall on the right side of the porch and ran toward the rear of the house. Jaafi heard gunfire. It sounded like an automatic weapon. He knew the only weapon

Abdulla had was a pistol. He ducked back into the safe house as bullets rained down around him. Yawer was still sitting on the porch down the street when two officers approached him. He was about twenty-five doors from the safe house and had heard the shots ring out.

"We need to get you out of this area, Sir." The officers took him off the porch and searched him. Once they found that he had no weapons or devices on him, he was given to a local officer back on the corner.

Yawer asked the officers, "What's happening?"

"We have a police emergency and it is for your own safety that we get you behind the police line." Yawer was being protected by New York's finest.

The National Guard, along with the NYPD, moved in to cover all the escape routes from the house. Fahim Wazir yelled his orders to his men. They would fight to the death he told them. El Jaafi had an unfinished mission. *Where is Yawer?* he thought. They had to escape this action so that they could continue to search for the documents that brought them back to the United States. He figured that Abdullah was lost to the cause.

Gunfire was loud and seemed to come from all directions. Fahim ordered his men to toss the nail bombs into the police who had mobilized around the safe house. As his men moved toward the windows they were chased back by a hail of bullets. It seemed hopeless for the terrorists. All the men who surrounded the house were ordered to let no one escape. The hope was that they could arrest these men. The reality was that they had to stop them at any cost. The military joined the FBI and NYPD and had brought the most sophisticated weapons available.

The news of the raid on the safe house had spread to the media gathered for the ballgame. FOX News was covering the game and had their TV blimp move into position over the suspected area for film footage. Television stations around the country picked up the feed and now it was being carried live across the country. More people would watch this than those who watched O.J. evade police on the LA freeway. It was close to six and the National Guard had covered all the entrances to Yankee

Stadium. They requested that the game be called off due to the possible terrorist attack. The American League president was being called by George Steinbrenner with the information. George didn't want to cancel the game but would do whatever he had to do to protect the players and fans. The fans that were arriving were told that they would not be let into the stadium until it was searched for possible bombs. All those who had entered were being removed and some protested because their tickets had already been scanned at the gate. Everyone was being told that a bomb scare was called in and the safety of the fans was more important than the game. "You will all be allowed back in once we have cleared the area." The officers were clearing the fans from the area.

Dino called the director from the van and told him that they uncovered the terrorist safe house and were moving in to arrest everyone. John Martin was excited. He would make sure that everyone knew that it was the FBI that uncovered this plot and that Dino's team led the investigation. He informed Dino that he had heard from Allisa Jones and she was headed to Washington with news of the missing documents that Dino had originally been assigned to help find. That information was confusing.

"Where was she calling from?" Dino asked.

"I thought you knew she's assigned to the LA Bureau and will travel here from California."

That information was a relief to Dino. It looked like the director would have news of both the secret documents that they were looking for and a key terrorist cell uncovered in New York. Dino was glad that he was off the hook about Allisa and Blair Adams being in Bridgewater. He would have his glory moment in New York.

The safe house was now ablaze with bullets coming from the terrorists inside and into the house from the National Guard. The Guard had a tank being mobilized and it was headed down the street into position. There were four military vehicles, including a rocket launcher, now parked behind the safe house in the alley. Don had the NYPD police chief and the commander of the National Guard with him as Dino and Steve watched from the FBI SWAT truck. They were still monitoring the action inside the safe house and although voices could be heard, nothing could be made out. There was a lot of yelling in Arabic. At times there would be a lull in the action and then it would resume with retaliation from inside the house. The SWAT truck had been moved further down the street as the action picked up.

Dino had a unit just like this one available to him in Philadelphia so he was experienced in its operation. He had told Steve that they should continue to monitor what was happening inside the house so that he could relay that to Don and the units surrounding it. He was hoping to get the men inside to see that there was no hope and to surrender.

The National Guard had now moved the tank to the front of the safe house. It had a short cannon-type of gun on the front that was about four feet long and maybe a foot and a half wide. Dino had never seen anything quite like it before. It had to be a new military weapon. The cannon on the front was raised and pointed at the target. Don had hooked up a loud speaker and called out to the terrorists, "This is the FBI. You are surrounded, toss your weapons out. We will give you five minutes and if you do not respond, we will blast the front of the house and kill everyone inside."

It was very quiet for what seemed like an eternity. Crowds had been pushed back as far as possible but the strain of onlookers pressed their way along the police lines. The NYPD police chief had ordered his men to make sure that no one got closer than two blocks from the action at the house. It was a mess. Over sixty thousand baseball fans and media were present for the big game and now they had to keep them away from both the stadium and the blocks that surrounded the house under siege. Reporters found their way to the front of the throng of people. They demanded some access or at least a response to their questions. Everyone was now aware that not only was there thought to be a bomb planted at Yankee Stadium but now there was a group of terrorists located just blocks away.

Don called out again for a response from the terrorists inside. "This is your last warning. You have two minutes to respond." Just then a man stepped out onto the porch and held a machine gun in the air. It wasn't clear if he was giving the signal that he was about to surrender or was he going to fire on the police and guard unit outside of the house.

"Death to the infidels," he screamed out as he pulled the machine gun into position to shoot.

Bullets flew from the gun, but all of them went straight up in the air as snipers positioned across the street on a rooftop shot him through the temple and the chest. More bullets rang out from the house and a package was tossed out from the porch. The bomb exploded with a loud blast that made everyone on the street hit the ground. Steel flew from the bomb and penetrated everything for fifty feet. It was a nail bomb just like the ones used in the subway attacks in London a few weeks previous.

The response was fast and loud. The smoke from the gun on the front of the tank left a small cloud that rose over the street. The noise came about ten seconds after the smoke was seen. It sent people running from their positions two blocks away. The devastation was unbelievable. The whole front of the house collapsed. The National Guard, in position both in the front and rear of the house, fired a hail storm of bullets into the house to ensure that anyone who survived was taken out.

Dino and Steve had dropped their listening devices and fell to the floor of the SWAT truck. Their ears rang with a terrible buzzing. What had happened? Who gave the order? Dino struggled to his feet and looked out the viewing screen that had the house on closed circuit. It was leveled. The Guard had moved in and was positioned all around the house with weapons drawn. Nothing was moving from inside. The tank had fired a devastating blast that exploded on contact. The explosion came from inside and caused the house to blow up and out from the interior. This caused total devastation and eliminated everyone inside. The block was covered in ash. There were some broken windows on the block and bricks and wood shattered all over, but this type of a device limited most of the extensive damage to just the target.

Dino climbed out of the truck and stood stunned as he looked at the blast area. It looked like a war zone. Nothing remained of the terrorists' hideout. Steve followed Dino and both of them held their hands over their ears. Their heads were still ringing from the blast.

People had run from the police lines when the first blast

took place. The bomb had been loud. When the second blast came from the cannon many people in the area fell into a crouching position. The FOX News blimp had been moved out of the area before the first blast to a position further away. It appeared that the guard had informed them that it would be dangerous to stay put. They caught the whole thing on film for the country to watch. Millions of people were glued to their televisions around the world. The incident had been fed via satellite to over one hundred world news agencies.

John Martin and the head of Homeland Security had tuned in along with the president in the Situation Room in the White House.

The president was startled, "Wow, what weapon did we use?" he asked.

His chief of Homeland Security explained the type of blast and how the military had developed this for urban warfare. The president was impressed when he saw how the damage was limited but had taken the target out. John Martin was telling everyone that he had one more surprise. He would be meeting with one of his top agents who may have discovered the critical material that they had been searching for.

****

Allisa was telling Blair how they should proceed. She would tell the director that she and Blair discovered the map and packet of information in a package sent to Blair from someone in Iraq. The package was not sent by Hunter. He must have hidden the documents to protect them when he went on his last mission. His original plans would have had him deliver them to his commander in Riyadh, Saudi Arabia. "Blair, I will make sure Hunter is known as a hero. He uncovered this critical information and you helped get it to me."

Blair was glad that she had trusted Allisa who would make sure that the information Hunter found was credited to him. She was proud of her husband and what he had accomplished.

"We're planning on telling the director that we found the

packet in Santa Monica and brought it to him first. Allisa doesn't want to get you or her friend, Baltazar, involved."

"Guess you're right," Thomas said. "Sounds like a good plan."

Thomas suggested that they use his car to go to Washington, but Allisa suggested, "We should rent a car to drive to the Capitol. I don't want to get anyone into trouble or cause further suspicions."

Thomas agreed and said he would drive them into Philadelphia to rent a vehicle. Blair wanted first to call Olly and her parents to fill them in. Allisa cautioned her to be careful and not tell them too much until they got the documents into the proper hands.

Thirty

The J. Edgar Hoover building in Washington that was the headquarters of the FBI was very impressive. As they entered, Allisa showed the guard her badge and stated that she had a meeting with the director. The military guard at the entrance called someone and they were both escorted into the lobby through a large metal detector. Allisa wore her FBI badge and made sure Blair had left the fake one in Bridgewater. Blair was given a visitor's badge that she pinned to her jacket. She held the package tightly when the military guard requested to scan it before they proceeded. She looked at Allisa and was told it was okay; they would give it back once they run it through the scanner. The package was handed back to her and the military guard escorted them down the long, winding hall to the office of John Franklin Martin, Director of the FBI.

The long corridor leading to the office of the director seemed to go on forever. Blair and Allisa had changed clothes before leaving the Adams' home. "We might meet some high-ranking personnel in Washington and we should look as professional as possible." This would be Allisa's moment. She had lost the confidence of the director just a few days ago when he gave her assignment to Dean Curry. Curry was so concerned that the information would not be found that he arranged to fly Captain Montgomery from Iraq to Santa Monica so that he might get the information out of Blair Adams. She hadn't told the director about bringing Mrs. Adams with her. This would be the icing on the cake. Not only did she solve the case and find the documents but she had the confidence and support of the person the FBI thought might be hiding the secret material.

This was so unreal to Blair. Here she was in the inner sanctum of the Federal Bureau of Investigation. They had

247

discussed their plan on the ride from Bridgewater. They were going to tell the director how they found the map and information in the middle of Blair's letters. They would also tell him that Blair had some Middle Eastern studies in college and had a little knowledge of what the map entailed. She was not able to interpret the foreign language but did understand a couple of the symbols on the map. They knew the FBI would have experts analyze all of the documents and take action according to what they held. Allisa wanted Blair to get credit for part of this. They had become friends. She told Blair on the ride that she should consider a career in the FBI.

"You'd be a great agent, Blair. You handled so many stressful things. You even came up with a plan to outwit everyone and get to LA and find the documents. Not everyone in the bureau gets involved in cases like this. Most agents live normal lives and never have a case that sees danger."

"I'll admit that as it went along and I watched you work, I did get a thrill out of the search. When I remembered about the package that came from Iraq it all came together."

The military guard had been walking about two steps ahead of the two women and they followed with confident strides. Blair was nervous and Allisa wanted her to be as calm as possible.

"We're going to be in a lot of meetings with key people, so just remain calm and keep to the facts." They approached an office that had a large entrance. The mahogany door had to be ten feet tall and four feet wide. The military guard knocked on the door and they heard a click, then it opened. There must have been an automatic release that someone pushed because no one was standing on the inside. The two women walked into an outer office. It had three large leather chairs and two couches with assorted side tables and a large conference table with twelve chairs around it. The guard positioned himself at the door as it closed behind them.

Allisa had been in the building many times in her career but never in the office of the director. Not many field agents ever made it this far. It seemed like something out of a movie to Blair. She said that once, in a play she was in, they had a set that was very similar to the room they were in.

"What was the play about?"

Before Blair could answer, the large inner door opened and John Martin walked into the outer office. He walked over to Allisa and shook her hand. "I'm so glad to see you again."

"Sir, I'm glad to be here. I want to introduce you to Mrs. Blair Adams."

John Martin knew who she was. He stepped back and smiled at Blair.

"Mrs. Adams, I'm so sorry for your loss. We all hope that all of our military men return from their assignments safely but sometimes that just doesn't happen." John Martin did not know how much Blair knew but wanted to remain on the safe side of his conversation when referring to her husband. He did not know Allisa was bringing her but when the closed circuit TV scanned both guests, he recognized who Blair was from some of her photos that the bureau had in her file from various activities she had been in. She was a beautiful woman. He thought she was even better looking in person. He wasn't sure why Allisa had brought her but noticed the package that Blair held under her arm.

"I'm glad to meet you, Sir. I know that my husband was a good soldier. He never told me about what he did or where he was when he was on any assignment, but now I'm able to put it together. He seems to have been an agent of yours and I'm certain he was a very good one."

Allisa was pleased that Blair had been direct with John Martin and had not said that Allisa told her about Hunter's FBI involvement.

"Mrs. Adams, your husband was an excellent soldier for us. He was very brave and always willing to help his country. I see that you have a package. Is it for me?"

"Yes, Sir, but we need to discuss the contents with you. We found the package after all the strange things started to happen to both Hunter's dad and myself. We have to be sure that your people understand the way the package got to me and that Hunter was a hero and probably an agent."

John Martin was surprised with the comments but impressed with Mrs. Adams straightforward approach. She was no

249

dummy, not the Hollywood starlet he had pictured when reviewing her file. She had attended the University of Mississippi and majored in both Journalism as well as the School of Performing Arts. *This is a smart cookie,* he thought. "Mrs. Adams, you're right. Your husband was working undercover and performed many successful missions for us. We are saddened by his loss, as you are, and he will be remembered as a hero. Can we have a seat and look at the package you brought me?"

Allisa was surprised at how calm Blair was and handling herself very professionally. Allisa figured that the director would intimidate Blair with his importance and the office would be overwhelming to her. They moved over to the conference table and John Martin pulled out two chairs for the women. He positioned himself in the middle seat at the end of the table. Blair sat on his right-hand side and Allisa moved to the seat on his left. Blair put the package on the table and said that she would explain the contents but Mr. Martin should understand that without Allisa's help none of this would have come to light.

"Sir, Allisa stayed in contact with me the last few days and suggested that I might have something that was sent to me of critical importance. I'd received this package a few days ago from Iraq. I went to the post office to claim it but it was the same day that I found out that there had been a second break-in at my apartment and men had been shot and killed. I left the package at my work and forgot all about it."

Allisa added, "I felt that Blair was being very honest with me about not having anything from her husband but we knew that the documents had to be somewhere. You told me that our people had not found anything in Bridgewater and it made more sense that the package would be sent to Hunter's wife, not his father."

The director just sat back listening to the developments as they unraveled the story.

Blair continued, "I remembered about the package yesterday and called Allisa right away. We got it from The Pub. I had left it there and had been too overwhelmed to even think about it. We found it in the office where one of the other employees had put it. This is the information we found inside."

The director moved to the edge of his seat as Blair started

to open the package.

"At first I could not understand why there wasn't a name on the return label. Hunter always put his initials on anything he sent to me. The handwriting was also different. It wasn't from him. We opened the package but the only thing we found were two bundles of letters that Hunter had saved. These are all letters that I sent him while he was away. We were looking through the first bundle when an envelope fell on the floor. Here it is." Blair handed Martin the manila envelope. He held it in his hands as Allisa added, "Sir, you will notice that there is nothing written on the envelope and we were not sure what was in it."

John Martin opened the envelope and his excitement rose as he saw a map on the top of the other notes.

"We are not sure what the map means but Blair said that she had a mid-eastern studies class and the two symbols showed that there was something hidden in these two spots."

"Shit, this is it!" Martin could not contain himself. He jumped up from his seat and the two women looked at each other. He grabbed his phone and called someone to get to his office right away. They were successful in weaving their story without the director asking questions. They were in the clear and the package would be his focus. Two men knocked on the door, Martin reached under the table and the door opened. They came into the office area and he introduced Allisa and Blair to them. He told them to sit at the table and look at the map and other papers inside the package. They all moved to the middle of the table and spread the documents out to review. The map was their main focus. They were talking fast and then looked at the director.

"You might want us to study these for awhile, Sir." He knew that Martin would not want them to tell him the contents with the two women in the room.

"You both have been through so much. How about if we get you into a hotel and let us go over these documents. I know you have had a long day already with the trip here from California."

"Sounds good to me, Sir," Blair answered. "But I must remind you that my husband did not send these to me and he was killed before he could get them to his commander."

"Mrs. Adams, I assure you that we know your husband was a hero and will be remembered that way. I will also tell you that you and Allisa have done a great service to your country. Allisa, you have my apology for not believing in you. You have done an outstanding job and I will be putting you in for a well-deserved promotion. Mrs. Adams, I would like you to get some rest. Allisa will go with you and I want to talk to you more about our organization tomorrow."

Both women walked to the door and John Martin instructed the guard to please escort the women to the lobby where he would have someone meet them and take them to a hotel. "We'll take care of everything," he told them. Allisa mentioned that they heard about the incident in New York and hoped that it had gone well.

"I'm not sure if you remember Dino Tuchy from the Philadelphia Bureau but he and his people were instrumental in that effort. We were very successful in removing a large terrorist threat in New York."

They were pleased that they had been successful in protecting Dino from being involved with Allisa in this mystery and that the director never questioned why Blair had not been seen for the past day and a half. The two women walked back down the hallway smiling at each other. The guard led them to the lobby where they were met by a woman who identified herself as Special Agent, Diane Roper, with the FBI. She said that she would escort them to the Marriott in Arlington. Allisa said that they had parked their rental car in the visitor's lot.

"It will be okay. Give me the license number and description and I will make sure they tag it as being good for the night."

"I think we would like to take the car with us to the hotel," Blair said.

Ms. Roper said, "Okay, I'll go with you and have someone follow us to bring me back."

They all walked to the parking lot and Allisa smiled at Blair. "You did a great job in there. I was very impressed and so was the director."

"Thanks Allisa, but I couldn't have done it without you."

They all got into the rental car and Diane gave them directions to the hotel.

"The director wanted me to tell you that he has called to reserve rooms for both of you and that anything you need should be charged to the room. We are taking care of everything."

Blair and Allisa had packed a small bag in case the question came up about their travel from California without any luggage. They also weren't sure how long they would be in the nation's capitol.

During the ride to the Marriott, Diane asked Blair, "Is this your first trip to Washington?"

"No, my parents brought me here before and I always enjoyed sightseeing around the area."

"If there is any place in particular that you would like to see, please let me know," Ms. Roper added. Blair was pleased with the results of the meeting with the director. She hoped that she accomplished what she had intended to and that her trust in him would be as fruitful as her trust in Allisa had been.

The view of the Capitol building from the Virginia side of the Potomac was grand. They could see the Washington Monument and the top of the Lincoln Memorial. Blair listened to Ms. Roper and Allisa talking about the colleagues that they both knew. The director was right; she was tired. She would call Hunter's dad when they got to the hotel and fill her parents and Olly in on the meeting with the director. The package was in the hands of the FBI and her mission was over.

Thirty-One

The view from their rooms was of the Potomac River and Blair could see some of the buildings in Washington. She could see the Arlington Memorial Bridge and the top of the Lincoln Memorial. She knew that they had done the right thing. She felt a rush of emotion as she looked out over the view. She had told Allisa that she needed some rest but didn't know if she could calm down enough to actually sleep. She had called her parents on the way to Washington and gave them an abbreviated version of the events that had happened. They wanted to come to meet her but she said she was okay and she would call them a little later. She'd also called Olly and told her everything that had happened. Olly was pleased that it was over and Blair was safe. Hunter's dad was happy that they had delivered the package safely, in person, and told their story to the director.

Allisa sat in her room and was very content with the direction the case had taken. She wanted to call Dino but she knew that wasn't the best idea. He was deep into the incident in New York and had been on the news channels constantly with a recap of the terrorist threat to blow up Yankee Stadium. He was a hero and would get the respect of every agent. She was sure that he would be promoted and she would probably never see him again.

Washington was beautiful in the spring. The trees were full of cherry blossoms and they had a fragrant smell that filled the air outside. The Marriott was located on George Washington Memorial Parkway and had a great view of the river and downtown Washington. Blair sat on a large leather chair by the window and just looked at the view. She remembered that when she was about ten, her parents had brought her to Washington and they went to see all the tourist sites. It was even more beautiful than she remembered. Her phone rang and she got up to answer it.

"Blair, I'm still so pumped up that I can't rest, how about you?"

"Me too!"

"Come on over to my room and we can talk."

Blair walked down the hall to Room 2412 and knocked on the door. Allisa opened her door and the women hugged. They had truly become friends and were bonded together by the events of the past few days. They moved over by the table in front of the window and sat across from each other on the two leather chairs. "Allisa, I'm so glad that you talked me into going with you to Bridgewater. You're a good friend."

"Blair, I felt you could handle yourself and what had to be done, but you surprised me. You're very strong and have a great sense of what has to be done. You adapted to the situation that came up and took charge when necessary." They both looked out of the window. The sky was deep blue and made the Potomac look clear especially from the twenty-fourth floor. The phone rang in the room and both women jumped. Allisa answered and a wide smile came across her face as she listened to the caller. "Sir, I'm glad that the information is that important to our effort. Yes, we would be glad to meet with you and the president."

Blair sat stunned as she heard her mention the president.

"When do you want to come get us, Sir?" She hung up and jumped up and down. Blair just looked at her and seemed in a daze.

"What else did he say?"

"They had experts look at both the map and the other documents and we may have uncovered a cache of weapons and a pile of gold that Saddam Hussein had hidden. The information is being fed to our forces as we speak and they are planning raids to check everything out."

"What about a meeting with the president? Are we meeting the president?"

"The director said that they informed him and he was very excited about the findings. He planned to award Hunter the Medal of Honor. He will want to present it to you at a special event."

Blair smiled as Allisa was talking. So much had taken place

255

and now the president wanted to meet them! "The director wants us to meet him for dinner about seven p.m. He said that the head of Homeland Security and a couple of other Washington dignitaries may also be there. Details of the dinner are still being worked out."

"I need something nicer to wear and these shoes would never do."

Allisa started to laugh and Blair laughed with her.

"You and your shoes."

"We can go downstairs, they have a few shops in the lobby area and we can just charge the things to the room. Remember, they said the FBI is taking care of everything."

****

Dino and Steve had been on a whirlwind tour of news media stations covering the mission in New York and the terrorist threat that they uncovered. Don was just a year from retirement and suggested that Dino take the lead in the case and handle the interviews. "You will have to follow up with this for the next year because of its implications. This is the first major terrorist cell that has been handled in front of the whole world on our soil." Dino was happy and always mentioned Don, the NYPD, and National Guard when he was giving details of the events. Steve would be promoted along with Dino and viewed as instrumental in the case.

****

Back in Bridgewater, the local police had to complete the final task of recording all the details of their involvement with the FBI. Captain Douglas had given Jon David credit with helping organize a joint effort to solve the investigation in his town. Jon had stayed back as instructed by Dino and made sure that all the loose ends were taken care of. He stopped in at Mr. Adams' house to thank him for his help. Thomas told him that Allisa and Blair had gone to Washington to meet with the director. They both sat and watched the news coverage of the events that had unfolded in New York, and now more information was being broadcast about a large-scale effort that was taking place in Iraq. Jon said, "Everyone was a winner in this." He was glad that this case was over and he would be heading back home to his wife and two girls. He was always happy to be going home.

****

Allisa and Blair had been in and out of the shops in the lobby of the Marriott and were pleased to find so many places to buy clothes and accessories. Blair wasn't sure how much would be proper to spend but Allisa said that they needed to be prepared to meet some very high-ranking officials. They had been able to rest and Diane had called to tell them that a driver would pick them up about six-thirty p.m. from the hotel. He would pull up out in front and take them to dinner. They met in the very ornate lobby of the Marriott. They were waiting for their driver to pick them up. They weren't sure where they were going but they both looked beautiful. People who passed by took a second look. Allisa thanked Blair for helping her pick out an outfit.

"You have a great sense of style."

"In my business, when you get a break you have to look the part. Besides, it's always easy when you're not spending your own money." Blair had only been lucky enough to be in a few plays and had one small part in a movie. She was once asked to be an escort at the Oscars by the studio and she made certain that she made a splash on the red carpet. The experience was unbelievable. She was to walk alongside one of the presenters for that evening. Until she got there she didn't know who she would be walking with. To her surprise it was Ron Howard and Tom Hanks. They were both up for an Oscar and Tom's wife was out of town. The studio just wanted a young actress to be seen with them as they entered the pavilion.

The driver pulled up in a limo in front of the Marriott. He got out and held a sign up with their names on it. When they came out of the hotel he opened the door for them and the women got in the back. They crossed the Potomac River and headed down Constitution Avenue to 17th Street. They had asked the driver where they were going but he said he wasn't supposed to tell them.

"It's to be a surprise." The driver turned right on Pennsylvania Avenue and entered the east gate of the White House. Both women turned to look at the other and then stared at the entrance. The driver opened his window and the guard opened the gate. He pulled around to a side entrance and got out and opened the car door for them.

When they got out of the car, John Martin was there to meet them.

Allisa asked him, "Why didn't you tell us where we were going?"

"The president was told about your involvement and that you were both here in Washington. He wanted to meet you and have you here for dinner. It all came up very quickly."

They entered past a metal detector and into a lobby. The house was just beautiful and both women were looking around when the president came into the lobby. They were speechless as he shook their hands and extended his thanks for the great service they had performed for their country. The president's wife came out and was very gracious to them. She also shook both of their hands. "You are both so beautiful. Please come in. Honey, you didn't tell me that they were so beautiful." They walked down a small hallway and the first lady had one of them on each side of her. "I hope that you like what the staff made for dinner. I didn't have time to find out what you like to eat so we had to come up with something. I hope it's okay."

"We are so honored to be here," Blair said.

Allisa then expressed that the evening was very special and what an honor it was to be invited to the White House.

At dinner the president asked the two women about themselves and he conveyed to Blair that he and his wife were sorry for her loss. Blair felt a rush of warmth come over her and she didn't know what to say. The president said, "John will give you more details about tomorrow but I plan to present you with a Medal of Honor for Hunter's work in Iraq. The presentation will take place on the lawn of the White House." He then told Allisa that she should be there too because she is the one who made sure the documents got to the right people. "You both are very brave young women and represent beautifully the people of the United

258

States."

The evening was magical. They had a wonderful dinner with the president and his wife and now were being told that they would be honored at a special event on the lawn of the White House the following day. After dinner they were escorted to the Lincoln Room for coffee and dessert. The president excused himself and the first lady entertained them while the president met with John Martin and the director of Homeland Security on a matter of importance.

John Martin returned to the Lincoln Room and said that he had called the driver to come back to the White House and take them back to the hotel. He walked the women out to the limo that was waiting for them. "You need to watch TV tonight for developments in Iraq; it's directly related to your information. We will be carrying out missions in Iraq and Pakistan over the next few days." That news was exciting. Blair was surprised that the government was able to move so fast on the information.

They asked him what time they were supposed to return to the White House the following day.

"We will pick you both up about ten-thirty; the president is calling a press conference for around noon on the White House lawn. Go down to one of the shops in your hotel if you need anything for the event. It will be televised."

"We already bought some items today. Are you sure we should buy something else?" Blair asked.

"What you have done is tremendous and I want to make sure you are given first-class attention. Please get something special for tomorrow's occasion. It will be carried live across the nation."

John Martin put his hand on Blair's right arm. "Blair, I would like to talk to you after all of this about joining our training group. You are a bright person and would make a great field agent."

"I appreciate your confidence in me but I love where I live and would not want to move."

"We could arrange to keep you right where you are; you would be surprised how many agents we have that are living what appear to be normal lives."

"Thank you. I'll think about it, but right now I'm so overwhelmed that I can't process anything else."

"I understand. Just keep it in mind. We can talk more about it tomorrow."

The women climbed into the back seat of the limo. The driver took them back to the hotel while they sat in the back talking a mile a minute. They had experienced so much that day and now tomorrow would bring even more excitement. Blair had to call her parents and Olly and she wanted to tell Hunter's dad what had happened. When they got back to the Marriott they went to Blair's room and turned on CNN. Details of events were unfolding about the discovery of weapons of mass destruction being found in Tikrit, Iraq, close to Lake Tharthar near one of Saddam's castles. The reports showed the 5th Army removing boxes and putting them in trucks lined up in a convoy to return to their headquarters. There was also information about a missile attack near Islamabad, Pakistan, where reported al-Qaida leaders were holding a meeting. The reporter said that key terrorist group leaders were meeting and that this would be a significant blow to al-Qaida in the region. The evening was full of news reports on every station and both women were pleased with what they had accomplished.

Allisa said, "I'm going to my room, Blair, and make some calls."

"I need to do that too," Blair said. She called her parents first and filled them in on the whole story. They were happy that everything turned out okay but wished she had gotten them involved. They knew that their daughter was strong willed and would follow the action that she thought was right. She had been through so much and now some positive news was great to hear. She talked to Hunter's dad and he was thrilled that his son was going to be awarded a medal for his work. Her next call was to Olly. With the time difference from the East Coast to LA she knew she would be able to get her at home. They discussed the events and Blair said that she wanted to talk to Blake and Ashley before the news came out. She didn't want them to hear about it from television first. They were great friends and had been there for her through it all.

The night had been a whirlwind of excitement. After talking to Blake and Ashley, she turned on the television. Blair did not have a television in her apartment. It seemed an expense that didn't make any sense to her. She was rarely home and when she was she loved to listen to music. It was hard to put the evening into perspective; first hearing news that the president was going to want to meet them and present Hunter with an award and then having dinner at the White House with the president and first lady. She knew that tomorrow would be a big day and the emotions she was feeling sent adrenaline pumping through her veins. She had to get some rest. She had made plans to call Allisa around eight to go down for breakfast and buy a new suit for the White House event. Blair watched the CNN broadcast that was unfolding a story about events in Iraq and details that the president would be holding a press conference for tomorrow. She turned the channel to a local station to see if they had any other news. The reporter said that the president would honor a fallen hero and two women who were instrumental in helping the war effort. He also said that there would be further details about military action in both Iraq and Pakistan. Sleeping would be difficult but Blair had to get some rest.

She got into bed and listened to a recap of the terrorist situation in New York. She smiled as Dino gave the reporters the timeline of events. He told them that his team had been following leads that took the FBI from California to the East Coast. He never mentioned her or Allisa but said that a couple of agents had been involved and was instrumental in solving the case. She turned off the television and turned over in bed. She wasn't sure what to expect from tomorrow but wondered how it could possibly top today's dinner with the president.

Thirty-Two

The morning sun was high as the alarm went off in Blair's room. It was seven and she had to shower. Blair knew that she was too excited to eat but wanted to talk to someone. She dialed Allisa's room. Like Blair, she was very hyper. She had been awarded special commendations before but never anything like this. They talked and decided to move their meeting time up. The shower felt great and she put on some clothes and walked down the hall to Allisa's room. She was waiting and they took the elevator down to the lobby. She had contacted the hotel manager and he arranged to have someone open one of the boutiques early for them.

"We need to shop for something for today's ceremony," she had told the manager.

Blair said, "I feel funny about buying all these clothes."

"With everything you have been through, it's the least they can do for you, Blair. Besides, it was an order."

She agreed and they headed down to the shop on the main level where they were met by a charming, young saleswoman who was happy to show them around. They were the only two in the shop and the woman knew that they were VIPs of some sort. The shop usually didn't open until noon but the manager said he would need someone to help a couple of dignitaries that the FBI had staying at the hotel. It was not unusual for them to get a request like this from a government agency.

Blair found a navy suit with a bright blouse. "I have shoes that will go with this." Allisa laughed. Both women were nervous and the laughter was great medicine to calm their nerves.

Allisa settled for a basic black suit. "This is something that I can use for meetings."

The saleswoman rang up their purchases and thanked them

for shopping at the boutique.

They had planned on having breakfast but neither of them felt hungry. "Why don't we just grab some coffee and Danish?"

"Sounds good to me," Allisa answered.

Afterward Blair said, "I want to go up to my room and get ready. Do you think that I should have something prepared to say in case I'm asked?"

"That's a good idea."

"I'd guess once the president finishes he will want you say something. You will have to wait until we get there; I'm sure they'll let us know."

"I can work on that but will you read it over before we go?"

They had become truly good friends and trusted each other's opinions.

They went to their rooms to get ready for the trip back to the White House. "See you about ten," Blair said.

They met at the elevator and headed to the lobby. They found a quiet spot near the entrance and Allisa reviewed the notes that Blair had prepared. "This looks very good. I think that the president will appreciate what you've written."

They saw the limo that had pulled up in front of the Marriott about ten twenty. They got into the back seat and were now feeling like veterans. Blair looked at Allisa and said softly, "To the White House, young man." They both laughed as the ride took them on the same route as the night before. The driver didn't hear what she had said but smiled when he heard them laughing.

It was a beautiful day. The sun was bright and the trees that lined Pennsylvania Avenue were all in bloom. Everything was perfect. They pulled into the gated area and the limo went to the same entrance they used last night. They noticed that a large crowd had gathered around the front gate of the White House. They asked the driver if that was normal.

"Anytime there is a press conference on the lawn of the White House, we have large crowds that gather hours before to get a view of the event. Sometimes we have more protesters than onlookers but today's crowd seems to be very quiet," he said.

They got out of the limo and John Martin was there to meet

them. He introduced them to the other men that were waiting in the outer lobby of the White House. One of them was the White House press secretary. He addressed them. "We will want to meet with both of you for a few minutes before the press conference. I want to go over the details of the event with you and if you have any questions, please, now is the time to ask."

Blair asked, "Who will be present during the press conference?"

"The president will make the presentation and Mr. Martin will also have some remarks. The president will cover events from last night before he introduces you."

"We saw a large crowd along the gated area and were wondering why so many people were out in front when we pulled up to the gate."

"After the events of last night and the CNN coverage it is not surprising to see this big of a crowd."

Both women knew that the president's approval rating was very low and the war had not helped. He hoped that this would be a turning point in his presidency and by allowing people to gather at the gated area, it would help him seem more of a people's president.

"Will I get a chance to say anything?"

"Yes, but I would need to see what you have in mind. Most times people being given an award just thank the president."

Blair gave him the note she had written and he looked it over.

"This looks good to me but I will have to give it to the president for his final approval," he said. "If he approves, they will give you a cue when you will be able to give your response."

They were escorted to an outer office. It was getting close to the time the press conference was supposed to start. Blair was nervous and asked if she could have some water. A young man brought each of them a bottle of water. He introduced himself and he returned the note that Blair had written. She got up and introduced herself and Allisa. "I have gone over your planned remarks with the president and there is no problem with what you plan to say. Please make sure that you look into the cameras when you're talking," then the president and his wife came in. Both women jumped up and exchanged hellos.

"I hope you are not too nervous," the first lady said.

"We should be okay," they both answered.

The president spoke to each of them. "Ms. Jones, you have been instrumental in this case and I want to recognize you for your efforts. The director said that he will be putting you in a new position that would keep you in Washington. I hope that is okay with you."

"Yes, Sir."Allisa was in awe and found it hard to speak. The two women smiled at each other as the president was talking to them.

"Mrs. Adams, you are a very brave woman and I cannot tell you how important your efforts and the information your husband found has helped our cause."

"Thank you, Sir. He was very dedicated to his country and his father will be pleased to know how that he will be honored here today."

"I called his father last night after dinner and invited him to be here today but he said that this should be your moment. We will send him a copy of the medal that I will present to you today. You both should have one."

Blair was speechless and had tears in her eyes. The first lady moved closer to the girls and gave them both a hug.

"My press secretary will be back in here in a few minutes and go over the details of the presentation. I've read your planned remarks Mrs. Adams, and they are very nice."

"Yes Sir, I gave them to one of your people and they said it was okay."

"I appreciate your wanting to contribute."

"We will be going out to the lawn in about ten minutes, Sir," the White House aide said.

They moved toward the West Wing of the White House and were told that the Secret Service would have men in position along the grassy area, that the military personnel stationed outside of the West Wing would open the doors, and that they should follow the president and first lady out to the lawn. There would be a small platform with microphones mounted on it and they should stand to the right of the president. His wife would be on his left-hand side. The doors opened and the president stepped out followed by his wife and the two women. Flash bulbs went off as they took their position on the platform.

The president addressed the crowd. His speech detailed the events of the past evening and those of the morning. He talked about the events in New York, Iraq and Pakistan. Reporters clamored for answers to questions but he said that he had a presentation to make first. "I would be happy to answer your questions after that." He then turned and introduced Allisa Jones and congratulated her on being instrumental in finding the critical information to help the war effort. He handed her a plaque and she posed with the president for pictures. He told them that she was a key special agent and would be promoted to a position at the Hoover building in the WFO, referring to FBI Headquarters and the Washington field office. "I have one more special guest to introduce," he said.

The president put his hand out to Blair and she stepped forward. "This is Mrs. Blair Adams. It was through her husband, Hunter Adams' efforts in Iraq that the information we needed was found. She made sure that information got to the proper people and it has been critical in our efforts. It gives me great pleasure to present Mrs. Adams with the Medal of Honor for her husband, Hunter, who was killed in the line of duty in Iraq."

Photographers were moving forward and pictures were being snapped of the presentation.

"I also want to present Mrs. Adams with a plaque of appreciation from the people of the United States for her efforts. We are sending matching awards to Hunter's father in Bridgewater, Pennsylvania. Mrs. Adams has some remarks she would like to make."

Blair had both the plaque and the Medal of Honor in her hands with the press snapping photos and asking questions. She moved toward the microphone.

"I want to thank the president and first lady for this honor. My husband, Hunter Adams, was a hero and his father and I are glad that he is being recognized for his gallantry. I am just a normal citizen who did the right thing. Regardless of your views, we are all Americans and when the opportunity is there to serve our country we have to step up. My husband died in the line of duty and he is being honored as a hero, but he's not the only hero we have. The brave men and women in our military and the civilian contractors who are helping to rebuild Iraq are all heroes. I want to share this award with all the family members who have lost someone in the conflict."

The press was in love with her. Why not; she was a beautiful young woman and represented family members across the country that had lost someone in the war. She stood next to the president and the photos would be on the cover of every newspaper in the country. This would be good for his approval rating and she would be in the limelight for a long time. As the people along the gated area watched many of them cheered. Flags were waved and Blair smiled. She knew that all her problems were over now.

****

Along the gated area one man seemed to stare at the event that had just unfolded. He had no expression on his face but seemed to be taking special interest in them more than anyone around him. He took a few pictures and made sure that he had a close up of this Mrs. Adams. He also took pictures of the FBI agent with her. Yawer watched Blair as she took the medal and plaque from the president. He knew that she had helped to destroy what his group had built and he vowed to get revenge.

Tony Aued

Acknowledgements

Thanks to Beverly Styles and Priscilla Mangold for their editing. Your work has made my story better for the readers. You did a great job.

Thanks to the members of the Shelby Writers Group. You are all an excellent source of help and support.

In appreciation for the cover art that Carl Virgilio helped to create. Your work brought the cover to life.

To Charles Allen, your FBI insight has been very valuable. You are a great friend

Special thanks to my son, Blake, for his reference material. Your professional help was greatly appreciated. The journalistic material and advice you gave me was very valuable.

Tony Aued

About The Author

Mr. Aued's novel created a local buzz when it was introduced during a preview book signing in Marine City, Michigan.

A review from Sheila Yancey of the Times Herald in Port Huron, Michigan, stated, "Aued weaves a riveting tale that reads more like a motion picture than a novel."

Locations used are the result of detailed research and trips by the author to make sure they are accurate.

Aued is a retired teacher who also had a corporate career that took him across many cities in the southeast and Midwest. He currently resides in Michigan with his wife, Kathy, and their dog, Baxter.

98353094R00164

Made in the USA
Columbia, SC
26 June 2018